THE FURTHER MEMOIRS
OF
SHERLOCK HOLMES

VOLUME II

The Further Memoirs of Sherlock Holmes

Volume II

CAIDEN COOPER MYLES

MX Publishing

First edition published in 2024
© Copyright 2024
Caiden Cooper Myles
Cover and internal illustrations © Copyright 2024
Marie-Charlotte Feret

Hardback ISBN 978-1-80424-533-0
Paperback ISBN 978-1-80424-534-7
ePub ISBN 978-1-80424-535-4
PDF ISBN 978-1-80424-536-1

Published by MX Publishing
335 Princess Park Manor, Royal Drive,
London, N11 3GX
www.mxpublishing.co.uk

Cover design by Awan

For BB

You are a constant source of faith, love, and encouragement.

Contents

Prologue

FTER so many years, I remain astonished that the public appetite for the adventures I shared with my friend, Mr. Sherlock Holmes, is undiminished. This incredulity is shared, and often exceeded, by Holmes himself. As we leave the second decade of this century, the idea that accounts of adventures from the end of the nineteenth should continue to find an audience, is nothing short of astounding. I am even given to understand that many of my readers did not witness the times of which I now write.

As with the last volume, this book contains accounts that had, for various reasons, been withheld. Two appear courtesy of the efforts of my friend's brother who was cajoled into obtaining government approval for their release.

John H. Watson, M.D.
London 1920

We found Gregson a few feet up the street, pointing a battered lamp at the body of his fellow policeman.

The Adventure of the Kidnapped Reporters

(Mid-1896)

T WAS some forty minutes after midnight. Sherlock Holmes sat in his chair, dressing gown draped about him, and one of his longer pipes clenched between his teeth. He wore a faraway expression, as if, spiritually, he were somewhere else. He had said nothing for more than an hour, simply content to watch smoke drift upwards like a ghostly serpent.

I had no objection to the silence and was working my way through the late edition of the *Evening Standard*. We had both risen late the previous day. I had descended to the sitting room at around ten o'clock. Mrs. Hudson had just presented me with boiled eggs when Holmes had walked in from his room, the first cigarette of the day already between his lips. He ignored his own eggs and poured a large cup of coffee before stubbing out his cigarette in the saucer. This behaviour no longer prompted any real reaction in our long-suffering landlady and she left, throwing me a glance of feigned despair as she shut the door.

As a result of our late start to the day, we were both very much awake despite the late hour.

The month before had seen the conclusion of the events I have chronicled as "The Adventure of the Hirsute Intruder." Holmes had, once again, found himself up against a criminal organisation, and had outsmarted it. For me, the prospect of another such sinister enterprise filled me with foreboding. For Holmes, it offered the opposite. He had spent a significant portion of the day going through past newspaper clippings, looking for patterns he could ascribe to this new malign force.

I lowered my newspaper. "Holmes?"

"Yes, Watson," he said, without turning his head.

"Only you could find pleasure in something which normal people would dread."

He turned towards me and smiled. "Dear Watson, I need criminals as you once needed patients. What am I to do with my talents otherwise?"

"You could employ your powers in a similar fashion to your brother," I suggested.

He snorted and rose from his chair. "Watson, although I have been known to sit in a chair for hours on end, it is not something I would seek to do permanently. I require physical, as well as mental, exercise."

"Have you managed to discern anything regarding this new organisation?" I asked.

He frowned and knocked out his pipe on the mantelpiece. "I have satisfied myself that it exists. Nothing more. That said, I lack anything that would convince a third-party."

"Do you believe it has any connection to the late professor?"

"It is possible, Watson. There is every chance someone has rounded up Moriarty's remaining lieutenants and made them into something cohesive. It is equally possible that this is a rival group that has been able to come to the fore. In any event, the identities of its leader and principal lieutenants need to be determined. After all, you cannot cut off the heads of the hydra if you do not know where it is."

"Do you think this new leader is as formidable?"

He frowned. "It is too early to say. One of our late friend's attributes was that he had no desire to be recognised. It was this lack of thirst for the limelight that protected him for so long. Our new adversary seems eager to communicate and this could be his undoing. I have no doubt we shall hear from him again."

Holmes was about to say more when the bell rang. We both looked at the clock. "I wonder who this could be?" he said.

We heard the weary footsteps of Mrs. Hudson make their way to the front door. She opened it and, almost immediately, there were heavy footsteps upon the stairs. The door burst open and two men entered the room, one in his mid-fifties, the other about twenty years younger. They were both dishevelled and evidently exhausted. The elder had encrusted blood on the back of his neck. Having entered the room they both seemed at a loss as to what to do so they just stood there, breathing heavily, and looking from one to the other of us.

"Gentlemen," said Holmes, unruffled, "how may I assist you this evening?"

After what seemed like an age, the younger of the men managed to say "Mr. Holmes, you need to help us. We've been kidnapped."

Holmes and I exchanged glances.

"Gentlemen," he said, "while you both look as though you have experienced some kind of ordeal, you do appear to be at liberty."

He was about to speak further when the elder of the men swayed and fell onto our hearth rug only narrowly avoiding the mantelpiece. The younger man looked horrified and bent down to check on his companion. After a few seconds, he tipped forwards, landing alongside the older man. Holmes nodded at me and we proceeded to convey each man to an end of the settee. There they lay like two rag dolls while Holmes and I looked on.

Holmes retrieved his pipe, seemingly unmoved by what had just transpired. "Perhaps, Watson, you can attend to their injuries while we wait for them to re-join us."

I performed a cursory examination while Holmes lowered himself back into his seat. The men both had a lump on the back of their heads. That on the head of the younger man was harder to see, due to a fuller head of hair, but was less pronounced than the older man's injury. The older man had marks around his wrists which were suggestive of him having been tied up. I examined them as much as possible and informed Holmes there was no evidence of any other injuries. I then managed to force some brandy into them. Both men opened their eyes but otherwise remained quiescent.

"Well, gentlemen," said Holmes, "if you are able, do you think you would be willing to tell us who you are and something of what has happened to you this evening?"

The younger of the two men spoke first. "I am sorry, Mr. Holmes. My name is Bill Gardner and I am a reporter with *The Graphic*. This is John Oldridge, my rival at *The Times*."

The man we understood to be John Oldridge did his best, with some difficulty, to nod his head by way of acknowledgement. The expression on his face indicated that it was painful for him to do so. Words were seemingly still beyond him.

Gardner continued. "I was at the office some hours ago when we received a tip that there had been a violent robbery at a house in Lower Norwood. My editor was keen that I get the story so I hailed a cab and headed to the address. When I arrived, I was perplexed to find no sign of activity. The street was quiet and contained several houses on each side, a reasonable distance apart. Despite the darkness, there were no lights on in the house. The nearest streetlamps were apparently faulty making it darker still. I paid the cabby, who went on his way, went through the gate, and approached the door. I was straining to see my way, and was beginning to think I had been the victim of a hoax, when I heard footsteps behind me and felt a pain in my head. I must have been knocked unconscious.

"When I woke, I realised at once that I was in a bedroom. I was bound at the ankles and wrists with rope. As my vision cleared, I saw Oldridge on the opposite side of the room. He was unconscious, and bound similarly. The room was lit by a single lamp upon the table next to me. I noticed my watch had been taken, not that I would have been able to reach it any case."

Holmes had remained motionless in his chair while Gardner spoke. He removed his pipe from his mouth and gestured with it towards the young man. "Could you hear any sounds?"

"None," said Gardner. "It was eerily quiet."

"What happened next?" asked Holmes, returning his pipe to his mouth.

I offered both men more brandy as Gardner continued. "I managed to sit up and looked around for anything that might assist me in freeing myself. As I struggled, I bumped into the table and knocked a glass from it which shattered as it hit the floor. My first concern was that the noise might attract our kidnapper so I closed my eyes and waited."

"Did anyone come?" asked Holmes.

Gardner squinted as if trying to focus. "No, Mr. Holmes. I briefly thought I heard footsteps downstairs but I am convinced I was mistaken. Satisfied that no one was coming, I proceeded, with some difficulty, to get hold of one of the shards and rubbed the rope around my wrists against it until it snapped. I had proceeded to freeing myself of the rope around my ankles when I saw Oldridge wake."

"Mr. Oldridge?" said Holmes.

The older man straightened himself on the settee. His voice was weak. "My story is much the same, sir. I received a similar tip-off and arrived at the address. I opened the outer gate, which I seem to remember needed oiling, and was attacked from behind a few steps from the front door. I remember drifting in and out of consciousness. I think I may have been hit more than once. I remember a loud bang, like a door slamming shut. It seemed to focus me and I saw Gardner here, as he said, pulling at rope around his ankles.

"Next thing I knew, he was by my side helping me free." Oldridge looked fondly at his young rival as he said this.

Holmes stood up and waved his pipe from one man to the other almost in the manner of a conductor. "Did you notice anything else?"

Oldridge frowned. "I do recall a strange smell. I couldn't tell you what it was though."

Gardner interrupted. "Yes, I remember that too."

"When did you smell it?" asked Holmes.

"I smelt it around the time I woke to see Gardner. I was also struck," said Oldridge, "by the poor state the room was in."

"How do you mean?" I asked.

"The bed was only a frame. Wallpaper was beginning to peel from the walls and the floor was without any rugs, and rather damaged. The house was clearly abandoned and unfit to live in."

"Having freed yourselves, what did you do?" asked Holmes.

"I helped Oldridge up," said Gardner, "and we made our way out of the room. I carried the lamp with one hand, as there was no other light in the house, and we made our way downstairs. The rest of the house seemed in a similar state of disrepair and when we reached the ground floor, we nearly tripped over some wood that was scattered about the hallway. We headed for the front door as we both wanted out of the house as soon as possible."

"But, Mr. Holmes," said Oldridge, "just as we got to the door, Gardner here turned his head sharply to the left and held the lamp out. As he did so I caught sight of a body."

"What body?" said Holmes.

"It was a sight I hope never to see again. It was the front parlour of the house. Just like the hallway, there were various pieces of wood scattered around the bare floor. In one corner, resting on some of this wood, and in a pool of blood, was the body of a man."

"I see," said Holmes. "Furnish me with all the details."

"Nothing to tell, Mr. Holmes," said Oldridge. "We didn't hang about. We got outside as soon as we could."

I looked at Holmes. His frustration was evident.

Oldridge continued. "I knew the location of the nearest police station so I said we should head there. Gardner here thought we should come to you and we argued about it. Our raised voices attracted the attention of a constable and I fear he took us for a couple of drunkards having a brawl. He blew his whistle and ran over to us. I began to try to explain what had happened, but it was clear the constable was not convinced. Gardner asked him who was on duty at the nearest police station and the constable said it was an Inspector Graham. Gardner asked that he be fetched with the utmost urgency and, to convince the constable, he helped me to the nearest working streetlamp so my head wound could be seen. The constable told us to wait while he went for the inspector."

"But you did not wait?"

"No, sir. Gardner said that, now we'd informed the police, we should inform you. We managed to hail a cab and here we are."

Such was the remarkable story. Having exhausted themselves, the two men fell silent. Holmes looked concerned.

"What is it, Holmes?" I asked.

Holmes got to his feet and went out to the landing. He shouted for Mrs. Hudson. Our stately, and evidently weary, landlady duly appeared, not looking pleased, and Holmes whispered something to her. He asked Gardner for the precise address in Norwood before disappearing into his room, throwing off his dressing gown as he did so. He swiftly emerged, ready to depart. I stood and followed. As we descended the stairs, and opened the front door, I said "What about Gardner and Oldridge?"

"Mrs. Hudson will look after them. It is vital we reach the scene without delay."

At that hour, cabs were scarce but we eventually secured one and were on our way to Lower Norwood. Holmes was clearly agitated. "I rather wish Mr. Gardner had won the argument."

"I beg your pardon, Holmes?"

Holmes turned to look at me. "It would have been better if Gardner had got his way and the two men had come straight to us. As it stands now, we are in a race to gather information."

"The house isn't going anywhere, Holmes."

"It isn't but Inspector Graham is."

"I don't think I've heard of him."

"He rose to prominence after you left Baker Street. The man's intelligence makes Lestrade and Gregson look like geniuses. A bit like Athelney Jones, he will stumble in there with a mob of constables, and we will be lucky if we can sort the wheat from the chaff."

A little over an hour later we arrived at the Lower Norwood address. It was clearly a prosperous street as the houses were quite large and at a good distance from each other. The events we had been told of would have seemed less plausible in a more working-class district where residents lived cheek by jowl. Due to the nearest streetlamps still being faulty, a dozen police lamps had been set up to illuminate the approach to the house.

We paid off our cab and endeavoured to enter. The constable at the gate forbade us entry but agreed to let the inspector know. A few moments later, a clearly self-important man emerged from the house. He was in his forties and I could see by the lamplight that his hair was greying at the temples. He walked the few steps to where we stood.

"Holmes," he said, putting his hands into his pockets in response to Holmes's outstretched one, "I shall want a word with those two reporters."

Holmes lowered his hand. "I'm sure you do, Inspector, and I have given instructions that they should remain at Baker Street for that purpose."

The inspector smiled. "That is appreciated, Holmes. Would you care to see inside and delight us with a theory?"

Given Holmes's description of the man, I had expected Inspector Graham to deny us entry. I made a note to ask Holmes about it once we were away from the house.

We stepped into the hall and Holmes's face fell. "Graham, did you move the wood?"

"Yes," replied the inspector. "It was dangerous. My men kept tripping over it."

Holmes looked at me and rolled his eyes. We turned right into the parlour. A pile of wood was stacked up by the window resulting in an almost clear floor. Holmes's face showed his frustration. "I do not suppose, Inspector, that you happen to know the prior position of the wood?"

"Does it matter?" said Graham. "The body is the important object here."

"Have you have managed to identify him?" I asked.

Graham looked at me. "I assume you are Dr. Watson, sir. As a matter of fact, we have. We know him well. This is William Scott, a reporter at *The Telegraph*."

"Holmes," I said. "Three reporters called to the same house."

"Indeed, Watson," said Holmes. "Most curious. Do we know why he was here?"

Graham looked irritated. "Scotland Yard does function in your absence, Mr. Holmes. We have spoken to his editor. There was a report of a violent robbery here which they dispatched him to investigate as their star reporter."

Holmes and I looked at each other. "You are aware, I take it, that the two other men were called here with the same story?"

"No, I was not," said Graham. "But it does not surprise me they said so."

"What do you make of it?" asked Holmes.

"What? No theory of your own, Mr. Holmes?" said Graham, with a smirk. "Very well, this is my working theory. We have someone with a hatred of all three reporters. He plans to kidnap them all but, for reasons we don't yet know, he only manages to overpower the first two. Mr. Scott here put up a fight with this result."

Holmes patiently listened and shook his head.

"You don't agree?" said Graham.

"It won't do, Inspector," said Holmes. "The others were knocked out before entering the house. This William Scott gets inside?"

"Well, he's clearly here," said Graham, pointing at the body.

"Watson," said Holmes, "would you take a look?"

I looked at the inspector. "Oh, go ahead, Doctor," he said. "The police surgeon has already made his initial examination."

I knelt by the body. Scott was face up, lying on a number of planks of various sizes. It was clear he had been struck across the forehead with some blunt object but the fatal act had been a swipe to the throat with a blade of some sort. I related all of this to Holmes who nodded.

Scott was face up, lying on a number of planks of various sizes

"May we see the bedroom where the other men were held?" he asked.

Graham shrugged and made no movement. Holmes left the room and headed upstairs with me in pursuit. At the top of the stairs there was a door to a rear bedroom. This room seemed in better repair than what we had seen so far but was little more than a box room. A similar, but slightly larger, room was adjacent. Holmes looked around briefly before heading to the other door along the landing which was at the front of the house.

The room we stepped into was clearly the room in which Gardner and Oldridge had been held. A bare bed was against one wall and a table against the one opposite. As the men had described, the room was in a poor state. If anything, Oldridge had been understated in his description. There were holes of various sizes around the room. One sizeable example, large enough for a child to fall through, was near to the table. Oldridge was right when he had described the room as dangerous. Holmes stepped over to the hole and looked down.

"Graham. Could you possibly get your men out of the house?"

"When we're good and ready, Mr. Holmes," came the response from below.

"Holmes," I said. "Do you suppose all the wood downstairs was intended to be used to effect repairs?"

Holmes paused for a moment. "That would be the most plausible reason, Watson."

He turned his attention to the glass fragments and pieces of rope that were around the table. "That is most curious," he said.

"What's that, Holmes?" I asked.

"Take a look, Watson. Tell me what you see."

I stood next to him and saw he was pointing at three pieces of rope. The first was about four feet long. The other two were the same length at just under eighteen inches each and they were both frayed at one end where, presumably, they had been joined prior to Gardner cutting them with the glass. I bent closer before looking back at Holmes.

"You don't see?" he asked.

"I'm afraid not," I replied.

"The longer piece is presumably that which was round Gardner's ankles. It is in one piece as he was able to untie it with his hands. The other two pieces, which were joined originally, are those Gardner cut through. Do you see what is curious about them?"

"I cannot say I can," I replied.

He tapped his temple with his forefinger. "Docket it, my dear fellow." He picked the rope and glass fragments up, before moving across the room to retrieve some others. "These are the ropes that bound Oldridge." He glanced around briefly and left the room.

I got to my feet, somewhat confused, and followed. When I reached downstairs Holmes was back in the front parlour, handing the rope and glass to Inspector Graham. "These are significant, Graham, try not to lose them."

The inspector frowned. "Anything else?"

Holmes pointed at an area of the floor close to the doorway. "Inspector. I don't suppose you can tell me if there was any wood here?"

For the first time since we arrived Graham looked less sure of himself. "Now that you mention it, Mr. Holmes. That's the one thing I did think odd. There was a large piece exactly there. Just the one. It seemed rather lonely where it was."

Holmes smiled.

About thirty minutes later we were once more in a cab and heading to the offices of *The Graphic*. On our way out, Holmes had examined the rest of the house and immediate surroundings. He informed me that he had found nothing of significance.

"You see the problem with Inspector Graham?" he asked, as we headed north. "The man has no notion about preserving evidence."

"It's a wonder he attained the rank of Inspector," I said.

Holmes smirked. "Like our other friends at the Yard, I have helped Graham out on more than one occasion. Although he accepts the help, he also resents it. I think he is all too aware he owes his rank to me."

"He did seem rather antagonistic towards you."

"Us, Watson. He will not confine his unpleasantness to me."

We arrived at the offices of *The Graphic* and were shown to the editor's office. The poor man was tired and seemed in no mood for further questioning.

"I don't know what I can add to what I told the police," he said.

Holmes smiled. "It always helps if I can hear first-hand. I am sure your account will be far superior to the recollection of Inspector Graham."

The editor managed a small chuckle. "Well, that's certainly true, sir. He's not the brightest. Same could be said for Gardner come to that."

"Were you here when he got the tip-off about the robbery?"

The editor stroked his chin. "Indeed, I was. It was around eight in the evening. He came into my office brandishing a piece of paper."

"A wire?" asked Holmes.

"No," replied the editor. "It was a handwritten note."

"Did you see it up close?"

The editor frowned. "Yes, sir. It was brief. It gave the address and the basics of the crime. It was sent by someone uneducated."

"What makes you say that?" asked Holmes.

The editor looked pleased with himself. "Because, sir, the word robbery was incorrectly spelt. It was also in rough capitals."

"Do you still have it?"

"No. Gardner took it with him."

Holmes thought for a moment. "Thank you. We shall be sure to let you know of any developments."

The editor stood and beamed. "Why thank you, Mr. Holmes. We will be discreet in any report."

I followed Holmes to the door. He placed his hand on the handle and, without turning, said "Your remark about Gardner being unintelligent. What did you mean by it?"

The editor resumed his seat. "Young Gardner has been something of a concern ever since he came to us. I'd have let him go long back if he wasn't such a good reporter."

"Go on," said Holmes, turning back to face the editor.

The man sighed. "When he first applied here, he talked about wanting to seek justice for the wronged. He considered the police, by and large, incompetent. He even took the occasional swipe at you, sir, alleging that your talents were largely the invention of the good doctor here."

Holmes turned and smiled at me. The editor continued.

"I'm not going to lie to you, Mr. Holmes. The press is all about a good story first and foremost. Justice is a nice by-product but it's not what we aim for."

"That is understood," said Holmes, with a degree of distaste.

"Gardner has got himself into all kinds of scrapes ever since he became a reporter. We were not his first employer. He worked at a local paper in Kent where he had brushes with the law in his quest to right wrongs he thought they had failed to address."

"Anything more recently?" asked Holmes.

"Yes," said the editor, "and only yesterday. After several months of good conduct, he picked a fight in a local public house of all places. He went straight up to a local criminal and insulted him to his face. According to people who were there, having given the fellow a piece of his mind, he just headed out whereby the rough concerned struck him down."

"He seems a foolhardy fellow," I said. Holmes said nothing.

As we exited the building, I could see that Holmes was intrigued. "What is it?" I asked.

"Too early, Watson," he replied. "We need to complete our round of interviews."

A cab took us to the offices of *The Times*. There we spoke with the editor who explained that a handwritten note had been dropped in, addressed to Oldridge, at about eight-thirty in the evening. The man who delivered it had reportedly concealed his face and promptly left without a word. The wording of the note was in line with the message received at *The Graphic*. In response to Holmes's questions, we learned that Oldridge was a competent reporter, with an exceptional reputation for integrity, but ill-health was likely to lead to early retirement. We had a similar story at *The Telegraph* except the time of the note arriving was closer to nine-thirty. We learned it was addressed explicitly to Scott. Scott was reportedly an excellent journalist who had been responsible, over a lengthy career, for significant stories around everything from murders to government scandals. His editor assumed Scott must have had a significant number of sources. To the editors of both newspapers, Holmes made similar promises about sharing information. None were aware that his cooperation was not exclusive.

"I think, Watson," said Holmes, "we should return to our guests in Baker Street. I fully expect Graham to be there now."

"Why?"

"He would have headed there as soon as possible after we left. He is an imbecile but tenacious. They are his only two witnesses and he will want their accounts. I instructed Mrs. Hudson to admit him and to also warn our guests that he would be coming."

"What conclusions do you think he will draw?"

"Erroneous ones, Watson."

It was around six-thirty in the morning when we arrived back at Baker Street. We negotiated our way past four constables who were loitering outside. Mrs. Hudson met us in the hallway. We could hear raised voices upstairs. Our landlady informed us the inspector had been present for almost two hours but that she had insisted his constables remain on the street.

"Bravo, Mrs. Hudson," said Holmes. "Could you possibly bring up some coffee?"

We stepped into our sitting room. Our two reporters were very much where we'd left them. Inspector Graham was standing in front of the fireplace, legs splayed, one hand in his left pocket and the index finger of the other waving in the faces of our guests. He paused as we entered.

"Ah. Holmes, Dr. Watson. Perfect timing."

I looked at Holmes's side table. There was a half-filled brandy glass. I looked at Holmes. He nodded and placed a finger to his lips.

"Perfect timing for what, Inspector?" he asked.

"I am about to make an arrest."

I was startled. "You are?"

"Yes, Doctor," replied the inspector. "I have developed a new theory since we last spoke. I am about to arrest both your guests on the charge of murder."

Both men on the settee paled. Oldridge spoke first. "On what grounds?"

Graham smiled the tell-tale smile of self-satisfaction. "My investigations have revealed that the three of you had been hated rivals for years. All competing for the same scoops but Scott always the more successful. I venture that, as the two lesser talents, perhaps in fear for your jobs, you decided to bury your differences and remove Scott.

Oldridge, we know you're in poor health and likely to be dismissed if you cannot justify your employment. Gardner, you have a record of getting into scrapes that bring your paper into conflict with the authorities. What better way to improve both your prospects than to get rid of the competition together?"

I expected Holmes to stop the inspector but his expression appeared to be one of pleasure. Graham continued.

"The evidence suggests you both lured Scott to that house and killed him. You fabricated the story about being kidnapped and were each other's alibi. But it all fell apart almost immediately."

"How so, Graham?" asked Holmes.

"My guess," said Graham, "is that these men planned to take advantage of Scott's excellent network of sources. They fell out over the division and began to fight only moments away from the scene of their foul deed. That's how they got their injuries. The constable stopped things from getting any further."

Holmes slowly clapped. "Very good, Inspector," he said. "I do have a number of questions before you take our guests away."

"Yes, Holmes?" said Graham.

"Firstly, why would two men quarrel so close to a murder scene and risk attracting attention?"

"They couldn't control themselves," replied Graham.

Holmes did not pause. "Secondly, why did they insist on sending for you if they wanted to conceal a crime?"

"Sheer bravado."

"Thirdly. How do you account for the sound of the front door slamming when both men were untying themselves upstairs before the body was found?"

"Sheer fiction."

"Finally, said Holmes, "how do two men, in a face-to-face fight end up injuring only the back of each other's heads?"

Inspector Graham could not muster a reply to Holmes's final question, which seemed to irritate him. His response was to hasten his arrest of the two reporters and take them away. Both men protested their innocence and Holmes promised he would uncover the truth.

"The truth," Graham had said, as he led the men out, "has already been uncovered. No assistance required from you, Mr. Holmes."

"The arrogance of the man," I said, as we heard the front door close.

Holmes was running his fingers up and down his pipe rack. He selected his briar-root pipe and proceeded to fill it. He took a match, struck it on the hearth and held it to the bowl. "I think this may be the apex of Graham's career."

"You cannot be serious, Holmes."

Holmes lowered himself into his seat. "As much as it pains me to say it," he said. "I believe this is the least mistaken he has ever been."

I stood aghast.

"Oh, do not misunderstand me," said Holmes. "Graham is *almost* totally wrong but normally he *is* totally wrong so it is a step in the right direction." He began to chuckle.

"He has arrested the right men?"

"If I am correct, the answer to that is yes and no," replied Holmes. "I have a theory that hangs together. What I don't have is the why, and that concerns me."

"What should we do?"

"I think we should return to Norwood in a few hours. If I know Graham at all he will have removed most, if not all, police presence."

He glanced at the clock. "Get yourself a few hours' sleep, Watson. We will leave just before midday."

After some badly needed rest, we found ourselves back outside the Norwood house. It was a lot less sinister in daylight. As Holmes had predicted, there was only a solitary constable at the gate. He was content to let us pass as he recalled us from earlier and he had been briefed by Graham to let us through as there was, in Graham's words, which the constable quoted, "Nothing for Mr. Holmes to find."

As we entered, Holmes was clearly irritated. I asked why.

"Nothing, Watson," he replied. "I think I find it frustrating that a man as idiotic as Inspector Graham can be so astute as to predict I would come back here and be so bold as to leave me a message."

On our way out of Baker Street, Holmes had picked up a bag. I now followed him into the front parlour. It was bare except for the bloodstains, and the wood piled near the window. Holmes proceeded to rifle through the pile and examine each piece. Eventually he found one that seemed to satisfy him and he placed it into the bag. As he rose, he suddenly let out a cry and bent down. When he straightened up, I could see he was holding a match. It was almost entirely consumed with only the smallest unburnt piece at the bottom.

"Ready, Watson?" he asked.

"Where are we going?"

"Lincoln's Inn Fields."

As we rattled our way towards our new destination, I tried to make sense of recent events. On our way out, Holmes had asked the constable if he knew where Inspector Graham was holding the two reporters. His understanding was they had been brought from Baker Street back to the local station in Norwood. Holmes asked the constable to get word to Graham that we would join him and begged that he be allowed to talk to both men before further action was taken.

"He will like that I begged," said Holmes.

"I assume that is pandering to his sense of superiority?"

"It's absurd of course, Watson," said Holmes. "Deep down he knows all too well that he owes most of his successful cases to me. Yet the man is stupid enough to bite the hand that feeds him."

"Stupid indeed," I said.

Holmes sighed. "Actually, Watson, I have to be honest and say it's my stupidity rather than his. He may not know one end of a crime from the other but he does understand me rather well. He predicts my movements, as you have seen, and he also knows the attraction of the problem to me. He knows I'll take whatever jibes he throws in order that I can be involved in the interesting problems that come his way. He understands my weaknesses just as much as I understand his."

"That's beginning to sound like respect," I said.

"Of a kind," acknowledged Holmes.

We arrived at thirty-four Lincoln's Inn Fields and Holmes asked me to hold the cab as he went inside. I stood on the street and smoked several cigarettes. He was not in for more than half-an hour before he emerged with a smile.

"Somerset House, cabby," he said as he leapt in. I barely had time to reboard myself before he had struck the roof of the cab sending it on its way.

I must confess I was getting more than a little irritable as we dashed around London. All my efforts to get Holmes to explain were rebuffed. "I don't have all the data yet, Watson," was all he would say.

Following our arrival at our latest destination. He spent about an hour going through records and emerged looking triumphant.

"I still don't have the why, Watson, but I think I have everything else. I require a clean collar before we head back to Norwood. We may even get a bite to eat somewhere on the way."

We returned to Baker Street. Holmes was right, we both needed a change of clothes. When I later descended the stairs, I found Holmes looking out of the window, pipe once more between his lips.

"Watson," he said, and gestured towards the table, "Mrs. Hudson has furnished us with some sandwiches. Would you care to?"

I was famished and practically fell upon the modest repast. I looked up to see Holmes staring at me, openly amused.

"Sorry, dear fellow," he said. "You've been so patient. Would you like some information before we go?"

"Most definitely," I said. "You've been frugal with it, as usual."

"Well," he said, "we need to be on our way but I'll say that the key points to consider are that, contrary to Inspector Graham's assertion, both men did indeed hear a slamming sound when in the house, and they both smelled unusual odours. You should take note of the rope that tied Gardner, and his wrists. Finally, Oldridge's integrity and poor health are vital points. Is that sufficient for now?"

"It most definitely is not," I replied. "But I know it will have to do. Are you bringing that?" I asked, pointing at the bag Holmes had taken to and from the Norwood House.

"It would be remiss of me if I did not," he replied.

The desk sergeant of Norwood Police Station sent a constable to seek Inspector Graham upon our arrival. The inspector appeared but, while he seemed as confrontational as ever, he also seemed somewhat less self-assured. We braced ourselves for a taunting but the inspector beckoned us to follow him to his office.

"You and I have our differences, Holmes," he said, as we sat down, "but we both share a desire to catch criminals do we not?"

"You certainly have a desire," said Holmes, acerbically.

"But not an ability? I guess I deserved that," said Graham.

"Despite that," he continued. "I feel I have the right men. Can you help me? The chief superintendent is putting pressure on me as the press is kicking up a stink over the death of one of their own and us holding their colleagues."

Holmes took pity on the hapless inspector. "I can half help you. Would you be so good as to fetch the glass fragments and rope I handed you in Norwood?"

A few moments later we were by the cells. Holmes asked to be shown to the cell of Gardner. We entered to find the man head in his hands on his bed. Upon seeing Holmes, he leapt up.

"Sit yourself down, Gardner," said Holmes. "The game is up."

"What do you mean?" asked the young journalist, who remained standing.

Holmes gestured to Graham who handed him the glass fragments and pieces of rope. They were carefully placed on Gardner's cell bed. The young man looked unmoved. Holmes reached into his bag and pulled out the large piece of wood. Gardner remained impassive. Finally, from his pocket, Holmes pulled out an envelope. From it, he tipped the blackened match into his hand.

Gardner's face fell and he sat back down.

Graham and I stood confused. "Holmes?" I said.

"My colleagues here don't understand, Mr. Gardner," said Holmes. "Would you care to relate events or would you prefer I do so?"

Gardner shrugged. Holmes began.

"You see, gentlemen," said Holmes. "From the beginning there were curious aspects to this case. Kidnap victims who never met their kidnapper and who easily escaped. A desire not to involve the police immediately replaced by a strong desire to involve them, and a house with damaged rooms and loose wood all over the ground floor for no apparent reason.

"We were asked to believe that all three men were lured to the house by someone who assaulted them under cover of darkness. But why attack two of them outside from behind and allow the third inside to attack him from the front?"

"So?" said Graham.

"We must begin with the tip-offs," said Holmes. "They were designed to be irresistible to both a reporter and his editor. They would not be ignored. However, all were targeted to specific reporters except Gardner's

"Gardner's editor simply told us that Gardner appeared in his office holding a note mentioning a violent robbery. No one saw it arrive. Gardner simply appeared with it. It seems clear to me that Gardner wrote it himself, being careful to disguise his handwriting.

"Once we assume that starting point you can begin to build the rest. Gardner, en route to Norwood, knows that two other letters are to be dispatched. One to Oldridge and one to Scott. They are dispatched in such a way as to ensure the men arrive in a certain order and a certain time apart.

"The house is already prepared. The street we know to be quiet and Gardner has taken care of the nearest streetlamps to ensure they are not lit. Under the cloak of darkness, he waits.

"But," said Graham. "If it was so dark, how would he see the others arrive?" A good question I thought.

"Perfectly straightforward," said Holmes. "Having been waiting there some time his eyes would have grown accustomed to an extent. The key item, which Oldridge mentioned, and Gardner, tellingly, did not, was that the gate needed oiling. When Oldridge opened the gate, it squeaked and this was all the alert Gardner needed to launch his attack."

"We didn't hear the gate squeak," I said.

"Because it was always open on our visits," said Holmes. "I saw little point in testing it. Gardner dragged his unconscious victim upstairs to the damaged bedroom. Not an easy task but one he had plenty of time to do."

"But why not kill him like Scott?" asked Graham.

"Because Oldridge was never going to be a victim," said Holmes. "He was going to be the perfect witness."

Graham and I were both astounded. Gardner no longer had his head in his hands and instead looked rather pleased.

Holmes continued. "Gardner remained with Oldridge in the bedroom and kept a watch on the street for Scott. This is one of two reasons why the front bedroom was used. If he saw a cab or heard one, which he would on so quiet a street, he would be able to get downstairs in readiness. As Scott was to be dealt with inside, there was no need to get outside. At least two or three times Oldridge began to come round. You will recall him telling us as much, Watson. Gardner, who sat behind him so as not to be seen, would, unkindly, strike his head against the wooden floor to induce further periods of unconsciousness.

"Gardner had a fair idea of when Scott would arrive, based on the timing of the note and the distance Scott had to travel. When he saw a cab approaching, he made his way downstairs. Remember the house was in darkness apart from the low light in the front bedroom. Scott would have knocked of course. Gardner here did not answer. He knew, being a reporter, Scott would certainly try the door rather than walk away.

"He waited for Scott to enter the house and struck him with a piece of wood. Scott staggered into the front parlour where he fell over.

"Now Gardner could have easily killed him then and there but he instead allows Scott to rise. At this point the match is lit. You can see this one was lit long enough to burn almost completely. I contend that Gardner lit the match; he wanted to be seen. This tells us this is vengeance as opposed to an ordered murder. Scott is given just enough time to recognise Gardner or, more likely, for Gardner to say who he is, before the latter struck the killer blow with the knife.

"Gardner dare not wait too long before striking the final blow. For one reason Scott was at a disadvantage at that moment but could recover if given too much time. Gardner also could not risk Oldridge having time to wake and witness the event. The deed done, he clears the wood from around the doorway, leaving the rest where it was."

"Why move the wood at all?" I asked.

"That's the clever part," said Holmes. "Having killed Scott, he makes his way back to the front bedroom. He must prepare the scene."

Holmes picked up the two shorter pieces of rope. "This was allegedly used to tie Gardner's wrists. It is clearly not true."

"How can you tell?" I asked.

"In one piece," said Holmes, "this rope would go round Gardner's wrists more than once. If he had cut through it, in the manner he claimed, it would be in more than two pieces. Furthermore, the chances of cutting a rope behind your back into two equal length pieces are slender at best. It is far more likely that, when he was preparing the room, he took both ends in his left hand and cut through them with his right. Tension would lead to the cut being at the mid-point. Added to this was an absence of any rope marks on his wrists when he arrived at Baker Street."

"Brilliant," said Graham.

Holmes continued "Oldridge is still unconscious at this point. Gardner moves over to him to apply smelling salts. This is the smell Oldridge later mentioned. Gardner quickly returns to the other side of the room and places the longer piece of rope loosely around his ankles. The other two pieces he places on the floor where Oldridge can see them.

"Oldridge is now conscious but groggy. He makes out Gardner sitting up on the floor apparently struggling out of ropes. Ropes he didn't know were never tied. He just assumed them to be because he had ropes around his own wrists. How am I doing, Mr. Gardner?"

"I can see I misjudged you, Mr. Holmes," said the young man.

Holmes nodded and continued. "Gardner sees that Oldridge is regaining his senses." Holmes pointed to the bed. "At this point he pushes that piece of wood, which is behind his back, through the large hole we saw near the table. The hit of wood-on-wood, as it strikes the floorboards, sounds much like a door slamming and a little bit of suggestion to a sluggish Oldridge would make it easy to believe. This was the reason for all the other wood. One large lump of wood in the parlour might attract attention but if it was one amongst many?"

"Clever," said Graham.

Holmes continued. "Gardner then takes Oldridge downstairs. You will recall, Watson, that Oldridge told us Gardner suddenly looked left with the lamp and they both saw the body?"

"Yes."

"Gardner clearly pretended to hear a noise and turn in that direction in order to ensure Oldridge saw the body. He knew Oldridge would put it together in the way he wanted. He would assume the slamming door was the murderer fleeing the scene after the deed. It would never occur to him to suspect his fellow kidnap victim.

"They get outside and must decide what to do next. Gardner knows they must report the body or he will look suspicious. This is where he insults me. He does not rate my talents, as you and I, Watson, learned earlier. He suggests coming to me. Oldridge wants to go to the police. They argue, as we know, and a constable appears. This is a potential nightmare for Gardner. Very coolly, he asks who is on duty.

"This is where he insults you, dear Graham. He clearly has even less respect for you. He believes you will destroy more evidence than you will uncover so he suddenly becomes enthusiastic about police involvement. He then involves me anyway in the hope that conflict will muddy things still further."

I had stood listening to this but could not contain myself.

"Holmes. It doesn't add up."

Holmes's face betrayed his surprise at my interjection. "How so, Watson?"

"Three issues, Holmes. One, why Oldridge as a witness; two, how did the notes get sent at the staggered times; finally, both Oldridge and Gardner had been assaulted when they came to Baker Street. I examined them myself."

At this point we all fell silent. Not because we were dumbstruck but because Gardner was laughing. Inspector Graham was not amused. "You would do well to either keep quiet or assist us."

Gardner was not in the least affected by the inspector's rebuke. "Go on, Mr. Holmes. I admit I was wrong about you but I am enjoying watching you put it all together."

Holmes was unconcerned. "For your first point, Watson, I refer you to Oldridge's editor. He spoke of Oldridge's unimpeachable reputation for integrity and his poor health. This made him perfect on two grounds. To begin with, he was not going to be capable of resisting Gardner's attack. Furthermore, as a witness, his word was unlikely to be seriously questioned thus ensuring Gardner was not suspected. You will recall how disturbed Gardner was when Oldridge collapsed at Baker Street nearly seriously wounding himself on our mantelpiece. If that had happened Gardner could have lost his unimpeachable witness and alibi.

"For points two and three we have one answer. Gardner's editor spoke of how he got into conflicts in the interests of justice. All of these were probably genuine except the one the day before his arrival on our doorstep. That argument in the public house was clearly arranged. He staged an argument and got his confederate to strike him from behind. The fact it was a day earlier and lightly done accounts for the fact the lump on Gardner's head was smaller than that of Oldridge.

It was already starting to go down which was harder for you to see through his youthful head of hair.

"I suspect the same confederate delivered the notes according to a plan. I very much doubt he knew he was abetting a murderer though. When this reaches the newspapers, I doubt he will rush to come forward."

Graham had gone through a variety of emotions while Holmes had been speaking. Anger at the low opinion held of him by Gardner and happiness as he realised how good he was going to look when he took the inevitable credit. Now he was frowning.

"All well and good, Holmes," he said. "But why?"

"Ah," said Holmes. "There we will need Mr. Gardner. The house was so perfect for his purpose, I theorised Gardner must have some claim on it. That was the purpose of our trip to Lincoln's Inn Fields, Watson. I learned the house is owned by a Mr. Geoffrey Thompson. A name which conveyed something to my mind. A trip to Somerset House revealed one G. Thompson, a widower, once married to a Jane Gardner. Your late mother I presume, sir?"

Gardner no longer looked pleased. "Yes, Mr. Holmes. I am gratified to see you put it all together but you have finally reached the hardest part of the story. I know I am for the rope but I regret nothing. What I have done was a duty as well as a pleasure. I am more than happy to tell you the rest so the world hears it.

"It all began twenty years ago. I was a boy of eleven. My two colleagues were star reporters in their thirties. My father was on the board of The Metropolitan Bank. Does that mean something to you, Mr. Holmes?"

Holmes snapped his fingers. "The Metropolitan Scandal."

Gardner's earlier cocksure posture had been replaced with acute sadness. "My father, along with his fellow board members, stood accused of investing customers' money for personal gain. It led to the collapse of the bank with thousands of people losing significant sums.

"My father was little more than the dupe of his fellow board members but was accused along with them largely thanks to the reporting of one William Scott, then at the *Evening Standard*. In several articles, he inferred and he suggested, always remaining just the right side of the law, until my father stood condemned in the court of public opinion. My mother hanged herself from shame and her death sent my father, although later exonerated, to an institution."

"No action was taken against Scott?" asked Holmes.

"None," came the bitter reply. "The silver-tongued villain managed to convince the authorities he had been misled by his sources and had acted in good faith. The fact he was wrong did him no harm. The improved circulation he achieved for his employers, who merely had to print tame retractions, made him highly sought after and his career went from strength to strength."

"What happened to you?" I asked.

"I was sent to my maternal grandmother in Kent," replied Gardner. "She was kind to me and suggested I adopt my mother's family name to avoid association with the scandal."

"So, you knew all that had happened?" asked Graham.

"I was eleven, Inspector. I was not stupid."

"Temper, Mr. Gardner," said Holmes, sternly.

"For as long as I can remember," continued Gardner, "I have felt the need for justice. I figured that the best way to Scott, and to be in the know, was to also be a reporter. As soon as I was able, I made every effort to get into journalism. You cannot just walk into Fleet Street though. You must work your way up. I started locally and made a name for myself for being the subject of reports almost as much as the author of them."

"I have a certain level of admiration for your dedication," said Holmes, "even if I cannot approve of your results."

Gardner bowed his head. "I truly appreciate that, Mr. Holmes. I sincerely regret misjudging you. Had I not brought you into this, I might have succeeded."

Holmes inclined his head towards Inspector Graham before turning back to Gardner.

"Quite," he said.

"When did Oldridge come into this," I asked.

At this question, Gardner brightened up. "That was one of my greatest strokes of fortune. Oldridge has many qualities but one glaring failing. He forgets people that are of no use to him. He and I crossed paths at the *Evening Standard*, about seven years ago, after Scott had moved on. As a young and inexperienced reporter, I was barely worthy of his notice. I shadowed him, and learned a lot, but years later, when we were both working for different papers, he didn't appear to recognise me. He enjoyed such a good reputation in Fleet Street, and with the police, that when I conceived my plan, and knew I needed an alibi, he was my first choice."

Holmes looked at the floor and tapped it with his cane absentmindedly. "I am truly sorry to see such potential go to waste. You have a sharp mind, sir, and it could have been put to such better use."

"I cannot agree," said Gardner. "I feel I put it to excellent use. My parents are avenged and a dangerous man has been prevented from ruining any more lives."

We left him there. A short visit was paid to Oldridge to inform him of his impending freedom. His happiness was, however, tinged with sadness. Surprisingly, he was not angry with Gardner. He went on to declare he would submit one last article to his paper before retiring.

Holmes was keen to return to the familiar surroundings of Baker Street. Upon our arrival, I realised how exhausted I was. I sat down and promptly fell asleep. When I woke, I found I was alone. It was now early evening and I could hear footsteps.

Holmes walked into the room. "Ah, Watson," he said. "I trust you feel refreshed. I have just been out for the evening paper." He held it out. "Would you care to?"

I took it from him and he took his seat. He lit a cigarette and reclined.

I read the paper quickly, still a little too tired to take in the finer points. My eyes alighted on something which arrested my attention. "Holmes!"

"What is it, Watson?"

I prodded the newspaper. "This."

He stood and moved to stand behind me. He gazed over my shoulder to where my finger lay. At that point it simply stated:

"To S.H. Very well done."

The Adventure of the Bedridden Widow

(Late 1896)

"WELL, well," said Sherlock Holmes.

"What is it?" I asked.

The morning post had just arrived and Holmes was standing by the window, reading one of the many letters. "I have a letter here from a Miss Isobelle Wolsey in which she asks to come and see me about her employer. She feels her employer's life is in danger."

"Does she name her employer?"

"Yes. It is not a name that means anything to me. Lady Sarah Dudley."

I knew the name. "I can help you there, Holmes. Lady Dudley is the widow of Sir Roger Dudley who died some ten years ago."

Holmes's eyebrows rose. "You never cease to amaze. How do you know this?"

"It comes within my sphere, Holmes. Sir Roger Dudley was a famous horse owner and trainer. It is a sad story."

Holmes sat and proceeded to light a cigarette. "Please enlighten me."

"He rose to prominence in the service of the Prince of Wales. He became successful and wealthy and bought a considerable estate in

Derbyshire. Soon after he left the service of the Crown, he was knighted."

Holmes frowned. "I cannot help but feel that the clouds are gathering."

"Quite so," I replied. "Lady Dudley was rather fond of high-living and she attracted something of a bad following. She was often tempted into making sizeable investments in schemes that usually did not go well. Sir Roger would not refuse her anything and she almost ruined him. It took its toll on his health and he eventually suffered a fatal heart attack. Due to the royal connection, it was in newspapers both here and across Europe. Gossips said that Lady Dudley had driven her husband to his death and she was universally derided."

"Anything further?" asked Holmes.

"It seems," I continued, "that Sir Roger, fearing his end, explained everything at length to his solicitor and the information was passed onto his son, George. He inherited a substantial sum from his grandparents, on his twenty-first birthday, which had been held in trust. Following his father's death, he was able to use this money to save the family home and clear most of his father's debts. Unsurprisingly, George Dudley blamed his mother and kicked her out of the house. He set her up in a modest house in Sussex called Eight Elms. He announced he wanted as little to do with her as possible."

"I imagine it was quite the adjustment for Lady Dudley to go from an open chequebook to nothing?" observed Holmes.

"Her son was not *that* cruel," I said. "According to reports, he provided an allowance that was sufficient to run the house, and leave her a little over, but she certainly could not lead the life she was used to. It is believed that she has chafed at this limitation ever since but keeps quiet, publicly, for fear of losing what little she does receive."

"And now it seems she is threatened," observed Holmes. "Relations between mother and son are certainly bad when an employee wishes to discuss her safety rather than her own kin."

The next day, we were called upon by Miss Wolsey. She stood a little over five feet, had light brown hair, and piercing hazel eyes. Her age appeared to be no more than thirty. The absence of any rings suggested she was unmarried – a fact I found surprising given her many advantages.

After the initial greetings, Holmes bade her to sit. "I thank you for your letter, Miss Wolsey. As you can imagine, I have questions."

"Of course," she replied. "Please ask them, Mr. Holmes."

"How did you come to be in Lady Dudley's employ?"

She frowned. "I know I described myself as such but, to be quite correct, I am actually employed by her son."

"Please explain."

"We are going back about five years. I had recently left the employ of Major and Mrs. Fairfax. I had been governess to their son but they had made the decision to emigrate to South Africa. I was offered a position with them over there but I had no desire to leave England. My mother is a widow and not in the best of health, so I wished to be as near to her as possible. Because of this I have rarely sought employment outside of Sussex.

"The Fairfaxes kindly furnished me with excellent references, before they left the country, and I moved back to my mother's house on the outskirts of Chichester. Once installed, I immediately made enquiries at the best employment agencies."

"Is your mother your sole relative?" asked Holmes.

"Yes," she replied. "I was an only child and my father died when I was fifteen. A result of this, and my mother's poor health, was that I became fiercely independent and self-reliant.

"Sadly, after several months, I had failed to secure a new position and my financial situation was becoming perilous. I realised I would need to consider alternatives to my usual occupation and approached further agencies.

"This decision bore fruit and I was called in to see Mrs. Hodges at her agency in the centre of Chichester. When I entered her office, I saw that a man was with her, seated near to the window. Mrs. Hodges introduced him as Mr. George Dudley.

"He strode over to take my hand. 'Delighted to meet you, Miss Wolsey,' he said. 'I understand you seek a new situation and I feel, having learned something of your past from Mrs. Hodges, and having read your excellent references, you would be ideal for a position with my mother.'"

"Did you know anything of the Dudleys prior to this?" asked Holmes.

"I had read of the death of Sir Roger," she replied, "but I had no idea, at that moment, that I was dealing with the same family. I asked what my duties would be.

"'My mother requires someone to act as her secretary,' he said.

"Now, Mr. Holmes, being a secretary was not something I was eager to entertain and I think this showed in my face. Mrs. Hodges spoke up. 'I think, Mr. Dudley, it would be an idea to inform Miss Wolsey of the salary attached to the position.'

"'Of course, Mrs. Hodges. The salary, Miss Wolsey, will commence at one hundred pounds a year.'"

I whistled.

"I was astounded, Mr. Holmes," said Miss Wolsey. "I had earned eighty pounds a year with Major Fairfax and that was considered above the going rate at the time. This was another prospect entirely. I enquired after my duties and was told they mostly consisted of dealing with correspondence and running the household."

"You accepted?" asked Holmes.

"Yes. I admit it was not a position I would have sought but the salary was astounding and I was in no position to turn it down. After all, I had my mother to think of as well as myself. As soon as I agreed, Mr. Dudley clapped his hands in delight. Then, bizarrely, he asked Mrs. Hodges if he might have a moment in private with me."

"That seems a little irregular," I remarked.

"I agree, Doctor. Mrs. Hodges was none too pleased to be evicted from her own office but I am forced to assume she had her mind on her commission. As soon as she was out of the room, Mr. Dudley picked up a chair and brought it close to me. He sat little more than four feet from me and leant forward. I felt a little uncomfortable, to say the least.

"He lowered his voice almost to a whisper. 'I could not say this in front of Mrs. Hodges,' he said, 'and I must ask that you treat what I am about to say with the utmost confidentiality.'

"I gave my word.

"'Miss Wolsey,' he said. 'My mother receives a modest allowance from me which is enough to run her household. Recently she succumbed to a mysterious illness that has confounded her doctors and left her bedridden. Because of this, she approached me for extra funds. I have reason to be cautious about these claims. My motive for engaging you is to act as I have laid out but also to report to me on the veracity of my mother's claims.'

"'You wish me to spy on your mother?' I asked.

"He grimaced as if he had encountered a foul stench. 'That is an unpleasant way of putting it. I simply wish you to monitor my mother's health over and above your other duties. You are clearly a strong woman and the kind of person capable of handling my mother. I will require regular written reports.'"

"You did not have second thoughts about the position?" asked Holmes.

"Naturally, I did. But, as I have said, I was not really in a position to refuse. I resolved to take up the post and give notice if I felt I was being asked to go too far."

"When did you begin your duties?"

"The following week. I had agreed with Mr. Dudley that I was to live at Eight Elms but could visit my mother at any time. It was a cab journey of about forty minutes from my mother's house to Lady Dudley's. The property is a large, isolated one even though it is not too far from Chichester.

"I was met at the door by Jeavons, the butler. I later learned that, aside from myself, he was the only staff member to reside in the house. All of Lady Dudley's other needs were met by people from the surrounding towns and villages who came to cook, clean, and maintain the grounds."

"How did your initial meeting with Lady Dudley proceed?" asked Holmes.

Miss Wolsey frowned as she recalled the occasion. "Due to her illness, Lady Dudley's bedroom is on the ground floor. It is towards the rear of the house and, from its design, I took it to be the former drawing room.

"The curtains were partly drawn so light was reduced. Propped up in a large, ornate bed was Lady Dudley. I was quite shocked."

"Why was that?" asked Holmes.

"I understood her to be around fifty-five years of age," said Miss Wolsey, "but she looked older. 'So, you are the woman my son has sent to spy on me,' she said.

"'I have been engaged to be your secretary, M'lady,' I responded.

"Propped up in a large, ornate bed was Lady Dudley."

"She smirked. 'You may call it what you like. I know my son's thinking.'"

"She seems to have the measure of her son," remarked Holmes.

"Her candour was quite alarming," said Miss Wolsey. "She proceeded to explain, or complain, that she had no money of her own. Her son had laid down a monthly amount and all bills had to be seen by him. One of my tasks was to ensure he received them regularly. She explained he had doubled the amount in view of her illness but it was not enough and he refused to consider more."

Holmes rose from his chair and went to the window. He stared down onto the hustle and bustle of Baker Street. I felt a need to fill the void. "Presumably it has gone well if you are still with Lady Dudley after five years?"

"Yes, Doctor Watson," she replied.

"In that case," said Holmes, from the window, without turning round, "why are you here now, fearing for Lady Dudley's life?"

Miss Wolsey sighed. "It is a strange tale."

Holmes turned. "Then kindly tell it."

"A few months after I had commenced working for Lady Dudley, she received a telegram from southern France."

"What did it say?"

"It was from a Mr. Banville of Marseille. He was a French solicitor. He requested a meeting regarding a family by the name of Turenne."

"How did Lady Dudley react?"

"She was confused, Mr. Holmes, and a little angry. She told me she had been close friends at school with another pupil called Annabelle Carstairs who had, many years later, met a minor aristocrat and successful businessman, by the name of Turenne, in London. They had later married and returned to his native France. Mrs. Turenne had never returned to England, and Lady Dudley explained that she had heard nothing from her."

"Did she agree to an interview?" asked Holmes.

"Yes. I wired back her acceptance and the meeting took place a week later."

"Did you meet this Mr. Banville?"

"Upon his arrival, yes. His English was not particularly good but he was able to make himself understood. I showed him into Lady Dudley and she asked me to leave. They spoke for almost two hours and he then left."

"It seems rather a long way to travel for a two-hour interview," observed Holmes.

"I agree. Lady Dudley asked to see me shortly after he left. When I entered her room, I could see she was excited."

"'It would appear,' she said, 'that my old friend and her husband have been killed in a carriage accident. Mr. Banville has informed me that, in Mrs. Turenne's will, I have been asked to act as a kind of legal appointee to their daughter Louise.'

"'How do you propose to do that from England?' I asked.

"'I am merely needed to counter-sign documents on occasion. Mr. Banville will act as my agent. It was that arrangement which he came here to discuss.'

"I suggested to Lady Dudley that it might be an idea to bring Louise to England. She was averse to the idea."

"Did she say why?" I asked.

"She said it would not be fair to take the girl from familiar surroundings after all she had been through."

"How old was Louise at this time?" asked Holmes.

"At the time, she was fifteen."

"Ah, so she would be twenty now?"

"Around that age, Mr. Holmes. Before I left her room, Lady Dudley informed me that she had a request."

"And what was that?"

"She said this matter was no business of her son as it did not concern finances or the running of Eight Elms. She ordered me not to report of it, and all letters or other communications from France were to be brought to her unopened. I was to see nothing further as it was not either my concern or that of her son."

"How did you feel about that?"

"I had no great difficulty with it, Mr. Holmes. As she said, it was separate from what I had been asked to do and did not concern her finances. I was there to report on her health and spending to her son. I was not there to do any more than that."

"Was there much communication from France?"

"Quite a lot at first. I understand this was for the initial legal papers required to put the arrangement in place. Once or twice, Jeavons and I were required to act as witnesses when Lady Dudley signed documents. After that, communication reduced to about one or two letters per month. Mr. Banville would send a monthly report on Louise and would occasionally ask for Lady Dudley's signature on further papers. To an extent, I am surmising, Mr. Holmes because I saw nothing. I often took Lady Dudley's replies to post in Chichester but the exact contents were unknown to me."

"And what of Miss Turenne?" asked Holmes.

"She writes to Lady Dudley to keep her informed about her life. I am told she has expressed, on more than one occasion, a desire to visit England and come to the house."

"Does she write directly?" asked Holmes.

"No. Her letters come via Mr. Banville."

"You are telling us Louise Turenne does not know Lady Dudley's address?"

"She knows which county, but that is all."

"I must confess," said Holmes, "that I find this unusual. Mrs. Turenne entrusts something akin to the guardianship of her child to her old schoolfriend, Lady Dudley, and the latter seems averse to direct contact."

"Lady Dudley has not welcomed any questions," said Miss Wolsey. "I tried, on several occasions, to raise the matter. I got told, in no uncertain terms, it was not my business. Her replies to Louise go back via the same route."

"Bizarre though this is," said Holmes. "It does not sound like a situation that would threaten Lady Dudley's life."

Miss Wolsey continued. "Six weeks ago, I took Lady Dudley an envelope that had come from France. She opened it and I could see there were two letters. She took out the first and began to read it. The blood drained from her face and she picked up and read the second. Her mood changed for the worse. I was naturally concerned and asked her what the matter was."

"'I suppose it will do no harm to tell you,' she said. 'As you know, you are not permitted to see any of my French correspondence. About six months ago I received a letter from Louise telling me she had fallen in love with a man she had met at a ball in Marseille. They had become engaged after a few months and, a few weeks ago, Louise asked me for money to pay for their wedding.'

"'Did you agree?' I asked her.

"'Yes,' she replied. 'At the same time, I asked Mr. Banville to make enquiries into this young man. It transpired he had a decidedly questionable past. I instructed Mr. Banville to inform Louise that I advised against the match and would no longer contribute towards any wedding. Mr. Banville has passed me this letter from her.'

"Lady Dudley handed me the second letter, Mr. Holmes. It was the first time I had seen any of them. As I read it, I could see the reason for Lady Dudley's distress. It was a vile letter, written in decidedly poor English. In it, Louise accused Lady Dudley of reneging on her promise and threatened dire consequences if the money was not provided by a certain date."

"Was there anything else in it?" asked Holmes.

"No. Lady Dudley said Mr. Banville was keeping a close eye on Louise. She took the letter back and placed it in her bedside table."

Holmes thought for a moment. "What date was given by Louise Turenne?"

"It was set at exactly one week later."

"So, what happened when the money was not provided?"

"A letter arrived from Mr. Banville to report that Louise had gone missing and was presumed to be on her way to England. Her fiancé was also missing and presumed to be with her."

"Do you know his name by any chance?" asked Holmes.

"I'm afraid not," replied Miss Wolsey. "Lady Dudley spoke little of the subject after Lousie's letter."

"So," said Holmes, "Mr. Banville reported that he believed Louise to be on her way, in the company of her fiancé, with the intention of doing Lady Dudley harm. What did her son think of this?"

"He didn't know."

"He was not told?"

"No. I was forbidden to do so."

"Why?"

"Lady Dudley was dismissive of Mr. Banville's theory. She said Louise did not have either the money or the temperament to carry out such a plan. 'She has more likely eloped with this young man and will get married in some run-down little church. She may do as she pleases. My duty is done.'"

"Yet," said Holmes. "I must assume Miss Turenne was more determined than Lady Dudley foresaw."

"Yes, Mr. Holmes."

"Please continue."

"One week later, Lady Dudley informed me she intended to engage a maid. She asked me to write to her son and seek the funds for such a position. He wrote back to say it was acceptable provided the wage was not above the going rate.

"I told Lady Dudley this and she dictated letters to a few agencies seeking girls who could fill the position. She was sent the details of some half-a-dozen and she arranged to see them three days later."

"What did you think of them?" asked Holmes.

"I did not meet them. On the day they were all due to be interviewed, I was asked by Lady Dudley to go into Chichester on a number of errands. They were the kind of errands Jeavons would normally undertake but he was not well.

"When I returned, Lady Dudley informed me she had seen all six girls but none had been suitable. She wrote to the agencies to enquire about further girls but quickly seemed to lose interest in the idea. When I asked about this, she said it was no longer a priority."

"Were there any further letters from France?" asked Holmes.

"That was curious, Mr. Holmes," said Miss Wolsey. "Lady Dudley continued to write to Mr. Banville. She was, she told me, enquiring as to whether Louise had been found. However, I don't recall her receiving replies. This seemed to annoy her and she sent Jeavons into Chichester to make enquiries at the post office. He came back and said they had received no letters from France. Telegrams also went unanswered. It occurred to me that Mr. Banville may have come to harm.

"Three weeks ago, I was having dinner in the dining room. Lady Dudley, due to her illness, always ate in her room. About ten minutes after sitting down there was the sound of breaking glass. I ran into the hall and encountered Jeavons who had clearly also heard it. We both ran into Lady Dudley's room. She was propped up in her bed and staring towards what was left of the French windows. On the floor was a brick.

"'It was Louise,' said Lady Dudley, who was visibly concerned.

"I ran to the windows. It was dusk but, in the distance, I could just make out a woman running away from the house. She was a long way off and appeared to be making for the wall at the end of the garden."

"How did you know it was a woman?" asked Holmes.

"I could see she was wearing a dress."

"This wall," said Holmes. "Is it high?"

"About six feet," said Miss Wolsey.

"Did anyone go in pursuit?"

"No. Lady Dudley said not to. Strangely, she immediately started to doubt herself. 'No, it cannot have been Louise,' she said. 'What was I thinking?' We were ordered to think no more of it. She decided it was a dangerous prank by someone local and we should arrange repairs in the morning. Jeavons was ordered to board up the French windows and they were later repaired." Miss Wolsey paused to drink some water.

"Please continue, Miss Wolsey," said Holmes.

"A few days later, Jeavons brought a note to Lady Wolsey. He said it had been handed to him by a boy. Lady Dudley opened it and started to tremble. I moved to a position where I could see it."

"What did it say?" asked Holmes.

"It simply said 'I am here.'"

"From Miss Turenne," I exclaimed.

"Yes. Even Lady Dudley started to reconsider her opinion of the earlier incident. I said we should involve the police but she still would not hear of it. 'Are you going to ask the police to search the county because of broken glass?' she asked.

"'But she threatened your life,' I said.

"'Not explicitly,' said Lady Dudley. 'Despite this note, we have no evidence Louise is even in the country. The police would laugh at us.'"

"Lady Dudley was not necessarily wrong," said Holmes. "The police would indeed be likely to put it down to a prank."

"They cannot do so now," said Miss Wolsey. "Several days ago, I was again having dinner when there was a loud bang. I ran to Lady Dudley's room and she was pale. 'Louise tried to shoot me. Jeavons has gone after her.'

"I ran to the French windows, which had a bullet hole in them. I could see a girl running away with a man in pursuit. 'Stay with me, Isobelle,' ordered Lady Dudley.

"Jeavons returned, out of breath, some minutes later. He said the girl had easily got away from him and had shouted abuse at him in French from the top of the wall before disappearing. The only word he heard in English, after she had dropped to the other side, was 'tomorrow.'"

"You must have gone to the police?" I said.

"Yes. There was no alternative now. The local inspector took the matter seriously. Lady Dudley is well-known in the area and is on good terms with the chief-superintendent. Inspector Hawkins was shown Louise's original letter as well as the later note. Taking the threat at face value, he put constables on duty around the house."

"And what happened?" asked Holmes.

"Nothing. The next day came and went without incident. The police remained in the grounds for three days with no result. Eventually, Inspector Hawkins requested an interview and suggested the withdrawal of the police presence. In his view, Louise had been scared off. I was concerned at this course of action but Lady Dudley agreed with the inspector. The police stayed one more night and withdrew in the morning. That's when I made my decision."

"Which was?"

"To come to you, Mr. Holmes. Louise seems intent on doing Lady Dudley some harm. The police have withdrawn and she is defenceless."

"What does her son think?"

"After the latest incident, I naturally wrote a report for him. He was sufficiently concerned to suggest she return to Derbyshire until such time as Louise was located."

"Something of a volte-face on his part," said Holmes.

"I thought it incredibly kind of him, under the circumstances," said Miss Wolsey. "But Lady Dudley poured scorn on the idea. 'I have no desire to return to that house.' I was ordered to decline the offer. Her son did not make it again."

"What does Lady Dudley think of my involvement?" asked Holmes.

"I have not told her. I suspect she will not be pleased."

Soon after this, Miss Wolsey left us. Holmes informed her we would be down as soon as possible the next day. After she left, he headed out to send some telegrams. When he returned, some hours later, he looked excited.

"That was a long time to send a few telegrams," I observed.

He smiled. "I thought it prudent to carry out some research into Miss Wolsey's story. The society pages of past newspapers rarely disappoint. It seems Lady Dudley and Madame Turenne were quite the society ladies, prior to their marriages, and considered great beauties.

"My researches have demonstrated that Sir Roger and Henri Turenne were business partners and spent considerable time in each other's company whenever the latter was in London. They encountered their respective wives at a ball in Mayfair and two unions were born."

"Yet," I observed, "the two women do not appear to have kept in touch once the Turennes left England? That is unusual for close friends."

"It is strange from end to end," replied Holmes. "Lady Dudley acts as legal representative for the orphaned daughter of an old friend but refuses to meet her. You told me her husband's death was reported across Europe. Did Madame Turenne not see those reports? In her place I would have thought long and hard about entrusting such power to a lady so accused, no matter how long our friendship. One is forced to assume she was aware of the reports but refused to believe them."

"I can see that," I said.

"But the anger in this girl is also curious. I can imagine she would be hurt at the refusal to meet her. A child orphaned at such an impressionable age would naturally thirst for knowledge of her mother from old friends. Having this denied would be painful but would hardly warrant threats of harm."

"But Lady Dudley denied her funds for her wedding," I said.

"True. But that would not stop her marrying. It would merely affect the size of the celebration. If Lady Dudley had prevented the marriage altogether, I might see the motivation. Now we are led to believe that both Louise and her fiancé are in England and conspiring to do Lady Dudley harm."

"What were the telegrams you sent?"

"As you know, Watson, I have my contacts at the shipping companies. I have enquired if Miss Turenne appears on any passenger logs. The first course of action is to determine if she is indeed in England. As we are heading to Chichester first thing. I have asked that the answer be delivered to Inspector Hawkins at Chichester Police Station."

Mid-morning the next day we found ourselves in Chichester. We took a cab directly to the police station. Holmes had wired ahead so Inspector Hawkins was waiting for us.

"Good morning to you both," he said, shaking our hands. "I am surprised you came all the way from London for this."

He led us inside to his office. We took seats and Hawkins slid an envelope across his desk. This telegram arrived for you, sir."

Holmes opened it and smiled. "Well, Inspector. It seems Miss Turenne and her fiancé have indeed landed on our shores. She and a Mr. Allard arrived in Dover only days before the first incident at Eight Elms."

The inspector frowned. "You have good contacts, Mr. Holmes. Naturally, I would have made the same inquiry if Lady Dudley had not dismissed the idea that Miss Turenne was in England."

"We have spoken at length with her secretary," said Holmes. "What do you know of Lady Dudley's current thoughts on the matter?"

"We have not discussed it since the day I withdrew the police presence from her grounds," said Hawkins. "As far as I know, she has not been troubled since. I did inform her we would drop by once each evening, just to check. I also said the time would vary just in case this Miss Turenne was watching the house."

"How did Lady Dudley react?"

Hawkins frowned. "She was not grateful, Mr. Holmes. She said it was pointless and asked the chief superintendent to withdraw the arrangement. He has delegated the responsibility on this matter to me, which has not pleased Lady Dudley. My intention is to keep it in place for a few weeks at most."

"Watson and I will go and pay our respects," said Holmes. "Before we do, do you have the letters from Miss Turenne?"

Hawkins opened his drawer and produced two pieces of paper. "Here you are, Mr. Holmes."

Holmes studied them. "The standard of English is decidedly below par. Both letters are in the same hand and neither is forged."

"How do you know?" asked Hawkins.

"The fluidity of the writing precludes it," said Holmes. "A forgery tends to be slow and methodical because the forger is focused on accuracy. A natural letter will show signs of speed typically absent in a forgery."

We took our leave of the inspector and obtained a cab to Eight Elms. It was a reasonable distance from Chichester and Holmes regarded the open country with suspicion. About half-an-hour later we arrived at the beginning of the drive. It was a strange kind of house, not more than one hundred years old judging by the style. It was large, I estimated it had around six or seven bedrooms, but would certainly be small to an aristocrat used to grander surroundings.

We knocked and were admitted by Jeavons. Miss Wolsey met us in the hallway as the butler went to announce our arrival. "Lady Dudley is not happy, Mr. Holmes. I honestly believe if she could dismiss me, she would."

"Can she not?" I asked.

"No, Doctor. My presence is one of her son's conditions for her allowance. I do fear that any trust that existed between us has gone. It may be in my interests to leave."

"Do not be hasty, Miss Wolsey," said Holmes.

The butler returned and asked us to follow him. We left Miss Wolsey and entered Lady Dudley's room.

"My secretary overstepped," said Lady Dudley, omitting any greeting. "I am in no danger and I am sorry you came all this way to no purpose."

"Good day, Lady Dudley," said Holmes. "Miss Wolsey wisely consulted me out of concern for you."

"I am not insensible to that," she replied. "I am sure she has told you the history. But days have gone by since the last incident and I am not convinced it is Louise Turenne."

"I have been able to confirm that Miss Turenne arrived in England," said Holmes.

Lady Dudley seemed shocked and angry. "You have?"

"Yes. In the company of a Mr. Allard. Is that name familiar to you?"

Lady Dudley looked confused. "Yes. I believe that was the young man's name."

"Is it possible to see the letters Louise sent you?" asked Holmes.

"No. You may not," she replied.

"May I ask why?"

Lady Dudley smiled. "It is not stubbornness on my part, Mr. Holmes. I simply don't have them any longer. I was so outraged by Louise's threatening letter, which the police now hold, that I had Jeavons burn all her past letters."

"That is unfortunate," said Holmes. "I had hoped they might contain further indications that might aid us in locating her. Is it possible to see Mr. Banville's reports?"

"Unfortunately," said Lady Dudley, "my butler burnt all Mr. Banville's reports, in error, as they were kept in the same drawer as Louise's letters."

"How unfortunate," remarked Holmes. "May I look around the grounds?"

"May I ask why?"

"I'll be candid, Lady Dudley. The police are disinclined to withdraw their men from you entirely. You are, after all, a lady of influence. I quite understand how you find that intrusive. If I can satisfy them as to the security of your house, I might be able to persuade them."

Lady Dudley smiled. "In that case, please proceed."

Holmes walked from the foot of the bed, where he had been standing to address Lady Dudley, to the French windows, which were at right angles to the bed and towards the far end of the room. He examined them before opening them and stepping outside. I followed him onto the rear lawn.

"I can just make out the route taken by the girl and Jeavons," he said. He set off and I followed. The lawn was extensive and it took almost two minutes to reach the wall.

"This wall is closer to seven feet in height," said Holmes. "How did this girl scale it with the butler on her heels?"

He looked around. "Aha."

I followed his gaze. There was a wheel barrow propped up against the wall.

"Hmm," said Holmes. "It seems rather rusty and weak." He placed a foot onto it and it almost immediately gave way. "I struggle to see this being used. Even if it were, how did she know it was there in the first place?"

We retraced our steps back to Lady Dudley's room. "Well, Mr. Holmes?" she said.

"I am satisfied it will be difficult for a further intrusion to be made. I will speak to the police."

"Thank you, Mr. Holmes." She gestured to the butler. "Jeavons will show you out."

The butler led us to the hall where Miss Wolsey had remained. Holmes took her to one side as the butler fetched our coats. "Can you let me have the details of the domestic agencies Lady Dudley applied to?"

"Of course, Mr. Holmes," she replied. She fetched some paper and wrote down the details.

"We returned to Chichester and the police station. Holmes instructed Hawkins to remove the police the following day and inform Lady Dudley. The inspector expressed concern but knew enough of Holmes's reputation to agree. He also handed my friend some further telegrams that had arrived while we had been at Eight Elms.

Holmes quickly read them. "I thought as much," he said, enigmatically.

A little later, we managed to secure a suite of rooms at a charming hotel. Just after six o'clock, we were relaxing with cigars, following an excellent dinner. Holmes took out a sheet of paper from his pocket. I asked him what it was.

"It is the list of agencies that Lady Dudley contacted in search of a maid. It has been bothering me why she wanted a maid, and went to the trouble of interviewing, only to give up on the idea."

"Do you intend to visit them?"

"Tomorrow," he replied, "there is no need to hurry."

About forty minutes later, Inspector Hawkins arrived. "Well, Mr. Holmes. Lady Dudley has been informed that, as you requested, after tomorrow afternoon, we will no longer be checking on her property. I am uneasy about it though."

"Worry not, Inspector," said Holmes. "Watson and I will be vigilant. Did you pass my message to Lady Dudley?"

The inspector nodded and departed.

"What do you know, Holmes?" I asked.

His face darkened. "I believe a terrible crime is contemplated. If a formidable lady is to be saved, we will need to be on our guard."

Holmes warned me that we would be visiting Eight Elms after dark the next day. I therefore rose later than normal, only a little before eleven. I met Holmes in the hotel reception before we headed out into the town. The hotel had stopped serving breakfast by the time we had risen, so we first went in search of a tea room. There I secured some sandwiches along with a pot of tea. Holmes accepted tea but declined anything to eat.

"If we are to visit Eight Elms tonight," I said. "What are we doing in the meantime?"

"After you finish your sandwiches," said Holmes, "we will call upon the agencies Lady Dudley was in communication with."

About thirty minutes later, sandwiches consumed, we headed for the first address. We entered a room in which a few ladies sat, presumably waiting to hear what situations were vacant. Holmes marched up to a young lady behind a desk and handed her his card. The lady looked startled before rising and walking to a door on which she knocked. She obeyed the invitation to enter and emerged a few moments later. "Mrs. Kendal will see you, gentlemen."

We walked into a spartan but smart office. A stern lady rose from behind her desk. "Good morning, gentlemen," she said. "I am Mrs. Kendal."

"Good day, madam," said Holmes. She invited us to sit and resumed her seat. "How can I help you?"

"I understand you were approached a few weeks ago about a vacancy for a maid at Eight Elms," said Holmes.

"We don't discuss our clients, sir."

"Please be reassured we are not seeking information about Lady Dudley," said Holmes. "I simply wished to know what the ladies who applied for the position said when they did not secure it."

Mrs. Kendal relaxed. Clearly, she did not regard the question as unreasonable. "I always ask my girls about their interviews. It helps me to better prepare them for future ones. As you can appreciate, gentlemen, I am only compensated when a position is secured."

"What did they tell you?" asked Holmes.

"A girl often on my books is Lilly Jones. She has been given notice a few times by past employers on account of her poor memory. But she is a hard worker so I do my best for her. When she came here, following her interview, she was confused."

"How so?"

"She told me she had barely entered the room when Lady Dudley began to doubt her suitability for the position. When Lilly asked why, she was told she was too short. It was a bizarre thing to say as height is not normally a key requirement to be a maid."

"Peculiar indeed," said Holmes.

"Another girl, Susan Murphy, said Lady Dudley had looked her up and down before rejecting her on the grounds she was too thin and did not look strong enough for hard work. Other girls told me similar stories. Only one, Jane Parker, came back to say it had gone well. She was positively beaming but said Lady Dudley had told her she would make a decision later. I received a note from Lady Dudley a few days subsequently to say she had changed her mind. Her reasoning was Miss Parker had been in court for petty theft and she did not want to run that risk. I communicated this to Miss Parker who did not seem too disappointed."

"Is it possible to meet this Jane Parker?" asked Holmes.

"I cannot help you," said Mrs. Kendal. "She secured a position through another agency, she told me, and has moved out of the county. I don't know where."

We bid Mrs. Kendal farewell. Back on the street, Holmes lit a cigarette and offered me one. "Lady Dudley certainly appears to be an eccentric woman. Not an uncommon characteristic for those of her class but odd, nonetheless."

A minute later, he dropped the cigarette and crushed it under his boot. We then made our way to the only other agency on the list.

Here we heard a similar story about girls seen and swiftly rejected. The proprietor of this agency, Mrs. Williams, told us one of her girls had briefly been considered before being rejected. Holmes, doing his best to make himself agreeable, managed to secure the young lady's details. We bade farewell to Mrs. Williams and headed straight for the address we had been given.

The house we arrived at five minutes later was a modest mid-terrace dwelling. An annoyed woman answered the door. "No salesmen," she barked.

"Excuse me," said Holmes. "We are not here to sell anything, Mrs. Martin. We wish to see your daughter, Alice, about a possible position. We were sent by Mrs. Williams."

The woman's face brightened immediately and she stepped out of the house. "Come in, gentlemen," she said, directing us inside.

We stepped into a cramped hallway. It was so narrow that the lady had to point us towards a room as she could not pass us to lead us there. We stepped into her front parlour. There were only two chairs.

"My girl has been looking for a position for weeks," said Mrs. Martin as she sat down. "Time and again she gets turned down. We need the money for the rent as my husband earns very little and I get a pittance for char work."

"We understand," said Holmes, "that Alice almost secured a position recently?"

"That she did, sir. She came back all smiles and said Lady Dudley was keen on her. Then, a few days later, we got a note saying the job was no longer open."

Mrs. Martin suddenly shouted for her daughter. We heard nervous feet on the stairs and a girl of about seventeen entered the room. "Yes, ma?" she said.

"These here gentleman may have a job for you."

Alice Martin looked at us like a frightened rabbit. "Yes, sir?"

Holmes and I had remained standing so Holmes requested Alice to sit on the remaining chair. She looked nervously at her mother as she did so. I was forced to wonder if she had ever been permitted to sit down in the room.

"Now, Alice," said Holmes. "I may have a position for you but I would dearly like to know what reason you were given for not getting the situation with Lady Dudley?"

Alice looked down at her feet. "When I went there, sir, I was told I was promising. Lady Dudley asked if I had ever been in trouble with the police. I said no, which is true, sir. She asked me about old employers and said she would be in touch with the agency."

"So, you had high hopes?" said Holmes.

"I did, sir. A couple of days later a note turns up saying there wasn't a position anymore."

"I am sure that was upsetting," said Holmes. "The position of which I speak is not with me. I am acting for another party. Would you have any aversion to working in London?"

The girl glanced at her mother and looked terrified. "London, sir?"

Mrs. Martin stepped in. "My little girl needs a job but I'm not having her in London. Horrible place."

"Alas, that settles the matter," said Holmes. "I'm sure you would have been ideal. I will report back to Mrs. Williams and be sure to let her know how suitable I found you. It may help you in your search for employment."

We made our excuses and Mrs. Martin ordered her daughter to show us out. At the door, Holmes took out his notebook and scribbled a few lines into it. He tore out the page and handed it to Alice. She read it and looked up. "Sir?"

"I know it is an unusual request, Miss Martin," he said, his voice rather low. "However, it promises excitement and will improve your prospects no end." He handed her a shilling. "Consider this an advance payment. I suggest you don't tell your mother."

The girl looked at the coin in her hand. "Very good, sir."

We walked a few hundred yards from the house. "What were you going to do if she had said yes to London?" I asked.

"There was little chance of that, Watson. Mrs. Martin is not a lady who likes to work. Despite professing to undertake char work, she does not have the hands a lifetime of such work would give. I suspect her husband brings in the money and her daughter is little more than an unpaid servant. It is her unwillingness to give up her daughter to a live-in position that has held the poor girl back. Hence, I knew a London situation would not be viewed favourably."

"Poor girl," I said. "What did you write in that note?"

"Wait and see, Watson."

We headed back to our hotel. "There's nothing more to do until tonight, my friend," said Holmes. "Make sure you are well-rested and meet me in the reception at seven this evening."

I met Holmes as arranged. It was now dark outside. We were soon joined by Inspector Hawkins. "I wish you'd tell me more about what we're up to."

"The less you know, Inspector, the better," said Holmes.

We climbed into a cab. Holmes gave the address of Eight Elms.

"Gentlemen, we are going keep watch on Lady Dudley. It will not be a long vigil. I expect it to all be done and dusted by ten at the latest."

He would say no more. When we approached the gate to Eight Elms, Holmes ordered the cabby to stop. We all alighted and Holmes paid the fare.

"It is important, gentlemen, that no one knows we are here. Keep to the grass and maintain the greatest possible distance from the house. We will walk round to where Lady Dudley's French windows are located. Fortunately, there are some shrubs nearby that we can conceal ourselves behind. No talking from here on in."

We did as he requested and, before long, we were behind the shrubs.

Thanks to a clear sky and an almost full moon, I was able to read my watch without requiring a match - the use of which Holmes had forbidden.

At a little after nine o'clock I spotted something. I tugged at Holmes's sleeve.

"I see her, Watson," he whispered.

Walking along the lawn, closer to the house than we had been, was a young girl. I could not make out her features but she was clearly around twenty years of age.

"Louise Turenne!" I exclaimed.

"Quiet, Watson," said Holmes.

The girl began to head for the French windows.

"Inspector," whispered Holmes, "are your men ready?"

"They are positioned as you asked, sir."

"Excellent. We must move now. Do not alert the girl to our presence. Follow in complete silence."

We rose from behind the shrubs and advanced towards the house. The girl was about twenty yards ahead of us and appeared to be trembling as she approached the window. Suddenly she stopped and we were forced to become as still as statues.

Equally suddenly, she ran towards the French windows. Her approach was erratic, running from side to side like a rugby player avoiding opponents in an effort to score a try. A gunshot was heard and she fell to the ground. I was horrified.

"Now, gentlemen!" said Holmes.

We ran at breakneck speed towards the girl who lay motionless on the grass. The French windows opened and Jeavons appeared, revolver in hand. He aimed it at the prone girl who was barely moving.

A shot rang out and Jeavons fell. I turned and saw the inspector holding his revolver. "Just in the leg, Doctor," he said.

Holmes reached the butler and seized the gun from the grass. "Help the girl, Watson."

I went to the prone body. She was shaking but uninjured. "Did I do it right, sir?"

I was shocked. "This is Alice Martin, Holmes. Did you put her up to this?"

"It was necessary, Watson." Without waiting, he advanced carefully on the French windows, gun raised. "Good evening, Lady Dudley."

I joined him in the room. Lady Dudley was sitting up in bed, clearly agitated. "What is the meaning of this, Mr. Holmes? The inspector informed me you had returned to London."

"It was what I wished you to think. Your plan has failed."

Hawkins ushered in a limping Jeavons who was ordered to sit on the floor. He pressed a handkerchief to his wound. Holmes unlocked the door to admit a frantic Miss Wolsey who had been banging on the other side. "Are you alright, M'lady?" she said.

"Lady Dudley is perfectly fine, Miss Wolsey," said Holmes. "The same nearly could not be said for this lady."

I turned at the sound of footsteps. Into the room stepped an attractive young woman. Behind her was an older gentlemen flanked by two constables.

"What is happening?" she asked with a decided French accent.

"May I present Miss Louise Turenne?" said Holmes.

The young woman was understandably perplexed. A condition I shared. "Why are you holding my guardian?" she asked, gesturing towards the older gentleman.

"Excuse me, Miss Turenne," said Holmes. "My name is Sherlock Holmes and Mr. Banville here does not have your best interests at heart."

"Nonsense," replied Miss Turenne. "He has taken me on a lovely tour of many English counties while we waited for the right time to come here."

"Had we not acted, Miss Turenne," said Holmes, "you would be lying dead on that lawn labelled as a madwoman."

The lady went to protest but Holmes held up his hand. "I will explain."

"That would be appreciated, Holmes," I said.

"Miss Turenne, you will soon turn twenty-one. At that point you gain full control of your inheritance. I regret to inform you that you will find it has been somewhat reduced."

"What do you mean, sir?" she asked.

"I mean," said Holmes, "that your two guardians have been helping themselves to your money since the death of your parents."

"I don't believe it," she said.

"You don't have to take my word," said Holmes. "You will soon have access to papers from your bank that will illustrate matters to you all too clearly. I have contacts in the French police who have long had suspicions about Mr. Banville here. A sample of his handwriting is being sought, and I am certain it will match the threatening letter and note sent to Lady Dudley.

"Did you know, Miss Turenne, that your parents' will leaves everything to Lady Dudley in the event of your death without issue?"

"No," she said, looking a little alarmed.

"You were close to the house when the police intercepted you. Did you hear the gunshot?"

"I did."

"Did you not think it odd that you had been asked to pay a social call on Lady Dudley at this time of night? Furthermore, that Mr. Banville here told you to come across the lawn rather than use the front door? Tell me, did he ask you to walk alone?"

"Yes, he did," she said, nervously.

"That was so he would not have any footprints near your body when you were shot by Lady Dudley's butler."

Miss Turenne looked unsettled. Holmes's words were starting to make sense to her. She looked pleadingly at Lady Dudley. "Is it true?"

I turned to look at Lady Dudley. Her face was contorted in anger.

"Get out of my sight," she shouted.

About an hour later we were back in the comfortable lounge of our hotel. Lady Dudley was under house arrest. The butler, after seeing a doctor, was in a cell and he had Mr. Banville for a neighbour. Louise Turenne had been installed in a hotel room to await an official from the French embassy.

"How did you figure it all out?" asked Inspector Hawkins.

"It began with three simple questions," said Holmes. "Why did a girl with an English mother have such poor English? Why did a solicitor come all the way from France to hold a meeting he could have handled by letter? Finally, why does a girl who is the heir to the estate of a successful businessman need to borrow money for a wedding?

"The answer to the first is she would not. What parent, is not going to gift their child their own mother tongue? Her mother was English and her father was an aristocrat conducting business in

England. It is likely they both spoke excellent English. The idea their daughter would not is absurd. You have since heard her, gentlemen. Her English is fluent.

"As to the second. Few are more aware of evidence than a solicitor. If such a man travels for a meeting when he could write, it suggests he does not want written evidence of what he wishes to say.

"The French police are looking into various matters I have drawn to their attention. They have already informed me that Mr. Turenne's estate was valued at close to one million pounds. His business is still operating, under a deputy, and continues to generate a profit."

"What do you think happened?" I asked.

"Mr. Banville is a good solicitor but I expect some weakness has left him close to bankruptcy. Mr. Turenne, unaware of this, appointed him to handle his estate. Imagine Banville's delight when he discovers Lady Dudley, whose high-living lifestyle and fall he had read all about, was appointed the girl's legal attorney and also a potential beneficiary of the estate. He sees a chance and writes to request an interview. Remember, according to Miss Wolsey, his English was poor but adequate.

"He arrives and starts hinting at what he has in mind. He was testing the water. If Lady Dudley had been honest and been offended, he could always claim to have made a mistake with his English to explain the offence.

"But he finds she responds positively so he becomes more and more candid about his idea. The plan is to use her power of attorney to plunder Miss Turenne's inheritance. Lady Dudley will sign the papers and he will move the money. They proceed to do this for five years and nobody suspects a thing."

"But why all this now?" I said.

"The clock was always ticking, Watson. At twenty-one Louise would take control and the power of attorney would expire. Then it would all come out. It would be hard to mask such a sustained period of theft. Lady Dudley knew from Banville that her old friend had made her the beneficiary of the will in the event of her daughter dying childless. Lady Dudley would inherit and ensure no questions were raised about the state of the finances."

"Is this why she refused to see Louise?" I asked.

"The reason is sadder still. I told you earlier, Watson, that Lady Dudley and Annabelle Carstairs had first met Louise's father at a Mayfair ball. The society columns strongly suggested Mr. Turenne was held in high esteem by both ladies. From this, I deduced that Lady Dudley settled for Sir Roger when her friend secured the affections of Henri Turenne - the man Lady Dudley really loved.

"She felt acute bitterness and wanted revenge against the friend she saw as having stolen the man she wanted. It speaks to her coldness that she kept this hidden from Madame Turenne.

"I think it is fair to assume she lied to Miss Wolsey when she said she was not in contact with her friend. I suspect there was a regular correspondence, kept from Miss Wolsey by Jeavons, which was filled with stories about Madame Turenne's life. Stories that further fuelled Lady Dudley's jealousy."

"But why refuse to see Louise?" I repeated.

"To Lady Dudley," said Holmes, "Louise was a reminder of a marriage that should not have happened. She wanted all such reminders to be gone and she also wanted the money to free her from a dependency on her son - who was also a reminder to her of an unwanted life."

"Such hatred," I remarked, sadly.

"Lady Dudley and Banville had had five years to both plunder Louise's money and come up with a plan to avoid detection. It was to paint Louise as a dangerous woman."

"How?"

"You already know. A letter arrived, supposedly via Banville, that threatened harm if money was not paid to fund a wedding. This created a motive. When we see examples of Banville's writing we will almost certainly see it matches that of the threat. Miss Wolsey saw the letter and mentioned the poor English. Lady Dudley had to show her as Miss Wolsey would then attest to the danger posed when questioned. When Lady Dudley told me all letters from Louise had been burnt along with those of Banville, I was immediately suspicious."

"I still don't understand how they were going to make it look credible," said Hawkins.

"Come now, Inspector," said Holmes. "The plan was cunning. Lady Dudley and Banville concoct the story that Louise is coming, along with her fiancé, to cause harm. In fact, Banville and Louise were enjoying a leisurely trip to England and a tour of the home counties. Banville travelled under a false name to masquerade as the fiancé in all records. Did it not strike you as odd that Louise Turenne would travel under her own name to commit a crime? It was all part of the plan to make her movements easy to trace and point to her unstable mind.

"Meanwhile, Lady Dudley needs to convince all around her that the threat is real. She decides to recruit a maid. An idea she later abandons after holding six interviews. She was looking for someone special."

"Someone to impersonate Louise," I exclaimed.

"Precisely, Watson. You will recall one was dismissed for being too thin, another for being too short. Only two fitted her requirements. They were Alice Martin and Jane Parker. Both were later told the position no longer existed. In reality, Jane Parker had been selected precisely because of the reason we were told she was rejected – her criminal past. Lady Dudley needed someone willing to break a window. Alice Martin was innocent and law-abiding. She was not likely to cooperate."

Inspector Hawkins spoke up. "So, she gets this girl to throw a brick through her French Windows. Miss Wolsey is in time to see a girl fleeing the house. I guess the idea was that when Miss Turenne was later killed, Miss Wolsey would be convinced it was the same girl she'd seen earlier?"

"Exactly, Inspector. This was later done again with the gun. Miss Wolsey enters the room to see Jeavons chasing after a girl. I'm prepared to wager that Jeavons fired the shot and pretended to chase this Jane Parker across the lawn. Very likely, when they got to the high wall, he helped her scale it. The talk of insults in French being a fabrication."

"But why did Lady Dudley keep asserting it was not Louise?" I asked.

"She wanted to plant the idea it was. However, if she did so too well, she would have a wall of police around her house and the plan could not be brought to its conclusion. She said it enough to convince those around her but then dismissed it consistently in an effort to get the guard withdrawn. That is why I asked Hawkins to withdraw it."

"Then Jeavons notifies Mr. Banville and he sends Louise to her death?" I suggested.

"Precisely. Had we not been on hand, she would have calmly walked to the French Windows, as directed by Banville, and been shot by Jeavons. They could have told the police anything and it would have been recorded as self-defence. Miss Wolsey would have aided this by attesting to Lady Dudley's version of events. Banville would have returned to France and resumed his true name and he and Lady Dudley would have divided the money."

"How will this all be proved?" asked Hawkins.

"Banville's handwriting will show him to be the author of the threatening letter and note. A fake passport will likely be found amongst his belongings as he will have needed it for his return journey. The French police will obtain the bank records that will show the plundering of the Turenne finances.

"Finally, if you manage to locate Jane Parker, you will be able to extract a confession of her part in this. She was almost certainly unaware of the intent to murder. Once she is aware she will likely tell all."

A few months later we read of the trial. Lady Dudley, Jeavons, and Mr. Banville were all jailed for attempted murder. The majority of the money taken by Lady Dudley was recovered and returned to Miss Turenne. Her overall losses were not too great and, with her father's business still running, she expected to make the money back in a few years.

Miss Turenne was kind enough to send Holmes a large cheque which he decided to accept. "Yes, Watson," he said, as he placed it into a pocket and patted it, "it is above my usual scale but it may help to look after me in my twilight years."

"Why did Lady Dudley not spend more of the money?" I asked.

"She could not," he replied. "She was pretending to be bedridden to obtain money from her son. Money she supposedly needed because she was ill. If Miss Wolsey noticed spending she could not account for, it would have got back to George Dudley and questions would have been asked. Lady Dudley had no wish to expose herself by spending money she was not supposed to have. This way she got even more money. Had the plan been successful, I'm sure she would have made a miraculous recovery and gone abroad where her son could not monitor her. Fortunately, we will never know."

I was not finished with Holmes. "I am not sure how I feel about the danger you put young Alice Martin in."

He smiled. "Don't let it trouble you too much, Watson. I advised her on how to reduce the risk of being wounded. That is why she ran the way she did. On my advice, she sold her story to the newspapers. She made enough money to escape her mother and is now working in London. Her future seems assured and she has a compelling anecdote to tell for the rest of her life."

The Adventure of the Monogrammed Napkins

(Early 1898)

"ATSON, make a long arm and pass me Debrett's."

My arm was not quite up to the task from where I sat. I put down my notebook, with a degree of irritation, and walked over to the shelf where Holmes kept a number of his reference books. I selected the most recent edition of that catalogue of the nobility and walked back to my friend who was waving a test tube under his nose in the manner that some might wield a glass of wine.

"Turn up the name Marden, would you?" he said, without lifting his head.

I opened the book and flipped through the pages. "There's a Sir Richard Marden, Baronet. His title has its origins in Sussex. Why the interest, Holmes?"

Without removing his nose from the test tube, Holmes passed me a piece of paper from the dining table. I saw it was a brief note and ran thus:

"Dear Mr. Holmes. I need your help regarding a recent dinner party. I will call at six, if convenient. Yours sincerely, Lady Caroline Marden."

I laughed. "You are giving advice on dinner parties?"

Holmes looked up, his face showing no signs of amusement. "I will admit my hopes are not high."

I looked to the mantelpiece. "It is five o'clock now."

He nodded. "That leaves me enough time to complete my present analysis." With that remark, he fell silent and I returned to my notebook. The aim of my afternoon had been to take some of my most recent notes and write them up for publication. However, I could no longer concentrate. Something about Lady Marden's note was seizing my imagination. Perhaps it was the absurdity of it, or the fact Holmes was even entertaining it. Consequently, the next hour passed slowly with the ticking of the clock seeming much louder than normal. The bell ringing finally put me out of my misery.

Following a short delay, the door was knocked on and opened by Mrs. Hudson. She stood back to admit a formidable looking woman who could only be Lady Marden. At almost six feet, she was somewhat above average height. She was around thirty years of age with dark brown hair and the most piercing blue eyes. She had an air of confidence that bordered on the intimidating. She looked from one to the other of us before settling her gaze upon Holmes.

"Mr. Holmes, I appreciate you seeing me."

Holmes offered a small bow. "I am at your service, Lady Marden. But I confess I struggle to see how I can assist you with a dinner party, past or future."

"Thanks to your colleague Dr. Watson," she said, "I am familiar with your cases, sir. I determined to couch my note in a manner which I hoped would arouse your interest."

"Please take a seat, Lady Marden," said Holmes. She took one end of the settee while Holmes and I took our seats. She wasted no time in commencing her story.

"The events of which I speak began approximately two weeks ago. My husband is connected to several business ventures and we host a great number of dinner parties for his business partners. Some three weeks ago he mentioned to me that we needed to put on an extra special dinner for a few of his clients. He leaves me to organise these events as they are not his strong suit."

"That would appear to be rather short-notice," said Holmes. "Was that customary?"

"No," replied Lady Marden. "I was more than a little put out that I only had a week to arrange everything, and he apologised saying the need for it had only recently come to his attention. The aim was to impress a potential new client who was due to leave the country the day after the dinner.

"I always ask my husband to tell me as much as he can about the people he invites to our house. This is so I can endeavour to tailor the event or the menu to suit them. Often, I invite additional guests if I believe it will help.

"There were to be eight guests, plus my husband and I, so I gave directions to the servants to set the table accordingly and use all our best china, cutlery, and linen.

"One week later it was the day of the dinner. The guests had been requested to arrive at six for six-thirty."

"Who were the guests?" asked Holmes.

"The man my husband was endeavouring to impress was one Mr. Carl Fredericks, who attended with his wife. The other business partners were Mr. James Clarke, who has, I believe, some connection to the shoe trade; finally, there was Mr. George Rosewood.

"The remaining guests were responding to my personal invitation. Firstly, Mr. Arthur Whittaker and his wife, who are friends of mine. The final two guests were Mr. Ronald Paget and Professor Henry Adams. Both men are in the art world, and my husband has done business with them in the past. When I informed my husband the professor was attending, he congratulated me but did not elaborate on why congratulations should be due."

"An eclectic guest list, Lady Marden," said Holmes.

She smiled. "That was intentional, Mr. Holmes. I find it stimulates the conversation. A dinner party that falls silent is not good for business."

Holmes rubbed his right index finger against his temple. "Precisely what happened to bring you to me?"

Lady Marden adopted a peculiar facial expression. I could not tell whether she was amused or irritated. She threw up her hands. "It is so absurd that I am not sure how to convey it."

"Please do so as it occurred," said Holmes.

Lady Marden took a breath. "The dinner proceeded perfectly well. Conversation was animated and our guests seemed engrossed. Mr. Fredericks was particularly involved, which pleased my husband. I was slightly concerned about Professor Adams who avoided conversation with all guests aside from my husband and Mr. Paget. However, the other guests seemed not to notice this, so I did not raise the matter.

"After post-dinner drinks our guests left. Perhaps unsurprisingly, the professor departed first. Richard congratulated me on the evening and said he and Mr. Fredericks would be discussing a business arrangement upon the latter's return from the Continent in a few weeks. He had also arranged some other transactions with Mr. Clarke. He could not have been happier with how the evening had gone.

"Events took a turn about an hour later. Richard and I were relaxing in the sitting room when our butler, Harley, asked to speak to us.

"'I am sorry, ma'am,' he said, 'we were clearing away and we cannot seem to locate all the napkins.'"

"Napkins?" said Holmes.

"Yes," said Lady Marden. "Following my earlier instructions, the servants had used our hand-made, monogrammed napkins. They were a gift to us from my husband's parents upon the occasion of our marriage. They have intricate embroidery, featuring our coat of arms as well as our initials, and are unique. Everyone had the use of one at dinner."

"And they had disappeared?" I said.

"Yes, Doctor," said Lady Marden. "Harley said they had determined that half of those laid out were missing. Our household staff are above suspicion so we were led to the inescapable conclusion that they had been stolen by one or more of our guests."

"Were they valuable?" asked Holmes.

"In financial terms, not particularly," said Lady Marden. "Because they were commissioned, they were naturally more expensive than plain napkins. Beyond that, their value lay in their rarity and the fact they were wedding gifts. That, however, is beside the point. A guest in our home had stolen from us."

"What did your husband think of the theft?" asked Holmes.

"He was annoyed but did not want to bring the matter to the authorities. He was of the opinion that the theft was trivial and I was letting a sentimental attachment cloud my thinking. He was naturally upset at the idea a guest had stolen from us but was determined we should drop the matter."

"That being the case," said Holmes, "why are you here now?"

"I am here, sir, because I am not content to let the matter drop. I have read many of Dr. Watson's accounts and the unusual seems to be something that attracts you. I therefore determined to lay the matter before you."

Holmes smiled. "That is certainly true, Lady Marden, but I fear your husband's interpretation of events is most likely correct. I have a number of other cases on hand at present, but I will give your matter some thought and advise you if anything occurs to me. If, in turn, anything further occurs to you, I would be grateful if you would inform me."

Lady Marden stood, rather abruptly. "I feared you might not be interested but I appreciate your tactful way of phrasing it. On reflection, I can understand your lack of enthusiasm but I hope you do not blame me for bringing it to you."

"Not at all," said Holmes.

With an obvious air of disappointment, Lady Marden departed.

"You were a little dismissive," I said, when I returned from showing her out.

Holmes shrugged. "Ah, Watson, always the defender of the fair sex." He took hold of his violin and scraped the bow absent-mindedly across the strings. "The theft of napkins from a dinner party may be vexing but I do not feel it warrants the attention of a detective. No matter how unoccupied that detective may find himself."

A few days later the newspapers were buzzing with the details of a daring raid on a West London gallery. Several paintings and small sculptures had been stolen. The aspect of the case that had everyone talking was not what had been stolen but how it had been carried out. Reports from a single eye-witness, who had clearly not entirely realised what he had been witness to, had stated that the people coming out of the gallery had all been wearing masks that covered almost the entire head, which was not in itself unusual for a criminal enterprise. What was unusual was that the gang had operated in total silence and with military precision. The witness had chosen to hide rather than act and had approached the police only after it was all over.

I had read the story to Holmes and it had interested him enough to wire Gregson, who was reported as being the lead detective on the case, to ask for more details. Gregson had wired back to say he would drop by Baker Street with further details as soon as he could.

It was around six in the evening when the, clearly weary, detective showed up at our rooms. Holmes directed him to the settee and poured him a brandy which he readily accepted.

"This one's an odd one, Mr. Holmes," he said.

"How so?"

"The organisation is the best I have ever heard of. According to our witness, one man sat outside with a cart, another kept watch, and three others went into the gallery, removing several items which were loaded onto the cart. Once this was done, the items were quietly driven away, and the remaining men dispersed calmly and quietly in different directions."

"Do we know what was stolen?" I asked.

"The newspaper reports were accurate, Doctor. Several paintings and some modest sculptures. Items the gang could comfortably and swiftly remove. Nothing was targeted that would be cumbersome to carry or drive away."

"Stolen to order?" asked Holmes.

"That's our thinking. All ports have been put on alert in case anyone tries to get anything out of the country. If anything is intended for a domestic customer, we might have a harder task on our hands."

Holmes asked Gregson to keep him apprised of any further developments and the detective departed looking disappointed. He was clearly at a loss and had presumably hoped my friend would offer some insight. I made this point to Holmes.

"Insufficient data, Watson," he replied.

A few days later, Holmes and I returned from dinner at Simpson's to find a few items had been delivered in the evening post. Holmes went through the modest pile and his eyebrows rose when he came across a small blue envelope. He turned it over.

"The Marden crest," he said.

"Lady Marden has something more for us?" I asked.

"It would appear so," said Holmes, without any enthusiasm. He opened the envelope and took out the enclosure. As he read it, his eyes widened in surprise.

"What is it?" I asked.

"It seems Lady Marden's home has been burgled."

"Good Lord," I exclaimed.

"She reports that, despite all the valuables in her house, all that was taken was two more of their napkins."

"More napkins?" I exclaimed.

"I must confess," said Holmes, "I am now rather interested in Lady Marden's case."

"Do I have your attention now, Mr. Holmes?"

Lady Marden looked remarkably satisfied for a woman whose home had been burgled. After receiving her letter, Holmes had sought an interview and we were now seated in her impressive sitting room.

"You must forgive me, Lady Marden," said Holmes. "The apparently opportunistic theft of napkins at a dinner party is a very different thing from a break-in."

"Indeed, it is," said Lady Marden. "What action do you propose to take?"

"I must begin by asking you more about them. You said they were unique."

Lady Marden stood and walked to the far side of the room. From a table she picked up a napkin and handed it to Holmes. "This is one of those remaining."

Holmes examined it. It was indeed most intricate and clearly a work of considerable effort and skill. Holmes rested it across his knees. "Do you, by chance, know when your husband's family commissioned these?"

Lady Marden clearly did not see the relevance of the question but, having gained Holmes's attention, was keen not to lose it. "My understanding is they were ordered about six months in advance of the wedding. A single lady was responsible and each one took some time to embroider on account of the design. She was so proficient that each napkin is almost identical to the last. About a year ago, I desired to add to the set so you can imagine how saddened I was to learn the lady had died. That is one of the reasons I find the loss of the napkins so upsetting, Mr. Holmes. They simply cannot be replaced."

Holmes considered this. "Surely you could find someone capable of producing a similar design?"

"My husband did make enquiries but he was told it would take quite some time and would cost a sizeable sum. I asked him not to proceed. For me, it simply would not be the same done by a different hand."

Holmes looked down at the napkin on his knees. "Would you mind if I retained this? It will help me recognise the others if I have one to compare with."

"Take great care of it, Mr. Holmes," said Lady Marden. "That's one of the last three in the set."

We left Lady Marden and hailed a cab to return to Baker Street.

"I have to confess, Holmes," I said, as we rattled our way through the West End, "that this is not something I thought would interest you."

"Nor I," he replied, "and it did not until the burglary."

"That is what seized your attention?"

"Yes. For one simple reason. If you are determined to steal from a set of napkins, why not steal all of them at once? Why steal some and then return for more?"

For the next few days, I was occupied by a colleague's practice, on the other side of town, which I had offered to run in his absence, so I saw little of Holmes. I was nonetheless eager to know how his investigations had progressed. One evening, when cases had finished early, I determined to ascertain the latest.

Mrs. Hudson informed me, upon my arrival, that Holmes had been out all day but that he had assured her he would return by seven.

Shortly before the stated hour, Holmes strode into the sitting room. "Good evening, Watson. I see you have been dealing with some cuts and grazes today."

I glanced down. "The iodine stains on my cuffs?"

"Quite so," he said as he disappeared into his bedroom. He emerged, moments later, in his dressing gown. "I take it you are loitering here for news?"

"I would be gratified to hear how the case is proceeding. By the way," I said, gesturing to the dining table, "the evening post has arrived."

Holmes briefly looked at the items on the table beside me before tutting and turning his back. He clearly had no interest in his correspondence. He often ignored it for days at a time, unless he was expecting something, so his disinterest was no surprise. He took hold of a pipe, filled it with tobacco, and sank into his chair, striking and applying a match as he did so.

"I really had no idea, Watson, how many purveyors of napkins there are in London. I was remiss to have such a gap in my knowledge. I believe I have visited some thirty in the past few days."

"What did you learn?"

"I learned that Lady Marden was quite correct about the rarity of her napkins. I took the example she kindly lent us and asked each shop owner what effort would be required to reproduce it to the same standard."

"And?"

"To a man, they informed me the napkin was of the highest quality and a single facsimile would take at least a week to produce and would be prohibitively expensive."

"So where does that information get us?"

"All in good time, Watson. At three of the places I visited, the proprietor informed me that he had received a similar question from a gentleman who was seeking to augment his wife's set."

"Sir Richard Marden?"

"Given his apparent lack of concern at their loss, I am inclined to doubt it. Nonetheless, a telegram to Lady Marden will do no harm."

I was intrigued by this fresh information. I stared into the fire while I thought it over. I raised my head in time to see Holmes staring at me. "What do you deduce, Watson?"

"Next to nothing, Holmes," I sighed.

He looked at me kindly or, perhaps, indulgently. "Come now. You have nearly all you need to reach the same conclusions as I have."

"Nearly?"

"Yes. The last item is that all these enquiries were made before the burglary at the Marden house."

"It has been a long day, Holmes," I said, feeling every ounce of my stupidity. "Perhaps you could simply tell me?"

"There is room for error of course," said Holmes, "but I would suggest the napkins were stolen to meet a specific need. As Lady Marden believes, one of the guests at her dinner had a purpose and opportunistically decided the Marden napkins would serve. They stole half of those accessible and slipped away with the other guests."

"So, why the subsequent burglary?"

"That appears simple enough. At some point in the days that followed, it was decided more were required. Someone connected to the theft decided to see if it was possible to reproduce the napkins to an acceptable standard. When they learned it was not possible, or not possible in the desired time, they fell upon their last recourse and arranged for them to be stolen."

"I do not see where this gets us, Holmes."

"For the moment, nowhere," he said. "However, keep it in mind for future reference."

An hour later, after we had partaken of several pipes and, in my case, several brandies, Holmes declared his intention of retiring for the night. He had been up since the early hours and explained that his schedule was to be similar the next day. I had no wish to delay him so began preparing to head back to my temporary accommodation. As I was putting on my coat the bell rang. The outer door was opened and we heard Mrs. Hudson commenting upon the hour to our caller. Despite having had Holmes as a tenant for some years, and thus the irregular hours of his practice, she still railed against late callers. Heavy, rapid footsteps on the stairs told of some urgency. We were both surprised when the door opened to reveal Inspector Gregson.

"Mr. Holmes," he said breathlessly. "Rat Parkinson has just been fished out of the Thames."

The name meant nothing to me but it clearly did to Holmes. The rodent prefix suggested a criminal to me but Holmes's expression was one of sadness. "Rat," he said, mournfully.

"Who is Rat Parkinson?" I said.

"A little before your time Doctor," said Gregson.

Holmes had stood and had detached his jack-knife from its customary spot on the mantel. He began to toy with it in a manner that suggested some anger. He stared at the official detective. "When, Gregson?"

"Little more than two hours ago. When I heard, I thought you would want to know."

"You both seem sad to hear of his death," I said.

"Don't get me wrong Doctor," said Gregson, "he was a wrong-un, but he was the last of dying breed. Thief for hire but honourable in his own way. He had actually been retired for years."

Holmes had reburied his blade into the mantel. His anger was no less evident. "Where did he wash up?"

"Near Limehouse. It did cross my mind if he might have been involved in the gallery robbery."

Holmes looked impressed. "That is certainly a possibility, Gregson. If so, I wonder how they tempted him out of retirement?"

"Why are you both convinced he is linked to this?" I asked.

The inspector took a seat. "It was in his line, Doctor. He was a cultured criminal. If you were in the market for something beautiful, Rat was your man. Intelligent enough to have gone to one of our great universities if he'd had the resources."

"Have you considered that this could be an insurance swindle?" said Holmes.

"Possibly," said Gregson. "The gallery's owner said he would be filing a claim with his agents."

"Who is the owner?"

Gregson took out his notebook and flicked through it. "A Mr. Ronald Paget."

"Holmes," I said, "that's one of the guests from the Marden dinner party."

"What dinner party?" said Gregson, his curiosity aroused.

"All in good time," said Holmes, impatiently. "Is the body at the mortuary?"

"I assumed you'd want to see it," said Gregson, "I have a carriage waiting."

As we made our way east to the mortuary, Holmes stared into the distance. To me it appeared that he had lost interest in the issue of the napkins and was fully focused on the art theft and the death of a criminal for whom he and Gregson clearly had some respect. As we careered down street after street, his gaze remained firmly ahead.

It was not long before we arrived at the mortuary. Thanks to the presence of Gregson, the usual formalities were dispensed with. The police surgeon led us to the appropriate slab and pulled back the sheet. Rat Parkinson had clearly been struck over the head. You did not require a medical degree to arrive at that conclusion. The surgeon's report told of an absence of water in the lungs making it clear that Rat was dead before he entered the river. Holmes studied the body but when he was finished it was clear he was unsatisfied.

"Gregson," he said. "Do we have any idea where Rat entered the river?"

"Some," replied the detective. "Based on the tide and the police surgeon's estimate of the time of death, we think he entered the river near the Embankment. We made enquiries and some witnesses recalled seeing a man earlier this evening, answering to Rat's description, loudly singing, not too far from the Needle. They took him to be someone intoxicated from a gathering. Other witnesses reported being accosted by someone similar who was abusive and smelled of alcohol. Of course, Mr. Holmes, you and I both know what is amiss with that."

"Rat did not drink," said Holmes.

"Why would he be drunk?" I asked.

Holmes returned to the body and bent down low over it. "I thought I smelt a faint odour of gin. Most has been washed away in the Thames."

"What are we to make of it?" said Gregson.

Holmes stroked his chin. "I think our friend, Rat, was deliberately drawing attention to himself in a way he knew would stand out. I fear he knew his life was in danger and he wanted to ensure his movements would be possible to trace. But why would he be at the Embankment?"

He had barely finished the sentence when I could see that an idea had occurred to him. "We must return to Baker Street at once."

"I have some things to do here, Mr. Holmes," said Gregson. "I will let you know if anything comes up. I trust you will do the same."

Holmes tipped his hat and left the mortuary. He moved fast towards the road and I was hard pushed to keep up. "Why the rush?"

As a cab responded to Holmes's hail, he turned to me. "I have neglected to examine the evening post to which you kindly drew my attention." With that remark he climbed into the cab. All thought of the next day's professional commitments left me as I climbed in beside him. He smiled and struck the roof.

Soon we were back at Baker Street. Holmes shot up the stairs and into the sitting room. Without pausing to remove any garments, he sat down and began to sift through the letters and packages. His attention seized; he took hold of one. "This is it."

"How do you know?"

"Charing Cross post-mark," he replied.

He carefully removed the outer packaging. Inside was a slim, but long, box. Holmes tentatively opened it and looked inside. As I watched, he turned it upside down and let the contents fall onto the table. I looked and was astonished.

Upon the table were a mask and a napkin.

... he turned it upside down and let the contents fall onto the table.

Holmes was not satisfied. He stared at the box and then, seemingly possessed, tore open every other letter and package. Those that did not meet with his approval, which was all of them, went into the fire.

I stared at the burning pieces of paper wondering what potential clients Holmes was losing by this reckless behaviour. "I am a little lost, Holmes."

He looked at me. "Rat was a good thief, Watson, but he never stole for himself. He was always commissioned. As Gregson suggested, we can safely assume he was part of this art theft. Unlike many of his criminal persuasion, he was educated and that was when his location became of interest."

"Why?"

"There are a number of post boxes in the vicinity of the needle but Rat was clever." He picked up the box that he had first opened. "You can see this is larger than it needs to be in order to hold a simple napkin and mask. They could have been folded and delivered in a box half this size."

"It does seem he was making things difficult for himself," I said.

"Not a bit of it. It was a stroke of genius," said my friend, whose expression was one of admiration.

"I do not understand, Holmes."

"Very likely not. Post boxes in this great city come in a number of sizes. Wall-mounted, those embedded into walls and, of course, the free-standing pillar boxes. They have gone through several designs since their introduction. They have different overall sizes and the aperture size can also vary." He held out the box. "This would only fit into the larger pillar boxes. Any attempt to get it into one of the smaller ones would have resulted in some damage to the box which you can see has not happened. We know Rat was in the vicinity of the Needle on the Embankment. This information narrows our field of search still further."

"I see," I said, only partially seeing.

"Here is my working hypothesis. Rat is involved in the art theft. For whatever reason, he believes his life to be in danger. He decides to alert me by sending these. He posts the package and then draws attention to himself. I suspect he poured some gin onto his clothes and gargled some. He wanted to be sure people would remember him. He knew Scotland Yard would alert me to his death. He left a trail of breadcrumbs to ensure we knew where he was immediately beforehand."

"What is the next move?"

"I think it is high time we visited Mr. Ronald Paget at his gallery."

The next day we presented ourselves at the Mayfair gallery. The contents of the gallery were certainly eclectic and contained much that I struggled to regard as art. The man who had greeted us upon our arrival treated us with a degree of suspicion as soon as he understood we were not there to buy. We offered our cards and they were taken off to an office upstairs. Holmes noted the expression on my face. "I believe, Watson, you are not intended to recognise some of the pieces here."

"I fail to see the point of art I cannot identify, Holmes."

"Good old Watson."

Suddenly, we heard an unfamiliar voice.

"I am pleased to see you take an interest, Mr. Holmes," said the man we took to be Ronald Paget. He completed his descent of the stairs and advanced with his hand outstretched. Holmes took it.

"I beg your pardon for being so tardy," said Holmes. "I was wondering if you could give me any details on the items that were stolen?"

Paget's face took on an amused expression. "It's an odd thing, Mr. Holmes. All the items were valuable but, as I'm sure you have heard, they were not the most valuable. In this trade that says a theft to order. Collectors passionate about these specific artists would be the first people to investigate."

"Do you think some items were decoys?"

Paget stroked his chin. "Clever, Mr. Holmes. That is possible." He looked at me and noticed I did not understand. He turned in my direction to complete his sentence. "Take one specific item and some others to muddy the waters."

"Indeed," said Holmes.

"It is a thought," continued Paget. "The most valuable was a Chinese dish. The most prominent collector of such items is an Austrian and he could easily have purchased it. In fact, I was expecting him to enquire about it any day. The paintings were the next most valuable. To be honest I am not sure which would have been the decoy piece. I suggest you speak with Professor Henry Adams."

"Ah, yes," said Holmes. "I understand you met recently at a dinner party."

"That is so. I was surprised to meet him."

"Why?"

Paget leaned towards us as if to share a confidence. "For some five years or more the man has been a relative recluse holed up in his old house with his equally old servants. I understand he became solitary following a significant illness or accident. He has conducted all his business via correspondence. The word is that he put considerable distance between himself, family, and other acquaintances. Therefore, to see him at a dinner party was a great surprise. He was a delightful person to talk to. That said, I can understand the rumours."

"Rumours?" said Holmes.

Paget, again, adopted a conspiratorial stance.

"Some of his rivals have said his quality of work has suffered since he went into seclusion. I must confess I found some of what he said to be below the standard I expected of such a renowned authority. Illness affects us all in different ways I suppose."

At Holmes's request, Paget supplied a detailed list of the stolen items and their approximate value. We said our farewells and Holmes and I made our way on foot eastwards towards the Embankment.

"It is time," said Holmes, "for us to walk Rat's last route. Then I suggest we try dropping in unannounced on Professor Adams."

For the next hour, I obediently followed Holmes around the streets near the Embankment. He pointed out the pertinent pillar boxes that were the most likely candidates for Rat's package. As we explored the immediate vicinity of the third such box, Holmes's eyes lit up. "Well, well."

I followed his line of sight. There was another gallery. On the face of it there was little to hold it apart from any other West London gallery. There was, however, a sign in its window that advertised the fact that the gallery was currently displaying some rare Chinese pottery on loan from a private, and unnamed, collector. Potential visitors were advised the exhibition closed the coming Friday. Two days' time.

"This is it," said Holmes. "This is the next target."

"Shall we go in and warn them?" I asked.

"No, Watson," he replied. "There is very likely an insider to facilitate matters. If we were to walk in with our story there is a good chance we would not be believed and the gang behind this would be alerted. Yes, we would prevent a crime here but we would not advance the recovery of the already stolen items or prevent future thefts."

"What do we do then?"

"We proceed to see Professor Adams. Afterwards we shall pay a visit to friend Gregson."

Holmes had done his research. Professor Adams lived in Runnymede in Surrey. It therefore took us a little time to reach his house. As we travelled, I was at a loss to understand Holmes's confidence that we would be able to see him.

The professor's home was impressive and not overlooked by any neighbours. It seemed perfect for a semi-recluse who still needed to conduct business in the capital. We rang the bell and a young man answered the door. Much to my surprise we were admitted to the professor's study and asked to wait.

I could contain myself no longer. "What kind of recluse is this Professor Adams?"

"A recluse who is emerging from his isolation, sir."

I turned in surprise to find a man standing in the doorway behind us.

"Mr. Holmes, Dr. Watson. A pleasure."

Thus, Professor Adams greeted us. He was a short, thin, and bearded man in his late-forties. In fact, as a doctor, I felt the term gaunt would have been more appropriate. He had the look of the kind of sudden weight loss associated with illness. Was this what Paget had been referring to? Despite his large beard it was possible to see the professor also had some rather unsightly loose skin around his neck. I assumed he was a vain man and the beard was an attempt to mask this skin.

He, in turn, was an observant man who read my expression at once. "Please do not concern yourself about me, Doctor. I lost a lot of weight following an illness gained in the tropics. I regularly see a specialist and am fitter than I might at first appear."

"I am glad to hear it, Professor," I replied. "All the indications are that your weight loss was quite sudden."

His face darkened and I feared I had gone too far. "Yes, thank you, Doctor." He waved us to two seats. "How can I assist you, gentlemen?"

As I sat down, I tried to take in the immediate surroundings. Professor Adams had clearly lived an adventurous life prior to settling into the art world and his later seclusion. There were various native artifacts, some clearly from the tropical areas he had alluded to, but there were also items from much colder climates.

"Do you ski, Professor?" I asked.

The professor instinctively looked over at the corner of the room where you could see a pair of skis, enormous boots, gloves, and a mask.

"I dabble, Doctor," he replied, looking concerned, "but I am assuming you came here to talk about art theft. Why else would the celebrated detective come to see me?"

"We were not entirely sure we would see you," said Holmes. "We hear you are a recluse but then you attend a dinner party?"

Adams smiled. "It is true that I cut myself off from society. My academic title is nothing to do with the art world. That is a hotly pursued hobby. My degrees are in anthropology - hence my travels. I have been accustomed to long periods in little company. On my return to England, I found it to be too busy for my liking. I based myself at a suitable distance to conduct my business but endeavoured to keep the world at arm's length.

"I have corresponded for a few years with Sir Richard Marden - advising him on the art world - and was surprised to receive a letter from his wife inviting me to dinner.

"It just so happened that I had been giving thought to re-entering the world, as it were, and a modest dinner party that involved no one who had ever dealt with me, aside from Sir Richard, whom I had never met in person, seemed attractive. When I learned Ronald Paget would be there, I was even more eager to attend."

"May I ask why?" said Holmes.

Professor Adams clearly thought the question an odd one. "Because he is an expert on Chinese pottery, a subject in which I have recently taken an interest."

"We have just come from the gallery," said Holmes. "I found Mr. Paget's comments about the items stolen to be interesting."

"I do not doubt it," said Adams. "Clearly stolen to order for patient buyers."

"What makes you say that?" said Holmes.

The professor leant back in his chair and placed his fingertips together in a manner not dissimilar to Holmes. "The authorities will be looking out for the items for some time," he said. "Those pieces will be removed to somewhere remote, and stored until they are conveyed to their purchasers."

Holmes nodded at the sense of the professor's theory. "Returning to your burgeoning social calendar, Professor; did you notice anything unusual at the party?"

Adams's face darkened. "Yes. I noticed that Sir Richard was doing business with some unpleasant people. If it had not been for the presence of Paget, Sir Richard, and his charming wife, I would have made my excuses."

"Were the other guests ill-mannered?" asked Holmes.

"Worse," said Adams. "They were ignorant. I cannot stand the ignorant. I did not come out of isolation to talk with fools."

The sudden change in the professor's mood took both Holmes and I by surprise.

"I seem harsh to you both I'm sure," he said. "But I say again that I cannot abide fools or ignoramuses. If you bother to go in for a subject, for goodness's sake become proficient in it. There was a fellow there by the name of Clarke. How that man sells anything to anyone is beyond me. The Whittakers seemed little more than country bumpkins. This country is full of people who are barely worthy of the air they breathe. The illiterate, the ignorant. I could go on but, as educated men, I am certain you understand me."

Holmes looked awkward. "I very much hope, Professor, that you will not hold my ignorance of art against me."

The professor smiled. "Of course not, Mr. Holmes. I do not expect everyone to be expert in my subject. I only ask that they be expert in their own. That is not too much to ask, is it? In modern society, we all need to be able to play our part."

"On the subject of art," said Holmes, "what was your opinion of the Mardens' napkins?"

Adams snorted. "One might think you phrased it that way to provoke me, Mr. Holmes. I believe Mrs. Whittaker admired them which prompted Lady Marden to give us the whole story of their creation. I understand them to be a unique set which is just as well. You would not want to see many of them. The best I can say about them was they fulfilled their function. In the long run, I am sure the Mardens will be pleased to see the back of them."

"So, you heard of the theft?" asked Holmes.

"Indeed," said Adams. "I had the news from Paget a day or two after the dinner. He had been told by Sir Richard who was bemoaning the fact that his wife would not letter the matter drop."

After a few more minutes of increasingly uncomfortable conversation, Holmes and I bade farewell to the professor. As his butler assisted us to don our coats in the hall, Adams expressed the desire to meet us again although he feared it was unlikely the occasion would arise for our paths to cross in the near future.

As we strolled towards busier streets in search of a cab, Holmes spoke. "Odd fellow, the professor."

"Odd!" I exclaimed. "I have to say I found him rather repellent."

"Me too, old fellow," said Holmes. "With his dislike of the ignorant one wonders how he ever managed to teach a class."

The thought had not occurred to me.

"But," Holmes continued, "I noticed a number of informative things in his study and in his conversation."

When we arrived back at Baker Street, Holmes disappeared into his room. He emerged, after a few minutes, holding a black jumper.

"What do you need that for?" I asked.

He smiled. "I like to be prepared. This coming Friday we are going to become members of the criminal class. Ensure you have similar clothing. Do you have a mask? No? I shall see you all right."

Holmes assured me there was nothing to be done before Friday. I spent the intervening days largely at the surgery and my club. When Friday evening finally came round, I endeavoured to present myself as requested. As I entered the sitting room, Holmes emerged from his bedroom dressed head to toe in black and holding a silk mask. I had done my best to do likewise although some of my outer wear was dark grey. Holmes looked me over before declaring I would do.

We spent the next hour smoking and talking, with the conversation not drifting once in the direction of the evening's planned activity.

A little after eleven, we were back on the street. Holmes asked me to hail a cab. As we got in, I noticed the cabby give us a disturbed look but we were soon on our way to the Embankment. We alighted at the Needle and waited on that small platform watching the Thames lap against the steps.

"Take these," said Holmes.

I looked down to see he was offering me one of the Marden napkins and a silk mask. "You borrowed another napkin?"

Holmes shook his head. "This one was in the possession of Rat. I fear I would strain Lady Marden's patience to breaking point were I to ask her for another. Ultimately though she will not be too disappointed."

I decided to check my understanding. "We are going back to that gallery you believe to be the next target?"

"Know, Watson. Know," he said with some impatience. "This gang has been commissioned to steal art. I strongly believe their focus to be on Chinese pottery. As we both saw, there has been an exhibition of the same that ends today. Tomorrow the items will be removed from the gallery either to proceed to their next venue or back to the collections of their owners. Tonight is the best opportunity for the gang to remove the items and gain a sufficient head-start on the authorities."

"What is the plan?" I asked.

"At my request, Gregson has kept the gallery under observation. The biggest risk we are running is that our watch is spotted and the theft called off. That is a risk I was compelled to take. Based on the descriptions from the newspapers, and statements Gregson shared with me, we can expect the members of the gang to arrive separately within no more than five to ten minutes of each other. As soon as we see them, we will move to join them. If my calculations are correct there will be six of them altogether. If they follow the same pattern there will be one to drive the cart, one to keep watch, and four to remove the required items."

I saw a problem. "Holmes. This gang presumably knows how many of them there are meant to be. Surely, our presence will alert them?"

Holmes nodded. "That is why we must join the gang before its final two members. Eventually they will realise the deception. At that point I will alert Gregson and his men will move in. You and I may need to exert ourselves to prevent any gang members getting away."

The plan explained, we left the Needle behind and walked towards the gallery. By this time, it was getting close to midnight. As we got closer to our destination, I had to take my hat off to Gregson. There was no sign of anyone watching the gallery. I remarked on this to Holmes and saw that it concerned him.

"Either Gregson's men have got better at this or they have been discovered. Let us hope it is the former."

We made our way around the area until we could see the easiest approach to the rear of the gallery. As we passed, we saw a cart, in a less well-lit part of the street, under the control of a masked man in black. The presence of a long scarf concealed the mask to a considerable extent. He appeared to be on his own. We walked on.

I was about to remark on the cart to Holmes when out of nowhere a young lad ran towards us before tripping over at Holmes's feet. Holmes bent down to help the young boy up. He touched his cap before running on in the direction we had come.

"A late hour for such a young lad to be on the open streets," I said.

"Yes," said Holmes.

We walked for another minute and stopped close to a street lamp. Holmes reached into his pocket and pulled out a small piece of paper. He looked at it briefly before returning it to his pocket. He was clearly pleased about something.

As we resumed our journey, he sensed my question. "That was Luff, one of Wiggins' new boys."

It had been a little while since we had made use of the urchins Holmes referred to as his Irregulars. The penny dropped. "He passed you some kind of message?"

"And I passed him payment," said Holmes. "Wiggins is training them well. I felt compelled to check I still had my watch."

"What was the message?"

"I had Luff liaise with Gregson. The message informs me that two men have entered the yard at the rear of the gallery. Gregson's men will endeavour to quietly intercept any others who approach. This allows you and me to make up the numbers."

We ducked into a doorway for cover. Holmes turned to me. "Watson. You remain here. I will advance up the street a little. Wait here precisely five minutes from now. When the time is up, put on your mask and proceed to the rear of the gallery. Don't speak and don't resist them. Copy any actions they take. Rest assured that when you are among them, I will be too." With that remark he strode off.

Holmes was soon out of sight. I checked my watch and could see I was going to be waiting for another four minutes. Never had it seemed so long a time. I was tempted to smoke but knew it would give away my position. I started to become uncomfortable so began to shift my weight from leg to leg.

I looked at my watch again. Two minutes to go. It occurred to me that as soon as we put on our masks, Holmes and I would not easily be able to tell each other apart from the gang members. If things were to get dangerous later, how was I to tell friend from foe?

I put my mask on and took a deep breath. With less than a minute to go I began to make my way slowly to my destination. It was quite a task to move slowly without giving the appearance of doing so. In no time at all, I was at the rear of the gallery. A door leading to a delivery yard was ajar. Pulse racing, I pushed it open and stepped inside.

I was seized as soon as I entered. A hand covered my mouth and another pinned my arms behind my back. In line with Holmes's instructions, I did not struggle. This was a wise course of action. Hands went into my pockets and pulled out the contents. They were examined and I found myself released. Everything was returned and I was directed into a corner of the yard. All of this was done without a word spoken.

I quickly determined there were three of us in the yard. A fear started to come over me. Holmes had stated there would be six people in total. One was outside with the cart. Another was also outside somewhere keeping watch. This meant only four people to break into the gallery. Clearly Holmes had not yet arrived. I had barely finished this thought when another man entered the yard and was subjected to the same treatment. The searcher satisfied; the newcomer was released. Now there were four of us, one of the gang members began work on picking the lock of the gallery's rear entrance. Whoever he was, he was impressive as the door was swiftly swung open. Just as the man was about to head inside, the yard door opened and a masked man walked in.

It was as if time froze. Each of us looked from one to the other. We were one too many. Still, no one spoke. The man who came in after me reached into his boot, drew out a whistle and blew it. At least I knew who was Holmes.

The man who had just entered the yard, turned, and fled. The man who had searched me fled inside the gallery and the man who had picked the lock of the door advanced towards Holmes and began to attack him. I swiftly moved to Holmes's aid and pulled his attacker off affording Holmes the opportunity to land a good left, sending his assailant to the ground, unconscious.

He pulled off his mask. "Well done, old fellow, but you did nearly blow the whole thing."

"How?"

"You headed over a trifle early. I was supposed to be here before you."

"Sorry, Holmes," I said, removing my own mask.

"Never mind," said Holmes. "Let's help Gregson clean up."

A constable entered the yard and Holmes directed his attention to the man on the floor. He was quickly handcuffed and dragged out. Holmes and I advanced upon the open door.

Inside it was dark. We shut the door and manoeuvred a heavy box against it. This done, we advanced slowly. More than once, Holmes tugged my sleeve to steer me away from walking into something valuable. As our eyes adjusted, it appeared that the ground floor was empty.

Holmes whispered in my ear. "We must head upstairs, Watson."

We advanced to the foot of the stairs. "Holmes," I said, "we need to arm ourselves."

Holmes paused and waited. I glanced around and noticed a thin vase. I seized it and passed it to Holmes.

Holmes led the way, holding the vase by its neck. Three steps from the top, a figure suddenly appeared and kicked out. His foot caught the vase and sent the base flying towards me. It clipped my shoulder before completing its journey to the ground. Holmes lashed out with the remainder and evidently found his mark as there was a scream of pain. The man hobbled out of sight.

"Are you alright, Watson?" said Holmes.

My shoulder throbbed. "I'm fine."

We reached the top of the stairs and turned towards the front of the shop in time to see our assailant hurl something through the front window. Having done this, he climbed out and dropped to the ground. As we reached the window and looked out, we could see him look up and salute before turning and running straight into the arms of Gregson.

At about three in the morning, we found ourselves sitting in Gregson's office. The evening had not gone perfectly. Of the six-man gang, we had failed to capture the lookout. Holmes chastised Gregson for failing to intercept the gang member that had, by his unwanted appearance, forced us to reveal ourselves.

With an apologetic expression, Gregson informed us he had some further bad news for us.

"He escaped!" said Holmes.

Gregson looked downcast. He hated having to admit to another failure. "Yes, sir. We liaised with our Surrey friends but Professor Adams' house was empty."

"Professor Adams?" I exclaimed.

"Yes, Watson," said Holmes. "He was the organiser of all this."

"I accept he was an unpleasant man, Holmes, but how could he be the organiser?"

Holmes lit a cigarette. "To begin with we need to understand that our reclusive Professor Adams has been engaged in criminal activity for some time. He coordinated everything from that house of his and was directly involved in nothing. If we look hard enough, I suspect we will be able to trace a number of art crimes back to that house.

"Let us suppose he lacks discipline, and gets bored of being so far removed from the action. He decides to get involved a little more. He is a man that enjoys an element of risk.

"This brings us to the dinner party. Adams elected to attend this party. He told us himself that the presence of Mr. Paget was one of the reasons he chose to go. He attends and, in speaking with Paget, learns of the Chinese pottery Paget currently has on display at his gallery.

"With a mind like lightning, he decides to have that pottery stolen. He has learned its value but he must act fast. He clearly has an established formula – it is not the first time he has done something like this. He assembles a gang to steal whatever he has set his mind to. The best form of safety is for the gang not to know who each other are. Hence, they are not only masked but are required to operate in total silence.

"That is why our dear professor loathes the ill-educated. For his plan to work he needs people who can work in silence; people who can read a plan and follow it to the letter. Your average London thief is not in that class."

For me, the penny had dropped. "So, the napkins were identification?"

"Precisely," said Holmes. "He needed a form of identification that was near unique. If you picked something common, infiltration would be easier. He quickly worked out that the initial theft would require five people so he stole five napkins."

"So why steal another two?" asked Gregson.

"For a detailed answer to that question," said Holmes, "we need to speak to the gang."

We descended to the basement. The five captured gang members were in adjacent cells. The first thing that struck me was the silence. "They are quiet."

"Yes," said Gregson. "Her Majesty's average guest tends to be somewhat vocal. These monks are taking their vow of silence seriously. As you asked, Mr. Holmes, they were all taken into their respective cells before their masks were removed. So, none of them knows who the others are."

"Excellent," said Holmes. "Where is the one who was so optimistic as to assault me in the yard?"

Gregson pointed. "Number one."

At Gregson's direction, the duty constable took out his keys and unlocked the cell. We all stepped inside. Perched on the hard bed along one wall was the first prisoner. He looked up nervously. Holmes bent towards him and whispered. "Hello, Wallace."

The young man smiled. "Bless you, Mr. Holmes."

Holmes stood up and raised his voice "So you thought you would get away with this did you?"

I was confused.

Holmes bent down and lowered his voice. "Tell me all, Wallace, and I'll see they go easy on you."

The young man clearly understood what was going on which was more than Gregson and I did judging by how Gregson looked and I felt.

Holmes turned to us. "Gregson," he said, keeping his voice low. "We will lead Wallace here back to your office. When we leave, we will make it sound as though we are leaving him here. Follow my lead."

He stood and we all walked carefully back into the corridor. Once outside, Holmes turned back to face the empty cell and said, at the top of his voice, "You will regret not cooperating."

He bid the constable to shut and lock the cell door. Now in the company of Wallace, we returned upstairs to Gregson's office.

"What on Earth was that all about, Holmes?" said Gregson as he handcuffed Wallace to a chair.

Holmes smiled. "Dear Gregson. Silence has been a distinct characteristic of these crimes. Even our newspapers latched onto that." He turned to the young criminal; his face serious. "Tell me, Wallace, were you part of the first gang that raided the Paget gallery?"

"Yes, sir."

"I take it you heard what happened to Rat?"

The young man lowered his head. "It was horrid, sir."

"Go to the beginning," said Holmes.

"I think you'd say was I recruited, Mr. Holmes," said Wallace. "I went into my local and the landlord gave me a letter saying it had been left for me the day before.

"It demanded that I go to a house in Spitalfields the next day. Said it would be worth my while. Whoever sent it clearly knew my habits. I was a bit rattled and no mistake."

"So, you went?" said Holmes.

Wallace nodded. "The door was answered by a young boy. He told me where to go. I went into a room at the rear of the house. There was a man behind a desk. He was a smart one as he sat in front of a window so I could not make him out.

"He went on to say he needed people for a job. It would pay well and was I interested? I naturally said yes. He said what I needed to wear, where I needed to be and what I was expected to help steal. He pointed to a table that was near to me and I could see a package. He told me to take it with me and open it when I was alone."

"What else?" asked Holmes.

"Well, this was the odd bit," said Wallace, "he said we would have to be masked throughout, and silent. He was clear that this was so no one would know who else was there. He said this was vital for our protection. I understood, it made sense."

"But events got sinister, didn't they?" said Holmes.

Wallace swallowed. "Yes. He said the man he represented would not compromise on this secrecy. Anyone who disobeyed the rules would be seen to."

"Any other details?" asked Holmes.

"No. I was shown out onto the street. I decided to take the package back to my lodgings. There I found it contained this strange napkin and some papers. I read the papers through and burned them."

"Tell me about Rat," said Holmes.

Wallace looked upset. "I knew Rat well. I'd even worked with him. Of course, when I turned up to that first gallery, I had no idea he was there. We all met where we'd been told to and we were checked on arrival."

"Who checked you?" I asked.

"The written instructions said to look out for a man who had white stitching around his left sleeve. He was to be recognised as the leader. The papers we'd been given contained details of a few hand signals that we had to learn. This chap would use them to issue any instructions that were not in the plans."

"Very good," said Holmes.

"We had been told to meet in an alleyway about one street from the gallery. When I arrived, I was grabbed and searched. I had the napkin in my trouser pocket as instructed. This was found and given back to me. When we were all there, we walked to the gallery. One of the others picked the lock and we proceeded to lift the items we'd been told to."

"So, when did it go wrong?"

"One man was carrying a sculpture of some kind and he dropped it. It landed on his foot and he swore. At that point I recognised Rat's voice. He knew his mistake at once and froze. The leader approached us and made the hand signal which meant to keep quiet and proceed with the plan."

"So," said Holmes, "you got what you had been ordered to, loaded it onto the cart and left the scene?"

"Yes, Mr. Holmes," said Wallace.

"What happened next?"

"Payment turned up at my lodgings the next day. Good money too. Whoever it was, they were willing to pay well for our services. I was more than ready to work for them again for that kind of cash. Following my original instructions, I posted the napkin to Charing Cross Post Office."

"Who was it addressed to?" asked Holmes.

"A Dr. Eve. To be called for."

Holmes smiled. "So, you then heard about Rat?"

"No, Mr. Holmes. I saw him."

"You saw him?"

"Yes. I walk out with this girl sometimes," said Wallace, winking as he did so. "With all this money in my pocket I decided to take her up west one evening, show her a good time. She wanted to stroll by the river so we got out of our cab by the Embankment. I was a little nervous, being close to the gallery so soon after robbing it but, of course, I agreed. She was going on about how pretty it was in the moonlight when we heard this racket.

"I soon worked out it was coming from a man who was wandering up and down singing at the top of his voice and using some pretty foul language to anyone who had the misfortune to get near him.

"Of course, Annie wanted us to get out of harm's way so we crossed the road. As we did so I got a good look at him and recognised Rat. He recognised me and I think, in that moment, he worked it all out. Seeing me in a part of town where I had no business to be, he realised that I had money and I had likely been part of the same gang. He winked at me, before turning away. I looked over my shoulder, after a few paces, and saw him wander onto the Needle. He was on it for a few minutes before stumbling back onto the Embankment. I knew what this meant but I carried on walking."

"What do you mean by that?" said Gregson who had hitherto maintained his silence.

Wallace smiled. "I guess I've got no choice but to give away a trade secret. The Needle is a place where some of us leave messages for each other. I pretended I'd lost something and walked Annie back to the needle. I quickly searched it and found an envelope weighted down with a small stone. Annie wasn't fooled, and demanded to know what was going on. I simply said it was a letter from a friend and I'd read it later.

"She was off with me for the rest of the night. She went on and on about secrets. It was quite a relief when I dropped her back at her mother's house. I returned to my lodgings and opened the letter."

"And what did it say?" asked Holmes.

"Very little," said Wallace. "It said he was being followed, that he'd figured out that the next job would be nearby and he was contacting someone about it. You, I'm guessing?

"I burned it as soon as I finished reading it. Then a message arrived to go to a house in Whitechapel."

"Same routine when you arrived?" asked Holmes.

"Yes. Almost exactly. Sure enough, the job was near the Embankment. I didn't know what to do. If Rat was being followed, they would've seen me. I felt unsafe. But I went just in case me not going would put Annie in danger."

I had to admit I was impressed by Wallace. Not by his story so much as his concern for his young lady. He was sensible to realise that someone who could arrange all this could easily get to someone vulnerable.

Holmes had sat back in his chair. "So, when did you find out about Rat?"

"Word gets around, Mr. Holmes. It was all over the pubs that he'd been pulled out of the river near Limehouse. Of course, no one apart from me knew what he'd been up to. I guessed that my best course of action was to act as if I'd not heard and that all was normal. I turned up at the gallery and had only been there a short while when you gents showed up and knocked me out. Sorry for hitting you, Mr. Holmes."

"No harm done, Wallace. I wonder sometimes who taught you to box."

We returned Wallace quietly to his cell. Holmes then went through a loud-voiced charade designed to give the impression that we had returned for a second interrogation. We gave a similar performance in each of the other cells. Holmes later explained that this was to give each prisoner the idea that they had all been interrogated and none had given anything away. If one of them was an insider, the mastermind would remain unaware of the breach of secrecy.

Holmes extracted a commitment from Gregson for the eventual return of the napkins before leaving him to his charges and, of course, the credit.

"Lady Marden will be unhappy about having an incomplete set," he said. "At least she'll get many a dinner party anecdote about the remaining eight."

Upon our return to Baker Street, I went and changed my clothes. I came down to find that Holmes was not in the sitting room. I sat myself down and could hear Holmes clattering about in his bedroom. After a few minutes, he emerged in his more usual non-burglar attire and sat down. "I have a confession, Watson. Something I could not yet tell our friends at Scotland Yard."

I was a little alarmed. "What is it, Holmes?"

"Professor Adams is dead."

I was shocked. "How do you know this?"

"You misunderstand. He has been dead for some time."

He stood and began pacing back and forth. "The clues were there."

"Slow down, Holmes."

"It was there for all to see. The man goes into seclusion. That part was genuine. Then rumours start to appear to the effect that he does not seem the academic he once was. Paget drew our attention to that. Paget also mentioned that he understood Adams to live with an old and long-established domestic staff."

"We only met a young butler."

"Exactly. When the professor presented himself to us, he was modest in size. There was no way he ever fitted into those skiing boots that were on display – even allowing for the weight loss you noticed. Then there was his own reference to desiring everyone to play their part. He practically struck me in the face with that clue and I missed it. The rumours about his loss of form were not down to a decline in standards but stemmed from the fact he was not the professor at all. He prizes expertise above all. We now know what his is. We just don't know who he is."

"How did he get away with the impersonation if he was so physically different?"

"That's the cleverness of it. All the professor's long-standing acquaintances were used to not seeing him. The only people to see the fake professor were people who had not met him before. Even Marden had only dealt with him by letter. It also explains the weight loss."

"It does?"

"Yes. Our professor is clearly a much larger man who was forced to slim down suddenly to play his new role. I imagine he is working furiously to return to his former size, the beard is almost certainly already history."

"Could this be the leader of this new group?" I asked.

"It is possible, Watson," said Holmes, as he moved to the window to look down on the street below.

At Holmes's suggestion, a thorough examination was made of the house of Professor Adams. Nothing was found that indicated where he or his servants had gone.

The Adventure of the Yellow Boxes

(Mid 1898)

VERY SO often a significant case would begin with a seemingly insignificant, yet bizarre, event. On this cool July morning, Sherlock Holmes had risen late, which was not unusual when he was without a case. I had finished my breakfast, and was on my second cup of coffee, when he emerged from his room, still in his nightclothes, and drifted towards the settee like a phantom. He lit a cigarette and stretched out.

"Anything interesting in the papers, Watson?"

"Not in your line," I replied. He grunted and stared at the ceiling.

"Don't worry, Holmes," I said. "Something will turn up." I sincerely hoped that would be the case as I knew all too well the alternatives Holmes would consider. He worked his way through six cigarettes in succession before returning to his room in the same manner as he had left it.

About an hour later, the bell rang. Holmes's door flew open and he emerged. He had dressed and carried several cigarette stubs on a saucer. He tipped them into the fire, gently tossed the saucer onto the dining table, and stood by his chair. I stood up and the two of us waited.

There was a knock at the door and Mrs. Hudson showed in a middle-aged lady. What was most peculiar about her was the bright yellow cardboard box she was holding. Holmes asked her to place the box on the dining table. She did so and turned back to face him.

"Thank you for seeing me without an appointment," she said.

"You are welcome, madam," said Holmes. "May I ask your name?"

"I'm sorry. My name is Mrs. Elsie Fairfield. I live in Stoke Newington."

"Please take a seat," said Holmes. Mrs. Fairfield sat and we did likewise.

"How may we assist you?" asked Holmes.

Mrs. Fairfield shuffled in her seat. It was clear she found what she was about to say uncomfortable, perhaps embarrassing.

"I am a widow. My husband died some five years ago. He was not a rich man but he was able to leave me an annuity which permits me to live a comfortable, but not extravagant, life. Three years ago, I moved to Stoke Newington, from our former home in Suffolk, because I desired the hustle and bustle of the city. I cultivate a small circle of friends and we have formed a modest book club which is located at our local community hall.

"Yesterday morning, I rose late and was a little flustered as I had all manner of household jobs to get done before heading to the hall for the latest meeting. We meet every Wednesday at eleven o'clock. We are currently reading *David Copperfield*, by the wonderful Mr. Dickens."

"You have no servants?" asked Holmes.

"As I said," she responded, tersely, "comfortable, but not extravagant."

I stole a glance at Holmes. He quickly looked at me before returning his gaze to the lady. If she did not rouse his interest soon, I knew I would be escorting her out. She continued.

"I busied about the house but was still running behind. Eventually, I chose to abandon my domestic duties in order to be punctual at the hall. I put on my hat and coat and opened the door.

"Imagine my surprise when I found a cab driver on my doorstep about to knock.

"'Excuse me madam,' he said, 'I was asked to deliver this to this address.'"

She turned and gestured to the box behind her. "At his feet was this bright yellow box. I had not ordered anything so I asked him if he was sure he had the correct address. He assured me he did and said a gentleman had given him the box about ten minutes previously and told him to deliver it immediately. He also passed on a message that it was from 'an admirer.'

"Given my small social circle, the idea that I could have a gentleman admirer seemed laughable. I was going to ask the man further questions but he appeared to be in a hurry. He touched his hat and left. I watched as he climbed up onto his cab and drove away."

Holmes's face showed his attention had been gained. "Did you, by any chance, observe if he were carrying a passenger?"

"I could not say, Mr. Holmes," she replied. "My eyesight is not the best these days and I am a little reluctant to resort to spectacles."

"What did you do?"

"Curious though I was, I was mindful that this event had made me later still. I brought the box inside, left it in my hallway, and made my way to the community hall."

"Did you notice if the box was addressed?" asked Holmes.

"No, it was not."

"And when you got home later that day?"

Mrs. Fairfield was getting more animated as her story progressed. "As you can imagine, my mind was barely on the book club. My friends chastised me more than once for my lack of attention. I did not explain myself as I recognised one of them could be behind the delivery. So, when I got home about two hours later, you can be certain the box had first claim on my attention. I carried it into my parlour and placed it on the table. It was tightly bound with string which required some effort to undo."

"And what was inside?"

Mrs. Fairfield stood and returned to the dining table. As we rose to join her, she opened the box. Inside we could see a modestly decorated clock. The kind that would sit nicely above a fireplace.

"A handsome clock indeed," said Holmes. "You found no note inside the box?"

"None at all."

"And there was no indication as to the identity of the sender?"

"None whatsoever." She gazed into the box. "Clearly my admirer has some money. This clock was certainly not cheap. All I know is it was not purchased locally."

"And how do you know that?"

She smiled. Perhaps she was pleased that Holmes showed interest in her deduction. "It is simply the case that there are no shops in my immediate area that sell clocks of this quality."

Holmes walked back to the fireplace and turned to face us. "Your mystery interests me, Mrs. Fairfield. Where can I reach you when I have news?"

The lady returned to the settee and reached into her bag. From it she withdrew a card and handed it to Holmes. He took it and placed it on his desk. "Good day, gentlemen," she said.

Inside we could see a modestly decorated clock.

I escorted her to the front door and watched until she successfully hailed a cab. Upon my return to the sitting room, I found Holmes examining the box and clock with his magnifying glass. "Any initial thoughts, Holmes?"

"In my limited experience, Watson, it is unusual for a gentleman who admires a lady to send her such an item."

I nodded. "Flowers or jewellery would be more common."

"As I have remarked before, Watson. I lack your formidable experience in such matters. However, I do know that an admirer who conceals himself rarely wins a lady's attention or affection. Remaining hidden is likely to achieve the opposite.

"The only distinctive thing about the box is its colour. This should make it easier to trace. The clock, whilst handsome, is commonplace and not as valuable as Mrs. Fairfield thinks. I suggest we begin by taking a cab to Stoke Newington."

Around an hour later we were in that area north of central London, a short distance from Mrs. Fairfield's address. Holmes and I walked almost to her door and stopped. He spun round to face the opposite direction.

"Mrs. Fairfield's house is a short distance from the main shopping street. That would appear to be the most likely direction from which the cab would come. Let's take a stroll down it and see if anything suggests itself."

Side-by-side we walked down the street. At face value it was a normal working day. Ladies could be seen talking in tea rooms and traders of all kinds were busy peddling their wares. After about five minutes, having failed to spot any shops selling clocks, we noticed a constable. He was standing outside a jeweller's. As we approached, our old friend, Inspector Hopkins, emerged. He wore a perplexed expression and appeared to be in a world of his own. He looked up as we approached. His expression became one of both surprise and gratitude.

"Good afternoon, Mr. Holmes," he said. "How did you find out about this?"

"Good afternoon, Hopkins. How did I find out about what?" asked Holmes.

"The robbery at this shop."

Holmes smiled. "I assure you, Hopkins, I know nothing of it. I am here in connection with another matter."

Hopkins removed his hat and scratched his head. "I don't suppose I could trouble you for an opinion on this could I?"

"Certainly," said Holmes. We stepped inside.

Inside the jeweller's all was calm. If it were not for the police presence you would have been forgiven for thinking all was well. Hopkins asked a couple of constables to leave the shop. He closed the door behind them and turned to address us.

"The crime happened yesterday, Mr. Holmes. The proprietor, Mr. Howlett, had left the shop a little after ten o'clock to pay his regular weekly trip to the bank. His normal practice was to leave his assistant in charge but, on this occasion, he had been informed that his assistant was unwell. Because of this, and the fact that the appointment at the bank could not be missed, Mr. Howlett had been forced to close the shop. He locked up and headed for the bank which is about ten minutes away on foot. When he returned around thirty minutes later, he found the door unlocked and half-a-dozen customers in his shop.

"A lady, who was waiting at the counter, remonstrated with him and said his assistant had been rude to her. She explained that he had suddenly run out of the shop about two minutes earlier and she had not seen him since."

"Go on, Hopkins," said Holmes.

"Mr. Howlett, still confused, apologised to the lady, and asked her what she had been enquiring about. They conducted their business and that was that. Later in the day, during a quiet moment, Mr. Howlett had occasion to go into his back room, where he keeps some stock. Imagine his shock when he found his safe unlocked and hundreds of pounds worth of jewellery missing. He immediately sent for the police."

"What did the assistant have to say for himself?" asked Holmes.

Hopkins frowned. "We sent a constable to his lodgings. His rather stern landlady informed us he had not left the house all day. The constable saw the young man in his room where he was laid up with some kind of stomach problem. We have only recently learned he is now missing."

Holmes rubbed his chin. It was quite the puzzle, and I could sense a loss of interest in Mrs. Fairfield's mystery.

"May I take a look around?" asked Holmes.

"By all means," said Hopkins.

Holmes proceeded to slowly walk around the shop. He looked in all the cases, the till, and, finally, at the front door. He opened it before kneeling to examine it with his magnifying glass.

"Most interesting," he said. "It has been expertly picked. It would be hard to do in broad daylight without looking suspicious."

He rose and went through to the back room where he examined the safe. This too, in his opinion, had been adeptly picked.

"Do we have a description of the assistant?" he asked.

"We know what he looks like, Mr. Holmes."

"You misunderstand me, Hopkins. Was a description sought before the young man was visited?"

"We asked about when we arrived and a few people reported seeing a young man run out of the shop. Early twenties, average height, average build, brown hair."

"Does that match the assistant?"

"Yes. But it also matches many other young men and we have the landlady's word that he did not leave his lodgings."

"How much was taken?"

Hopkins opened his notebook. "A dozen watches, ten signet rings, twenty necklaces, and the same number of ladies' bracelets."

Holmes rubbed his chin. "If I were you, Hopkins, I would endeavour to trace the other customers in the shop when Mr. Howlett returned."

"Why?"

"I suspect some, if not all, of them carried the items in their pockets and calmly walked out of the door under his nose. The supposed assistant may have taken some items but he would have rattled rather a lot if he had fled carrying that much. Do let me know how you get on."

He walked out of the shop. I looked at Hopkins, he was opened-mouthed in shock.

I caught up with Holmes a few paces down the road. "What was that all about?"

He smiled. "Hopkins is likely to come up empty-handed. It won't go down well with his superiors. The job was clearly executed by a gang. To rob a jeweller in broad daylight, with no one getting suspicious, takes nerve. One man picked the lock, probably shielded by his accomplices. I suspect the man impersonating the assistant, whoever he may be, literally ran the shop whilst his confederates emptied the safe. You noticed that nothing was taken from the front of the shop? That was to delay the discovery of the crime. The bogus assistant then ostentatiously fled the shop, presumably to ensure he became the focus of any witnesses. His allies remained posing as customers. Our Mr. Howlett returns to what appears to be a busy shop. He does not notice what has happened because the front of the shop looks in order and the customers keep him from entering the back. Only after they all leave does he discover the theft. I would wager that most of them, with the likely inclusion of the lady, left with many items each over the space of many minutes."

"The nerve," I said.

"Clever," said Holmes.

We continued our walk down the street. At the end, roads went left and right. Holmes looked in both directions. "Aha," he said, as he headed right.

I followed. In the distance I could see a bank. However, it turned out this was not his destination. A short distance from the bank was, what appeared to be, a taxi rank. Two hansom cabs stood there. Holmes walked up to the first.

"Good afternoon," he said, idly toying with a shilling. "I don't suppose you carried a yellow box to the nearby home of a lady yesterday?"

"Don't know what you are talking about, sir," said the cabby. Holmes studied him, presumably trying to ascertain whether or not he was telling the truth. Suddenly, the second cab took off. I had to move to avoid being clipped by it.

"How unfortunate," said Holmes, as he joined me. "I can only assume that is our man. I fear, Watson, that I have made a small blunder. If that is indeed our cabby, he will be watching out for us. I may need to get one of Wiggins' boys to let me know if he comes back. It was remiss of me not to get its number before I approached."

We availed ourselves of the first cab to take us to Baker Street. When we arrived, Holmes went directly to his bookshelves and fetched down a copy of the commercial street directory. He sat at the dining table with it, a pencil, and his notebook.

"What are you doing, Holmes?" I asked, after more than twenty minutes of silence.

"I am writing down the details of giftshops in London," he said. "It is most likely that our yellow boxes were purchased from such an establishment." He sighed. "So far, I have identified more than thirty. Sadly, all will need to be visited. Another job for Wiggins."

The put-upon Mrs. Hudson was dispatched with a note. It occurred to me, not for the first time, that I had no idea where these notes went. A reminder, if one were needed, that I still did not know everything about Holmes's methods.

The next morning, several dishevelled young girls turned up at Baker Street in the company of Wiggins. This was the first time I had seen girls, and it tugged at my heart-strings that they too should be out on the streets. I expressed this to Holmes.

"Don't you worry, Watson," he said. "Wiggins takes good care of them all. Our society, as you know, tends to ignore children. You have to learn to use society's prejudices against it. A young girl staring in shop windows is likely to cause less suspicion than a boy."

Holmes gave Wiggins his instructions. He was to send the girls to all the shops on the list. They were to see how many were selling yellow boxes. Wiggins was to bring a report by the evening. I then let them all out. As I watched them run down the street, laughing, I felt nothing but concern. I was immediately struck by the fact that I had rarely felt so for the boys.

I returned to the sitting room. Holmes had taken down one of his larger pipes and was filling it.

"What now?" I asked.

"For the moment, nothing. We need to wait until we receive Wiggins' report, or something else occurs."

Wiggins did not report by the evening. He sent one of his boys with a note to say it was taking longer than expected. Holmes tutted. His mood became even more sour when he learned from the same note that the cab had not been seen since it had sped off. He crumpled the note in his hand and threw it on the floor.

"This delay is inconvenient. I dislike being at the mercy of events."

Fortunately, mid-morning the next day, Wiggins turned up with his report. Of the thirty or so shops Holmes had identified, only ten seemed to be stocking yellow boxes. Holmes took note of the ten in question. He seemed pleased to have something to work with. He handed over a number of pennies, telling Wiggins to be sure to share them out according to the usual rate. Wiggins saluted and dashed off down the stairs. We heard Mrs. Hudson shouting after him to close the door. Holmes chuckled.

"At last, something to go on. Shall we?"

Moments later, we were on the street where it had begun to rain. I dashed back into the hall to obtain an umbrella. Holmes and I sheltered under it until we secured a cab.

For the next few hours, we made our way between the ten establishments identified by Wiggins. We learned that, at one of them, several yellow boxes had been purchased about two weeks previously. They were available in packs of two and had to be assembled by the purchaser. We also learned they were the least popular colour with customers tending to prefer red or blue.

Regrettably, the proprietor had not been able to furnish any useful details about the buyer other than it had been a man. Holmes's disappointment was evident. As we exited the last shop, he stopped and hit the pavement with his cane in frustration.

"Never, Watson," he said "has something so seemingly trivial been so hard to advance."

"You once asserted," I remarked, "that such a situation makes a problem more stimulating."

He managed a smile. "Touché, Watson. Indeed, I did. I have a feeling that something obvious is eluding me and it is rather vexing."

In an effort to cheer Holmes up, I suggested an early dinner at Simpson's. To this he agreed and we spent a couple of charming hours eating fine food and discussing other matters.

When we arrived back at Baker Street, we were surprised to find Hopkins waiting for us. His face told of his exertions. He gladly accepted the brandy I poured him and resumed his place on the settee.

"Is this about the robbery?" asked Holmes.

"Robberies, Mr. Holmes."

"Another one?"

"I'm afraid so."

"Another jeweller?"

"Yes. On Charing Cross Road."

"Go on," said Holmes, as he lit a cigarette.

"The owner of the shop goes by the name of Peabody. He always closes his shop for lunch at one o'clock and heads to the Golden Lion pub for a dram and a sandwich. Today was no different. He locked up at one and headed to the pub which is only a modest distance away but takes a good five or more minutes to get to on such a busy street.

"When he returned, his shop was open. Customers were browsing the cases and a slightly irritable gentleman asked him where he had been as he was waiting to pay. Does it sound familiar, Mr. Holmes?"

Holmes nodded.

Hopkins continued. "He saw to all the customers and closed the shop. It was only a short while later that he noticed several expensive items were missing from the back. He reported it at the local station."

"How did you hear about it?"

"I was back at the Yard updating the superintendent about the progress, or lack of, with the Stoke Newington case. He drew my attention to this one and suggested I take charge in view of the similarities. Can I persuade you to visit in the morning?"

Holmes nodded. "Certainly, Hopkins. My other matter is at a dead-end. This will be a pleasant diversion." We agreed to meet Hopkins at the jeweller's the next morning. I was pleased to get to bed as we had covered a lot of ground.

The next day we presented ourselves at the address. Hopkins let us in and explained that the proprietor had taken himself off to his sister's house in Brixton and we could find him there if we wished.

Holmes performed an examination of the premises. "A highly similar operation," he said. "The lock has been forced. However, it is an older lock so probably easy to do without drawing suspicion. Based on your report, Hopkins, it seems our gang entered as individuals and some posed as browsing customers while the others located the items they sought. Did someone pose as the assistant?"

"Mr. Peabody did not have an assistant," said Hopkins.

"Now that is interesting," said Holmes, without elaborating. "As with the first jeweller, nothing at the front appears disturbed. This gang is calm. I suspect we will find that they have done this many times. Perhaps in other parts of the country. It would be worth you looking into that, Hopkins."

The inspector looked somewhat daunted. "I shall do so right away."

We left the shop and walked the short distance to Shaftsbury Avenue. We engaged one of the many idle cabs and headed to Brixton to meet with Mr. Peabody.

A rather formidable lady opened the door to Holmes's knock. She was not impressed by his card. Fortunately, Mr. Peabody heard the exchange and asked her to let us in. We took seats in the modest front parlour. Mr. Peabody asked his sister if she would prepare some tea. She left the room with evident reluctance.

"You must forgive her, Mr. Holmes," he said. "I am the younger of the two of us, and she has always endeavoured to protect me. How can I help you?"

"With regards to the jewellery you lost," said Holmes, "I understand it was only a few, rather expensive, items. I also understand, from the police, that they were quite rare. Had you had them long?"

Peabody stared at Holmes intently. "A gentleman came into my shop about three months ago seeking similar items. He said they were intended for his wife and that I had been recommended to him by a friend. I explained I had nothing answering to his specifications. He said he would be prepared to leave a substantial deposit if I could secure the pieces he sought. Under the circumstances, I accepted.

"I contacted my many suppliers and secured two pieces within a month. The other arrived only last week. Once I had them all, I communicated with the gentleman concerned and he had arranged to come and view all three pieces a week from today."

"Why did he take so long if he was so eager?" I asked.

"He lived somewhere near Newcastle and was rarely in London."

Having ascertained that Mr. Peabody could tell us little more, Holmes and I elected to take our leave before the formidable sister returned with the tea.

"This gang takes preparation seriously," he said. "In the case of Mr. Peabody, they clearly got him to stock specific items that they wanted to steal. Perhaps they had studied his shop and knew it would be easy to rob once those items were present. Let us get back to Baker Street."

He hailed a cab. As we rattled along, he stared ahead. "I think I will carry out some research of my own, Watson. This gang is so well-practised that they must have done this elsewhere. With Hopkins and I dividing the work between us, we must find something."

Holmes's plans were destined to be foiled. Upon our arrival at Baker Street, Mrs. Hudson informed us a young lady was waiting to see us.

"I don't know, Watson," said Holmes. "For days, nothing. Now, everyone wishes to see us."

He ascended the stairs with impatience. I took off my coat and followed. I was two steps behind him when he opened the door to the sitting room.

The lady on the settee evidently did not hear the door open as she remained seated. Holmes gave a small cough and she jumped to her feet. She was a pretty, young woman of around twenty years of age. Red hair, a rather worn blue dress, and dark green eyes.

Our attention, however, was seized by the yellow box that sat next to her on the settee, which had become visible as she leapt to her feet.

"Please resume your seat, young lady," said Holmes. She sat down.

Holmes took his position by his chair and stared at the young woman. "May I ask your name?"

"Alice Shaw, sir," came the swift reply.

"And what brings you here?"

She jabbed her thumb to her right. "This here box."

I could see Holmes wanted nothing more than to open the box. However, he remained composed. "Please go on."

"I work at a hat shop on Great Newport Street," she said. "Yesterday afternoon, I was in the back room having my lunch when a man comes in. He looked a little shabby and was carrying this box. As I came out, he approached me and said he had been asked to deliver it to the shop."

"Was there a message?" asked Holmes.

The young lady seemed taken aback. "Well, yes, there was. He said it was from a gentleman admirer. Then he was off, straight out the door."

"Can you tell me anything more?"

"Yes. I ran outside in time to see him climb up onto a cab and speed off."

"Did he have a passenger?"

"Not that I saw."

"And what did you find in the box?"

She laughed. "It's the silliest thing." She reached in and pulled out a tiny box. This she opened to reveal a modest pair of earrings which were clearly of minimal value. "Daft isn't it, sir? A huge box for so small a thing."

The young lady had a point. The box was the same size as the one we had seen earlier. The clock it had contained had been approximately the correct size which was far from the case on this occasion.

"I assume there was no written note?" asked Holmes.

"No, sir."

"Did you get the number of the cab?"

"No, sir. I didn't see the need to."

Holmes tutted. "Why did you bring this to me?"

She shrugged. "I heard you were interested in strange things. I like the earrings and would like to know who my admirer is."

Holmes smiled. "If nothing else, they will serve as a souvenir of a bizarre event. I will inform you if I learn of anything else."

The young lady walked to the door. There she turned; her face concerned. "Do you think I'm in any danger, sir?"

"I very much doubt it."

Miss Shaw shrugged and walked out. I showed her to the front door.

Back in the sitting room, I found Holmes rubbing his hands. "Have you had an idea?" I asked.

"Just a small one," he replied. He went to his shelf and got his commercial directory. "But I must turn my attention to this and my files."

For the new few hours, Holmes pored over his hundreds of newspaper clippings. He had contacts around the country who would send him newspaper reports of all manner of crimes. Each would be studied, cross-indexed, and filed in such a manner that he could easily lay his hands upon them.

From behind my newspaper, I watched as he scanned each clipping and would either put it back where he found it or it would join a pile on the dining table. I presumed these were the ones that had some bearing. Suddenly he stopped and clapped his hands.

"Well, Watson. There certainly have been similar crimes elsewhere in the country."

He was about to say more when the bell rang. Holmes's face fell. "Who can that be?"

We heard footsteps on the stairs and a knock at the door.

"Come," said Holmes.

The door opened slowly and the face of a young man appeared. "May I speak with Mr. Holmes?"

I gestured towards my friend whose face was one of irritation.

"I'm so glad to find you at home, sir. I have a problem I wish to put before you."

"We are yet to learn your name," said Holmes, impatiently.

"Oh, yes," he said. "My name is George Gibson."

"And what is the nature of your problem, Mr. Gibson?"

The young man swallowed hard. "I am being watched, Mr. Holmes."

Holmes frowned. "By whom?"

"I don't know. Three mornings ago, I woke up and opened my curtains. My room is at the front of the house where I lodge. I looked down onto the street and could see a man staring at the house. He looked up at me before calmly walking away."

"Forgive me, Mr. Gibson, but that is hardly sinister in itself," said Holmes.

"I understand, but when I returned from work for lunch later that day, I passed the same man in the street. He glanced at me but I got no sense he recognised me. He was talking to another man who I could tell was Scottish from his accent."

Holmes's frustration was increasingly evident. "Mr. Gibson, can I ask you to come to the point?"

Gibson leant forward. "On my way home after work, I saw him again."

"And where was this?"

"About twenty yards down the street."

"Did you challenge him?" asked Holmes.

"No, I was too scared. I am not a strong or confident person."

"And why have you come to me now, if all this happened a few days ago?"

"Because I saw him again today. He passed outside the newsagent where I work. He seemed to be looking across the road."

Holmes stood up. "I am sorry, Mr. Gibson. I have many calls upon my time at present. Nothing you have said is suggestive of wrongdoing. Seeing a man outside your lodgings once is not suspicious. Neither is seeing the same man several times in a busy commercial street. He probably works in the area. I think you are concerning yourself unnecessarily. By all means, let me know if there are further sightings of this gentleman. For now, however, I must ask you to excuse me. Kindly give your address to Dr. Watson on your way out."

Holmes gestured towards the door and Mr. Gibson turned. I opened it and followed him. As he descended the stairs, he meekly uttered multiple apologies for taking up our valuable time. At the front door, I noted down his address. The young man walked unsteadily down Baker Street, looking over his shoulder every few yards.

I turned back to see that Holmes had followed and was half-way down the staircase.

"What a strange fellow," I observed. "I think you were a little harsh."

"Perhaps," said Holmes.

I was about to close the door when I heard a shout. A young lad appeared and held out a piece of paper. Holmes came to the door, took the paper, dropped a few pennies into the outstretched hand, and closed the door.

"Ah," he said. "It would seem that our Stoke Newington cabby has returned to his usual place. Watson, do me a service and make contact with Hopkins. See what his researches have unearthed."

"Now?" I asked.

"If you would be so good."

I seized my overcoat. "What will you be doing?"

He began to climb the stairs. "Acting on this," he said, waving the note.

I made my way to Scotland Yard where I was able to meet with Hopkins. He was in his office, surrounded by telegrams and official reports. He, too, had uncovered similar crimes. The earliest appeared to have been in Glasgow a year previously. Others had taken place in Wales and the north of England. In each case, the proprietor of a jewellery shop had returned from some errand to find his shop open and full of customers. Only later had each discovered they had been relieved of valuable stock.

Poor Hopkins looked perplexed and asked what Holmes had uncovered. I told him that Holmes had gathered together a similar picture. I left him looking downcast, and returned, with his information, to Baker Street.

Holmes was not there when I arrived. It was late evening and Mrs. Hudson informed me dinner was ready. With nothing else to do, I took a seat and proceeded to devour the lamb chops that she had lovingly prepared.

About an hour later, I was drinking a nice glass of port when I heard the door open and close. Slow feet ascended the stairs and the door was thrown open.

There in the doorway was a shabby looking man holding a whip. "Cab for Dr. Watson."

"I didn't order a...," the penny dropped. "Holmes?"

He broke into a laugh. "You're getting better, Watson."

"Stoke Newington, I presume?"

"Indeed," he said, as he walked into his bedroom, tugging at the false whiskers until they began to peel away. "It has been most informative."

"What did you learn?"

Holmes returned, minus his shabby overcoat, and took his usual seat. "Our elusive cabby's name is Fred Johnson. He was more than willing to tell his tale to a professional brother. On the day in question, he had dropped a fare a few minutes earlier and had driven to that rank in Stoke Newington. It seems our Mr. Johnson loves a mug of tea and there is a tea shop nearby where he has an understanding with the lady proprietor. He was bringing a freshly purchased mug to his lips when a man ran up to him with a large yellow box and asked him to deliver it to Mrs. Fairfield's address.

"Johnson declined, as he values his tea-breaks. At this refusal, the man became positively distressed and said it was vital the package be delivered immediately.

"Johnson's first instinct was to get another cabby to take the commission but there were no others on the rank. So, in an effort to get rid of the man, he said he would take the package for a guinea. It was an absurd rate he assumed would bring an end to the matter. Imagine his surprise when the young man handed him two.

"When he saw he was being offered two guineas for such an easy commission, he took it. He got onto his cab and told the man to put the box inside. Instead, the man handed it up to him saying that he wanted him to keep an eye on it because of its value. Johnson obliged and balanced it on the roof of his cab until he delivered it to Mrs. Fairfield."

"What does that tell you?" I asked.

"Well, it dovetails with Mrs. Fairfield's story – not that I doubted her. It is also suggestive."

"Did you get a description of this man?"

"Yes. Young, around twenty-five. Just less than six feet. Slim build. Dressed in slightly battered clothes."

"It doesn't strike me as all that useful."

"Except in one respect," said Holmes.

"Which is?"

"That so poorly dressed a man is unlikely to wish to pay two guineas to deliver a box a few hundred yards down the road when he could carry it himself. It must have been important to have it taken by cab. Why does he wish to hide himself from someone he supposedly admires?

"Then we come to the second instance. Miss Shaw has a similar box delivered from an admirer, by cab. Is this man wooing multiple women from a distance? To what purpose? There must be a purpose. It is also beyond coincidence that the two events have taken place in the vicinity of robberies."

Holmes reached for a cigarette. As he smoked, I told him of my conversation with Hopkins.

"That is good," he said. "That tallies with what I have learned. So, it would appear these crimes began in Glasgow before moving to the east coast. They then made their way south to Wales. Now they are in London. These people are clever. They are not loitering anywhere long enough for a pattern to be noticed. Until now."

"But how do we prevent the next one?"

"That I am not sure of," said Holmes.

Holmes sat up late into the night. The room soon became filled with smoke and I was forced to open all the windows. Eventually, I determined he was not going to come to any conclusions at a sociable hour. I announced my intention of retiring. He nodded and I headed upstairs.

I had barely taken off my waistcoat when there was a knock at the door. I opened it.

"My dear Watson," said Holmes. "Would you oblige me with Mr. Gibson's address?"

I got hold of my notebook and handed it to him.

"Thank you," he said. "Sleep well." He then dashed downstairs.

The next morning, I descended late for breakfast. It was almost midday and Holmes was sitting at the dining table. He was clearly lost in thought as the long ash on his cigarette testified to the fact that he had been motionless for many minutes. As I walked into the room, he smiled.

"Good morning, Watson." I do believe we stand a chance of bringing this to an end."

"Really?" I asked, astonished.

"It is by no means certain. But there is a chance." He tapped the commercial directory he had used previously. "I decided to re-examine Mr. Gibson's account. Based on his description and address, I have located the newsagent where he works."

"And?"

"Across from it is a jeweller."

"Sorry, Holmes, I don't see."

"You will recall him saying that he believed he was being followed. Also, that he saw this man multiple times, once in conversation with someone Scottish."

"Yes."

"Use a little imagination, my friend. We know these crimes began in Scotland. They have moved south. Let us assume that this Scottish man is part of the gang. He is seen in conversation with the man Mr. Gibson thinks is following him. Mr. Gibson later notices this man taking an interest in a jewellery shop."

"It all seems a little tenuous, Holmes."

He stood up. "Perhaps. But there was no harm in testing it. I sent a message to the jeweller, whose name is Henderson. He confirmed he takes a daily break for his lunch at midday. I trust you see the similarity?"

"Yes, I do."

"He confirmed that he has not suffered any losses as yet. Now, it could all be coincidence. Perhaps Mr. Gibson has quite the imagination and these men are just innocent citizens but what if they are not? Just suppose that they are gathering intelligence and Henderson is their next target. It cannot be many days before the attempt is made."

"What do you propose to do?"

"I propose to force the issue."

"How can you do that? You can hardly tell this gang when to act."

He rose and went to the window. "I believe I can and I have already set the wheels in motion. Nothing will happen today but I will make it happen tomorrow."

Holmes refused to be drawn further on his plans but his confidence was clear. The frustrated man of the past few days had been replaced by a man of increasing confidence. In the evening, a note arrived from Hopkins saying all was in place.

The next day, at eleven o'clock, Holmes informed me it was time. He picked up a flat package on his way to the door. I followed him into a cab. Our destination was Kilburn High Street.

"Mr. Gibson's lodgings are very close to Kilburn High Street and the newsagent where he is employed is on that very road. The jeweller, Mr. Henderson, likes to take a walk every day at midday. He walks north of his business and has lunch at a coffee shop which is approximately ten minutes away. He returns promptly by one o'clock. His habits would have been his undoing, but they will save him on this occasion."

The cab dropped us off at the bottom of the high street. Holmes turned to the south and pointed with his cane.

"A minute or two down there is Mr. Gibson's lodgings." He turned round. "A five-minute walk to the north brings us to where he works. Across from there is Henderson's jewellery shop. Follow me."

We headed north. After five minutes we came across a newsagent. I could see the jeweller's almost directly opposite. At Holmes's request, we continued our journey north.

"It would not do for us to be seen loitering in the immediate area. The gang might well be watching. Mr. Henderson's coffee shop of choice is a modest walk from here."

We continued our walk north. Holmes suddenly stopped. "Have you noticed, Watson, that this street is well served by cabs and the traffic flows freely with minimal congestion?"

"Yes, Holmes," I replied. "It's a busy commercial street. Surely that is no surprise?"

"Quite so. But it is important."

We stopped by a public noticeboard, a considerable distance past the jewellery shop, and pretended to study the various notices and advertisements. Holmes took out his watch. "It is five past twelve. We should soon see Mr. Henderson."

"How will you recognise him?"

"He kindly gave me some personal particulars that will aid me."

We waited a few minutes. "There he is," said Holmes.

I turned and identified the man. He walked in our direction, on the opposite side of the street. Soon he was past us on his way for his lunch."

"Look," said Holmes.

I immediately saw another man. He was young and kept about twenty feet behind Henderson. Under his arm he carried a large, flat package. In his other hand was a bag. He continued to follow Henderson and, after a minute or two, both were out of sight.

"Good," said Holmes. "Follow me." He turned and crossed the street.

"This will do," he said.

He unwrapped the package he had brought with him. It was one of the yellow boxes. Holmes quickly assembled it. "Flag down a cab, Watson."

It was mere seconds before one came into view. "Where to guv'nor?"

Holmes handed him a shilling and a piece of paper. "Please deliver this box to this address."

"Certainly, sir," said the cabby. "Just pop it on the seat."

"If you don't mind," said Holmes. Could you carry it with you? I wouldn't want it unsupervised."

He handed the box up to the confused cabby. "It's very light, sir."

"Don't worry about that," said Holmes. "It must not be delivered too early. Please don't depart from here for five minutes. Here's another shilling for your trouble."

The confused cabby confirmed he understood.

"Quick, Watson," said Holmes, as he headed south.

I had to maintain quite the pace to keep up with him. Soon we were nearing Henderson's shop. Holmes carried on past it for about twenty yards and stopped outside a greengrocer's shop.

"Ah good, there's Hopkins," said Holmes.

"Good afternoon, Mr. Holmes," said the inspector. "My men are positioned where you asked. All are in civilian clothes."

"Good. Now we wait."

We stood for a few minutes. Then we saw the cab come into view. As it passed us, Holmes smiled. "That will have caused some consternation. Now, Hopkins."

The inspector took out and waved his handkerchief. A number of men moved into position at the front of the shop. I saw some were armed.

"It is time we put in an appearance."

We walked into the shop. The customers turned to look at us. Each and every one of them looked flustered.

"Can I help you, gentlemen?" said a young man behind the counter.

"Yes," said Holmes. "Would all of you kindly empty your pockets?"

"I beg your pardon," said an older man who was looking at a case of watches.

"I believe your hearing is in good order, sir," replied Holmes, with a smile. "Is that a Perthshire accent?"

"I don't need to listen to this," said another man. He made for the door. Hopkins blocked his path. "I am a police officer. Please do as you have been asked."

The man backed away. He turned from side to side as if in search of an escape.

"I don't understand, gentlemen," said the man behind the counter.

"All will become clear when Mr. Henderson returns," said Holmes. He nodded at Hopkins who knocked on the window. The door opened, all his men filed in and produced truncheons and revolvers.

About an hour later, a man entered the shop and was visibly stunned to find it full of armed men. Holmes introduced himself and informed us this was Mr. Henderson.

"I am much obliged, sir," said Holmes, "that you followed my instructions."

Henderson smiled. "Why would I not? You have saved me a small fortune and I am happy to do my civic duty."

Holmes nodded. He moved closer to the Scottish gentleman. "You must be Angus Robertson. No, no, don't trouble yourself by denying it. I admire your scheme but it has run its course."

"I don't know what you are talking about?" replied the visibly angry Scot.

Holmes gestured to one of Hopkins' men who focused his revolver on Robertson. Holmes dived into the man's pocket and pulled out a necklace. "Yours?" he asked, with a smile.

Robertson grunted. He knew there was nothing he could say.

Over the next few minutes, the other people in the shop were relieved of various items including rings and watches. They were all taken by Hopkins for evidence, much to the discomfort of Henderson. This was only placated when Hopkins wrote out a receipt.

A few hours later, Hopkins joined us at Baker Street. He informed us the gang was not talking.

"No matter," said Holmes. "You have sufficient evidence to bring them to justice for this crime. If you circulate the descriptions to your colleagues up and down the country you will find someone who can start tying them to the other crimes."

"How did you figure it out?" I asked.

Holmes smiled. He took out his favourite pipe and filled it. "An idea formed in my mind when Miss Shaw told us where she worked. We had two cases of people receiving unsolicited gifts in close proximity to the site of a robbery. That, I thought, was beyond coincidence.

"In both cases, the owner of a business had left, on foot, to conduct some activity. Firstly, it was a bank transaction; secondly, it was a simple break for lunch. As soon as the owner was out of the way, the gang would move in.

"Once inside, they went about their business, being sure to have someone on lookout. The gang, once alerted, would need to restore the shop to order and have enough time to pose as normal customers before the return of the owner."

"Why would they not all leave as soon as the alarm was raised?" asked Hopkins.

"Because more than half a dozen people leaving a shop in a hurry would attract someone's attention. This was not only about executing a robbery; it was also about delaying its discovery. That required them to act calmly and slowly as opposed to swiftly and rashly."

"So, how did they do it?" I asked.

Holmes smiled. "I have to admire it, I really do. They identify their target. They watch the comings and goings of the people working there. In the case of the Stoke Newington robbery, they noticed that either the owner or assistant was always there. They also took careful note of when money was taken to the bank. I suspect they paid the assistant to stay away that day. Mr. Howlett is forced leave his shop locked but, essentially, unguarded. A member of the gang follows Howlett. They know it will take him approximately thirty minutes to go and come back. As soon as he is a safe distance away, the gang effects an entrance and begins taking what they came for. I have no doubt they made many innocent visits beforehand to ascertain what was there.

"Our man follows Mr. Howlett to the bank and sees him go inside. Later, he emerges, having conducted his business, and begins the journey back to his shop - a journey of around ten to fifteen minutes.

"The man who followed him can hardly run past him to the shop. If he did so, he would possibly draw attention to himself. He would also not arrive sufficiently in advance of Howlett for the gang to prepare. So, what does he do?"

Hopkins and I waited.

"He sends a signal. He approaches a cab driver. He hands him a sizeable sum of money and asks him to deliver a box to an address. He ensures the box is conveyed on top of the cab which renders it, thanks to its size and colour, highly visible. The cabby must pass the jewellery shop on his way to his destination. Another gang member, who is studying cabs, sees the bright yellow box. Something of that size and colour stands out, at a distance, in any amount of traffic. Because the cab is faster than the walking Mr. Howlett, the gang has plenty of time to stage the scene. The pretend assistant flees to make himself the obvious suspect. The others restore order to the shop before calmly waiting. They keep the confused Mr. Howlett busy for many minutes before walking off with the contents of his safe."

"Amazing," said Hopkins.

"But why the choice of gifts?" I asked.

"That was another stroke of genius," said Holmes. "A cabby would remember carrying a large empty box to an address. It had to hold something to be believable."

"But why a clock and earrings?"

"You have to understand," said Holmes. "That these boxes were destined for locations, not people. Both cabbies said as much. They never had the name of the recipient. They just had the address."

I was not satisfied. "But why a clock and earrings?"

"Simple, Watson. Let's take the second occasion first. Having selected a shop for the box to be delivered to, they determined that it was staffed entirely by women. A pair of earrings were therefore sent along with the message that they were from a gentleman admirer.

"In the case of Mrs. Fairfield, it was a private address. The gang did not want to knock on the door, or make enquiries, in case they were remembered. So, they chose an item acceptable to either sex. Do you have it, Hopkins?"

The inspector produced a bag.

"This, Watson, is the bag carried by the man who was following Henderson." Holmes reached inside it and produced a modest box. He opened it to reveal a set of six silver spoons.

"Once again," he said, "an item equally acceptable to a recipient of either sex. As the destination was a private address, they had not made any enquiries that might arouse attention. If we had not intervened, our man would have put this inside the yellow box he was also carrying, under plain wrapping paper, and given it to the first available cabby. You will recall me observing, Watson, that Kilburn High Street was especially blessed with them.

"When young Mr. Gibson, came to see us, I was a trifle dismissive. Later, given his talk of a Scottish man and the fact these crimes commenced in Scotland, the possibility struck me that his address might be under consideration to receive a yellow box. A study of the commercial directory revealed Mr. Henderson's shop."

Hopkins smiled the smile of man who had found a gap in the story. "I'm sorry, Mr. Holmes, but how could you know it would be today?"

Holmes's smile, although brief, was broader. "I couldn't. So, I communicated with Mr. Henderson. I knew his shop was likely being watched. I simply got him to place a sign in his window yesterday to the effect that he would receive a large amount of new stock this morning. There was little chance of the gang striking earlier and missing out on a haul. I arranged for a cart to deliver a number of boxes first thing this morning to complete the deception."

Holmes, his account over, leant back in his seat and puffed away contentedly. Hopkins stood.

"Thank you, Mr. Holmes. I have a mountain of paperwork and other forces to make contact with. If you will excuse me?"

Holmes said nothing. Hopkins and I made our way to the front door. The inspector stepped outside and turned to face me.

"You know something, Doctor," he said. "It seems Mr. Holmes may have had some difficulty with this one had it not been for Mr. Gibson. Without him coming to see you, the Henderson robbery may well have been a success." He touched his hat and was on his way.

When I returned to the sitting room, I pointed this out to Holmes. He sat up in his seat.

"Hopkins makes a fair point, Watson. Let us pay Mr. Gibson a visit at his lodgings. If nothing else, I owe him an apology."

At just before half-past six we arrived at Mr. Gibson's address. A rather stern landlady introduced herself as Mrs. Maxwell, invited us in, and led us to her front parlour. There, she invited us to sit.

"If Mr. Gibson owes you money, gentlemen, I'm afraid you are unlikely to see it repaid."

"I don't understand, madam," said Holmes.

"He came here two weeks ago, with the most excellent references and a single suitcase, seeking a room. He told me he was about to start a job nearby and desired a room close to his work. I took a modest deposit and he moved in there and then. This morning I found him gone with no form of explanation. He owes me three-days rent."

We commiserated with Mrs. Maxwell and made our excuses. From her house, we headed to the newsagent where Mr. Gibson had worked. It took a few minutes to rouse the proprietor, who lived above the shop, before we were admitted. There we learned that a note had been left by Gibson to say he had been forced to return to his family and was profoundly sorry. No forwarding address had been given. When we were informed that he was owed wages we suggested those wages be given to his former landlady.

Back on the street, Holmes looked concerned. "What is it?" I asked.

"Nothing, Watson," he replied. "Nothing."

The Adventure of Bramble Cottage

(Late 1898)

N OCCASION, a telegram or letter from a potential client would seize the attention of my friend either because it was unusual or because it was banal. On this particular occasion, it was the latter.

The letter had arrived in the afternoon post two days earlier. In the weeks running up to its arrival, Holmes had been juggling several small matters which, in response to his observation, I conceded were of insufficient public interest to warrant escaping from the pages of my journals. When those matters had been brought to a conclusion, Holmes had become bored. To distract him, I had suggested going to see a play which had been the talk of the West End for the previous few months. The play was called A Man through Time, and the lead actor, Edward Harrison, played a man at various stages of his life. It required him to employ his formidable vocal abilities as well as his talent for deploying greasepaint.

Harrison had only recently returned to the production. Some weeks earlier, at the height of its success, he had stopped performing, citing an illness which affected his voice. Without its star, the show had become something of a commercial liability with Harrison's understudy playing to half-empty houses. It was rumoured that Harrison had been threatened with legal proceedings by his backers if he did not return to the stage.

Harrison had certainly had a tumultuous career. Some ten years previously he had been saved from bankruptcy when a mysterious benefactor had rescued a production that had failed to attract the ticket sales he had hoped. The decade that followed had seen him restore his reputation by, essentially, starting again.

Holmes, to my total lack of surprise, had been less than enthusiastic about attending the performance. I only succeeded in convincing him by suggesting he might learn useful techniques he could apply on cases. He had ultimately conceded that there may be some merit in the idea.

Following the performance, we had succeeded in seeing Harrison in his dressing room. Holmes had questioned him, perhaps to excess, about his various guises and had the poor actor demonstrate a number of techniques to him over the course of an hour.

It took all of Harrison's formidable acting talent to pretend he was disappointed to see us depart. Holmes had expressed a desire to dine at Simpson's. Sadly, the staff had been unable to accommodate us so we had adjourned to nearby Rules in Covent Garden. About an hour later, over cigars, Holmes had expressed disdain for the play's plot but suggested he had indeed learned some techniques that he could put into practice. It was the day after the performance that had seen the arrival of the letter.

"Sometimes, Watson," said Holmes, as he lit a cigarette, "the challenging cases have the most unremarkable beginnings."

"You refer to that recent letter, I suppose?"

"Indeed," he said. He lifted the paper from the arm of his chair and proceeded to read it aloud – and not for the first time. "Dear Mr. Holmes. I beg to discuss the matter of my uncle's disappearance from

Bramble Cottage. May I call upon you at two o'clock on the fourteenth inst.? Yours sincerely, Rebecca Tomlinson."

"It is certainly a concise letter," I said, as I looked at my watch. "Well, the appointment is but forty minutes from now. Soon, we will know more."

A few minutes past the stated hour, the bell rang. Soon after, Mrs. Hudson showed a beautiful young woman into the sitting room. She advanced towards Holmes, with a boldness I think he found unsettling, with her hand outstretched. He gave her the briefest of handshakes before she extended me the same courtesy. The warmth of her gentle grasp, through her lace gloves, brought a smile to my face and an unexpected warmth to my cheeks.

"Do sit down, Miss Tomlinson," said Holmes.

She took one end of the settee. I took the other, and Holmes resumed his usual seat. "I must confess, Miss Tomlinson," he said, "that your letter tells me little."

She removed her gloves and brushed a stray lock of dark hair from her eyes. "I do apologise, Mr. Holmes, but I was in a state of some anxiety when I wrote it. The police showed little interest in my uncle's disappearance, and I fear I may have wasted too much time."

"I am all attention," said Holmes as he stretched out his legs.

She took a deep breath. "The events of which I speak centre around Bramble Cottage. It is located in Sussex, near Pulborough. Don't be fooled by the name, Mr. Holmes, Bramble Cottage is a house of considerable size. Its name derives from the modest original building but it has been extended by its various owners over the last three centuries."

"May I ask the business of your family?" said Holmes.

"We have been in the jewellery business for generations," she replied. "The house was acquired by my late grandfather some forty years ago."

Holmes nodded. "From your letter I note your uncle lives there. Is he the only resident?"

Miss Tomlinson's eyes betrayed her sadness. "Aside from the staff, alas, yes. Our family's recent history is one with more than its fair share of woe. My Uncle Peter is the head of the family. He had a wife, Sarah, and two children – Thomas, and Alice."

Holmes frowned. "Am I to presume they are no longer with us?"

"That is correct, Mr. Holmes. On a trip to Switzerland three years ago, my Aunt Sarah died when she accidentally fell from the balcony of their hotel. Only five months previously, they had lost their son in a horse-riding accident which had left the whole family bereft. They tried to continue with their lives but the heart had gone out of them, with my aunt being the most affected. The Swiss holiday was an attempt to revive their spirits and my uncle blamed himself for my aunt's death – saying he should never have arranged the trip.

"Upon his return from Switzerland, he arranged her funeral to which the entire extended family were invited – with the exception of my father."

"Why was your father excluded?" I asked.

She turned to me and smiled weakly. "My father is not the most pleasant of men. He was deeply resentful of how the family fortune was divided following the death of my grandfather. He demanded an allowance from my uncle which was subsequently granted. My father was forever complaining it was insufficient for his needs and my uncle would always reply that it was more than he deserved.

"I was angry with my father and pointed out more than once that my uncle was suffering. My father was heartless. His brother's suffering was not important when compared to his personal financial needs." She paused to gather herself.

"Please go on, Miss Tomlinson," said Holmes.

The lady took a handkerchief from her bag and tucked it into her sleeve. It was clear that she expected to need it. "My uncle struggled to keep his spirits up following the funeral. He wore black constantly and socialised little. All his time was focused on Alice who had been deeply affected by their bereavements and required constant attention.

"They seemed to be getting back on their feet when an unwelcome presence entered their lives."

"You intrigue me," said Holmes.

"Have you ever heard of The Brotherhood of the Compassionate Heart?"

Holmes rose and went to his files. "It recalls something to my mind." His fingers danced along the spines of several files before he alighted on one and leafed through it.

"Yes. Here it is. An organisation based in Sussex dedicated to charitable works. There was some suspicion around whether or not they were a criminal enterprise. No supporting evidence was unearthed."

Miss Tomlinson appeared to be impressed. "It is interesting to hear you say that, Mr. Holmes. They conduct themselves like a religious order and occupy a mansion, called The Cedars, about two miles from my uncle's house. They are led by a man who calls himself Brother Alaric."

Holmes's eyebrows rose. "And how did this group come into contact with your family?"

"Alice told me that Brother Alaric had called at Bramble Cottage about three days after my aunt's funeral. He was dressed in the habit of a monk with cowl up, concealing most of his face. Alice said that this remained up throughout his visit. My uncle agreed to see him and they held an interview in his study. According to Alice, who loitered nearby, they spoke for around thirty minutes before my uncle began raising his voice. The servants were summoned, and Brother Alaric was escorted swiftly from the house protesting he had been misunderstood."

"Do you know precisely what was discussed?" asked Holmes.

"Alice told me that Brother Alaric had offered to comfort the family. Counselling the bereaved was a common activity for his group. However, the conversation had eventually moved onto financial matters with Brother Alaric seeking significant, and perpetual, donations for his mission. My uncle saw this as a brazen attempt to benefit from his grief, and responded accordingly.

"The next day, a note arrived from The Cedars, in which Brother Alaric endeavoured to address the misunderstanding. He invited my uncle to visit to see the work of the group first-hand. My uncle was averse to the idea but was persuaded by Alice, who was less inclined to assume deception, to give Brother Alaric an opportunity to explain himself. At the same time, she issued an invitation to me to come and stay with them. I was to arrive a little after midday.

"I was in ignorance of all these events when I arrived at the cottage. Alice was there to greet me and explained everything when I observed her father's absence. She further explained that she regretted cajoling him into the visit.

"'Let us see what he says when he returns,' I said.

"My uncle returned to the house about two hours later. He was angry but his mood improved as soon as he saw me.

"'I'm sorry, my dear Rebecca,' he said, after a brandy. 'I had no desire for you to see me in such a temper. I understand Alice has told you about these people?'

"I confirmed she had.

"'As a rich man, I encounter a lot of people seeking money for nothing. Yet, I don't think I have met anyone more obviously so than Brother Alaric.'

"Uncle proceeded to explain that he had taken a lengthy tour of the house and spoken to several of the order's members, all of whom wore the same clothes and always kept their cowls up. He had been told of their good works in the local community and further afield. I asked him why he was annoyed.

"'I am annoyed, my dear niece, because it was all words. They offered no evidence of their claims and declined to identify any of their other benefactors. This Brother Alaric sought money again and I declined again. He expressed the hope he would win me over at some point and I said I considered it doubtful.'"

At this point, Holmes stood and went to the window. He looked out onto Baker Street for a few seconds before turning round to face our guest. "Please continue."

Miss Tomlinson's eyes began to moisten. "Just over a year ago, I received a letter from my uncle. It contained the most distressing news."

"The death of your cousin," said Holmes.

Miss Tomlinson showed no surprised. "Yes. Alice had hidden it well but she had been more deeply affected by the death of her mother and brother than anyone had realised. She had, over a period of time, extracted arsenic from fly-papers, and used it to end her life. She was but eighteen months away from turning twenty-one."

"You appear to be of a similar age," said Holmes.

"Yes. We were born a week apart. In some ways we were more like sisters. In his letter, my uncle gave me the details of the funeral. Imagine my surprise when I arrived at the church to find several men dressed like monks."

"I take it they were members of this brotherhood?" asked Holmes.

"Yes. It was Brother Alaric himself and two of his senior followers. They seemed to know who I was and introduced themselves. I was stunned, as you might imagine."

"How did your uncle react?"

"He was accommodating. He said he had come to appreciate that their motives were genuine and he had invited them to attend. He also said he had plans to discuss how he might assist them in the future."

"Quite the volte-face," said Holmes, as he returned to his seat.

"A few weeks later," said Miss Tomlinson, "I was invited back to Bramble Cottage. My uncle said there was important information for me to hear. Naturally, I accepted the appointment.

"I arrived and was admitted by the butler, Wilson, who escorted me to my uncle's study. What I found there surprised me.

"Several members of the order were there as was Frederick Sampson, my uncle's solicitor. My uncle was sitting behind his desk. To my astonishment he was dressed in similar clothing to the members of the order. He rose and embraced me before returning to his seat and raising his cowl. In that state it was not possible to distinguish him from the other members of the order.

"Mr. Sampson spoke, 'Miss Tomlinson,' he said. 'Your uncle has called you here in order that you should understand the terms of your grandfather's will.'"

"What was your grandfather's name?" asked Holmes.

"He was also Peter Tomlinson," she replied. "He did much to create the family's present wealth."

"Please continue."

"Mr. Sampson opened his case and took out a document. 'Under the terms of your late grandfather's will. A sum of money was put into trust to be divided equally amongst his grandchildren upon their twenty-first birthdays. The will stated that your uncle was to be the trustee. As you are the last grandchild, and are less than two years away from the required age, it is important that you know the entire sum will come to you.'"

"What was the value of this fund?" asked Holmes.

"Two hundred thousand pounds," said Miss Tomlinson.

I whistled. It was the kind of money people would do a lot to acquire.

"What else did the solicitor have to say?"

"Nothing. He put all his papers back into his case and bid us good day. My uncle rose from his desk and came round to see me. 'I know you are confused, Rebecca.' He gestured to the robed figures. 'After much reflection, I have decided that the best thing I can do with my remaining years is to assist Brother Alaric with his charitable endeavours. As you can see, I have gone a step further and have begun taking the necessary path towards entering their order.'

"At this point one of the hooded figures stood and removed his cowl. It was Brother Alaric. 'Dear Miss Tomlinson, your uncle has given me permission to tell you that he is rewriting his will to leave Bramble Cottage to the order upon his death. As you have heard, this will not be to your disadvantage as you are provided for.'

"My head was in a whirl and I could not formulate a response. Brother Alaric bowed, bid us all farewell, and left with his followers in tow. I turned to my uncle. 'What is happening here, uncle?'

"'I know you find it hard to understand, my dear, but it has taken this level of loss for me to realise where my path lies.'

"'But to give them Bramble Cottage!' I exclaimed.

"'You and I both know that your father would only sell it if he got his hands on it.'"

"I take it that, to put it kindly, your father is not the best with money?" said Holmes.

She nodded. "He used to be good but he reacted badly to the death of my grandfather and found solace in gambling and drinking. He shows no inclination to work and lives solely off the allowance from my uncle."

"What happened after this meeting?"

"I made a point of visiting my uncle regularly from that day onwards. This was not only to see him but also to ensure that this brotherhood was not taking advantage. My uncle was delighted to see me but he was always wearing this garb. He would take the cowl down occasionally but, as time went on, it was removed less and less."

"What did your uncle's household staff make of events?"

"My uncle has a loyal household some of whom have served him for more than twenty years. I did ask Wilson, the butler, what he thought. His response was to say that the staff would remain loyal to my uncle and support him. He did assure me that he shared some of my concerns and would notify me if he ever felt my uncle was being taken advantage of.

"Two months ago, on one of my many visits, I was struck by the changes to the house. It had become more spartan, as if my uncle was selling off some of the contents. It saddened me greatly. By this time my uncle wore his cowl constantly. I felt like I'd lost him and broke down in tears. In a moment, he wrapped his arm around me. He took down the hood to reveal a grief-weathered face. 'My countenance shows every mark of my grief,' he said. 'My desire is to hide my deep sadness from the niece whom I love.' With that remark the cowl was replaced."

Holmes fetched a pipe from the mantelpiece. He filled it and lit it before resuming his seat. "I feel I understand the background. Please proceed to what has brought you here today."

Miss Tomlinson asked for some water and took a few sips before placing the glass to one side. "About five weeks ago, my uncle wrote me a letter. In it he asked that I not visit for two weeks. He was having a guest stay and desired no visits until his guest departed. I was a trifle hurt but did not object. I wrote to agree and that was that. Following the end of those two weeks, I went, by arrangement, to see him. I was admitted by Wilson, who seemed on edge, and went to the study where I found my uncle at his desk, cowl up as usual. I asked him who his visitor had been and whether he had enjoyed being a host – something he had not done for some time. He answered in a manner that suggested he was suffering from a cold.

"'Are you unwell, uncle,' I asked. 'No, no,' he said, in a rasping tone, 'but please excuse me a moment.' He left the room and was gone for a few minutes. He returned with a glass of water, sat down, and removed the cowl before drinking. When he spoke, his voice was back to normal.

"'May I know who your guest was?' I asked.

"'It was one of the gentlemen from the hotel in Switzerland,' he said. 'A man by the name of William Frost. He was one of the few Englishmen at the hotel when your aunt passed. He had helped with the return of her body to England. We had exchanged addresses at the time. He recently wrote, asking after my health, and I invited him to stay.'

"This was the first I had heard of Mr. Frost. My uncle, understandably, had not been prone to talking about the events surrounding my aunt's death. 'I would have liked to have met him to express my own gratitude,' I said.

"'I am sorry, Rebecca. Perhaps you can if he visits again,' was all my uncle would say before he replaced his cowl, which, from that point, I never saw him without, and the conversation drifted onto other matters.

"A few hours later, my uncle sent one of his valets to fetch a cab to take me to the station. As I made my way home, I could not shake the notion that my uncle was holding something back from me.

"I had only been at home a week when I received a letter from my uncle, inviting me to visit again. I arrived on the requested date. As I stepped down from my cab I could see my uncle's loyal dog, Freddy, staring out of the window. He didn't even seem to notice me; his attention was fixed beyond me. I lightly tapped on the window and he looked at me before resuming his stare into the distance.

"My uncle greeted me in the front parlour and we began to talk about his activities with the order. On several occasions I called out to Freddy who remained at the window. Once or twice, he came over and I stroked him. As soon as I stopped, he would slink off back to the window. I asked my uncle what the matter was. He paused for a while, and sighed, before answering.

"'He has been like that for the last few days,' he said. 'I had to let Stevens go.'

"'But he has been your valet for years,' I replied. 'What was the reason?'

"My uncle seemed uncomfortable with the question. 'I'd prefer not to discuss it, Rebecca. He often brought a bone for Freddy from our local butcher. I suspect the old boy is pining for him.'

"There was a knock at the door and Wilson entered. 'A telegram for you, sir.'

"My uncle opened it and said, 'Please reply that all is well.'

"I remember Wilson's face fell. He nodded and left the room. My uncle and I had dinner together before a cab arrived to take me back to the station. When I left, Freddy was still in the window staring out."

Holmes had sat up in his seat in the last few minutes of Miss Tomlinson's account. "Did you tell your father any of this?"

"He didn't even seem to notice me; his attention was fixed beyond me."

Miss Tomlison grimaced. "As little as possible, Mr. Holmes. He would always question me on what had taken place on my visits. I was clever enough to realise that he wanted to know of anything unusual, anything he could use against my uncle. Of course, the news that my uncle had joined this order was of great interest to him. I feared he would attempt something and I recall warning my uncle not long after the meeting with his solicitor."

"What did your uncle do?" asked Holmes.

"He knew my father well and doubled his allowance."

"He doubled it?" asked Holmes.

"I remember when father got the telegram. His face lit up. He could not conceal his glee. I raised the matter soon afterwards and uncle said it would stop my father from trying anything."

"What next?" asked Holmes.

"About a week ago I was back at Bramble Cottage. When I arrived, I did not see Freddy in the window. I was initially relieved until I mentioned it to my uncle.

"'I'm sorry to tell you, my dear, that I was forced to have him put down.'

"I was shocked. 'But why? He was not unwell.'

"'No, but he was very old, my dear. I was advised it was the kindest thing to do.'

"It was said so calmly that it unsettled me. My uncle escorted me to the garden where a wooden cross could be seen in the borders. 'Wilson buried him there for me.'

"I asked for a few minutes to reflect. I had loved Freddy and was concerned that I clearly felt his loss more than my uncle appeared to. As we stood there, we heard a cough. We both turned to see Wilson.

"'I am sorry, sir, but an urgent message has arrived for you.'

"My uncle took the telegram and read it. Although I could not see his face, it was clear the message greatly disturbed him. His voice cracked as he spoke to me. 'I'm so sorry, my dear, but I must ask you to curtail this visit. You will not be able to visit me for at least the next few weeks. I will remain in contact by telegram.'

"With disturbing speed, I was reunited with my coat and helped into a cab that arrived about thirty minutes later."

"Most odd," said Holmes.

"I was greatly disturbed by the abrupt end of my visit and the demand that I not return. I assumed it was the Brotherhood exerting its malign influence. I decided to go back at the first opportunity. That opportunity came two days later. When I arrived at the house, a bemused Wilson told me my uncle was not at home. He saw the look on my face and admitted me to the house in order that I could determine it for myself. Uncle was nowhere to be found. In response to my questions, Wilson simply said my uncle had left the house not long after my last visit and left no details of where he was going or when he would be back.

"I left the house and headed directly for The Cedars. They declined to admit me until I threatened to go to the police."

"Did you manage to see Brother Alaric?" asked Holmes.

"Yes. He received me in his study. He seemed genuinely alarmed when I demanded to see my uncle. 'I can assure you, Miss Tomlinson, he is not here. He has not attended his most recent class for his admission to the order. If I do hear from him I shall, of course, let you know.' It was at this point that I approached the police.

"Their response was to say my uncle was entitled to go wherever he wished without informing me and, unless I had evidence of a crime, they could not help me."

"Fools," said Holmes, under his breath. "What do you wish me to do?"

"I need to know if my uncle is safe and well. He is a rich man and is surrounded by so many people who would benefit from his demise."

Holmes paused. "Very well. I will make some enquiries. Do you live with your father presently?"

"Yes, Mr. Holmes."

"If I wished to communicate with you, could we keep it from him?"

She thought for a moment. "I will give you the address of my old governess. She is fond of me and will not betray a confidence. I often visit her and can retrieve letters there."

She asked for some notepaper which I provided. She wrote down the address and handed it to Holmes who placed it in his pocket. I helped her into her coat and escorted her to the front door.

I watched her hail a cab and sighed as she departed.

Holmes looked at me as I entered the sitting room. "A trifle young for you, old fellow," he said.

I flushed with embarrassment. "You have it wrong, Holmes. But her countenance did rather remind me of when Mary first visited us."

He smiled reassuringly. "I understand. Remember, she is a mere factor in this problem. Do not be swayed by your fondness for a pretty face."

Holmes decided that he needed to send a telegram. He was out for around thirty minutes before he returned with a paper. "There's nothing else I wish to do today," he said. "Tomorrow we will visit Bramble Cottage and The Cedars."

The next day we were on a train heading towards the Sussex countryside. Holmes had received a telegram before we left but only now opened it.

"I thought it important to establish the accuracy of our client's story as she had most of it second-hand herself." He waved the paper. "This is from my contact in the Swiss Police. He confirms that Mrs.

Tomlinson fell from a balcony at the hotel as we were told. He adds that it was never viewed as an accident, and Mr. Tomlinson was briefly suspected of murder."

"Murder!" I exclaimed.

"After an investigation, it was later determined to be suicide and Mr. Tomlinson was permitted to return to England with his daughter. My contact adds that my telegram was curiously timed as they are investigating a similar death at the hotel which happened just two weeks ago."

Upon our arrival at the station, we took a cab out to Bramble Cottage. It was an impressive house, just as Miss Tomlinson had informed us. You could just about make out the original modest building at the centre of the impressive edifice. Substantial gardens surrounded the house and the distance from the gate to the front door was around a fifth of a mile.

As we got nearer to the main entrance, we could see an angry man being prevented from entering the house by the servants. He was cursing and lashing out. He saw us arriving and, with some harsh words, got into the cab that had, presumably, brought him. The cabby sped off with his passenger shouting abuse from inside.

"That would be our client's father," said Holmes.

"How do you know?"

"You can see something similar in the face."

"Can I help you, sir?" said a tall, imposing man, as we descended from our cab.

"You would be Wilson?" said Holmes.

"Yes, sir."

"My name is Sherlock Holmes. This is my friend, Dr. Watson. We have come at the request of Miss Rebecca Tomlinson to investigate the disappearance of her uncle."

"I am sure Miss Tomlinson is mistaken," said Wilson.

"You know where he has gone?"

"No, sir."

"Then you don't know he is safe and well," said Holmes. "You presumably wish no ill towards your employer?"

"No, sir."

"Then you will kindly admit us so that we can search for anything that may assist."

The butler thought for a moment. It was clear he was not sure of the best action to take. After some time, he gestured towards the door. "After you, gentlemen."

We stepped inside. Wilson followed, closed the door, and proceeded to take our coats.

"Was that the other Mr. Tomlinson?" asked Holmes.

"Yes, sir."

"Why was he so angry?"

Wilson's lip curled into a clear look of contempt. "He sought to gain entry to remove some of the master's papers. We have standing orders not to admit him."

"He seems to be rather unpleasant."

"I could not say," said Wilson, whose expression, in contrast, said everything.

The butler proceeded to escort us around the house. We began by entering the study. Above the fireplace was an impressive oil painting of a middle-aged man. He was clean-shaven with his hair greying at the temples. Holmes studied the plate at its foot. "It says Peter Tomlinson." He turned to the butler. "Your master?"

"No, sir," said Wilson. "It is Mr. Tomlinson's late father but they are much alike."

Holmes nodded, turned to me, and lowered his voice. "It is useful to know what he looks like, should we encounter him in future."

He turned back to the butler. "What is your opinion of the Brotherhood of the Compassionate Heart?"

The butler frowned. "I cannot say that I care for them, sir. They seem to be intent on getting the master's money."

"According to my understanding," said Holmes, "they have succeeded. They will inherit this house upon his death. That will mean an end to your position."

Wilson smiled. "The master has ensured our future, sir."

"In what way?"

"I am not permitted to discuss it, sir. Would you like to see the other rooms now?"

For the next two hours, we walked from room to room. The butler was always no more than five steps behind us. It was in the master bedroom that Holmes spent the most time. He opened all the drawers and looked in the wardrobe.

"Wilson. When your master left the house, did he take much with him?"

The butler appeared hesitant. "He took one case, sir."

"Approximately what size?"

The butler gestured with his hands. Holmes nodded.

We left soon afterwards, informing Wilson that we were headed for The Cedars.

As our cab moved away, Holmes turned to me. "Wilson has a lively imagination. The size of case he indicated was far too large for the clothes that were clearly missing from that room. Mr. Tomlinson appears to have taken enough clothes for two to three days at most."

"What does that tell you?"

"It tells me that Wilson lied. It also follows that he knows more than he is saying."

In contrast to Bramble Cottage, The Cedars was an unimpressive building. Although it was at least a century newer than

Bramble Cottage and, like that house, it had extensive grounds; it was clearly in a state of some disrepair. As we approached, we could see monk-like figures, hoods raised, walking solemnly in the grounds. They moved in a manner that suggested, to my military eye, that they were guarding rather than contemplating. We handed in our cards and were swiftly admitted. Our coats taken, we were escorted towards the rear of the building and into a spartan study. From behind a desk a man rose.

"Good afternoon, Mr. Holmes. My name is Brother Alaric."

"Good day, sir," said Holmes. "May I introduce my friend, Dr. Watson?"

Alaric nodded in my direction. "I presume you are here to accuse me of harming Mr. Tomlinson? The local police have been here already."

"I was under the impression they were not concerned in the matter," said Holmes. "Did you harm Mr. Tomlinson?"

Alaric flushed red. "Of course not. It was not in our interests."

"It is a matter of opinion," said Holmes. "We know you stand to inherit Bramble Cottage. But Mr. Tomlinson is middle-aged so it could be a long wait. A wait you might not be willing to endure."

Alaric seated himself and invited us to do the same. "I will not permit you to provoke me, Mr. Holmes. Mr. Tomlinson has undertaken to donate generous sums to us in the interim. So, as you can see, we have nothing to gain and everything to lose by harming him."

"I notice that your cowl is down," said Holmes. "Is it not a requirement of your order that faces be concealed?"

"Sometimes," said Alaric. "We are to be seen as one brotherhood, a collective. We are about the order, not the individual. The concealment of our faces is a way of ensuring this when we work in the community. Within these walls, or in private, showing our faces is permitted."

"Is yours a religious order?" I asked.

Alaric stood and walked to the window. "Yes and no, Dr. Watson. I have studied monastic ways, and the Brotherhood is run along similar lines. But we are not recognised by the church."

"I presume," said Holmes, "you do not have much in the way of assets if you are courting wealthy benefactors?"

Alaric had been looking out of the window since rising from his desk. He turned to face us. It was evident that he was struggling to master his temper. "You persist in being direct, Mr. Holmes. The order owns this house and grounds. We have some tenants who provide a certain amount of income. However, benefactors are key to our continued existence. We make no charges for the services we provide."

"Were you surprised when Mr. Tomlinson reversed his earlier hostility?"

"Ah," said Alaric. "You have been speaking to his niece. A charming young lady but she continues to see us as her uncle first did. I can understand that. I read of her aunt's passing and immediately went to offer our services. I regret that I moved too quickly onto the subject of donations. It was, in hindsight, a callous act on my part. Fortunately, Mr. Tomlinson was able to change his mind about us."

"And how did you accomplish that?" asked Holmes. "My understanding is your olive branch was not well received."

"You refer to his first visit here," said Alaric. "You are correct. He was courteous and patient. He listened to me and spoke to other brothers. He was told about our practices as an order as well as our charitable work. Nevertheless, he remained unmoved. If anything, his opposition to us increased. He just masked it a little better."

"When did things change?" I asked.

"A week or so after the death of his daughter. He turned up here, the image of contrition. He apologised profusely and expressed his intention of donating to us and leaving us his house. The offer, however, came with the condition that we admit him into the order."

"And you accommodated him?"

Alaric frowned. "I did not wish to. He did not meet our criteria for admittance. He was above the maximum age. We require a level of youth and fitness from our members which he did not meet. But, between us, our situation, financially, was so parlous that I decided to waive our usual criteria."

"Naturally," said Holmes, with something approaching a smirk.

Alaric was not impressed with Holmes's sarcasm. "I don't seek your approval or criticism, Mr. Holmes. In my opinion, which I later put to a vote at our governing council, a relaxation of the rules was advisable if our work were to have a future. What value has principle if it leads to people going without aid?"

"When did he begin the process of admittance?"

"Directly after his daughter's funeral. He was issued his habit when he arrived. I recall that he didn't like the first one and asked for one in a bigger size – claiming it was too tight. We obliged but it took him some time to get used to it as the cowl was a little too large for him which had the effect of making it hard for him to see. I almost laughed because I found it odd that a man who wore quite expensive clothes should suddenly be happy with apparel so basic."

"Were there academic studies to undertake?" asked Holmes.

"Indeed. Here his enthusiasm was less pronounced. He often questioned the purpose of the training. If it had not been for the financial inducement, we would have rejected his application. Instead, we chose to indulge him for the sake of the order."

Holmes rose. "When did you last see him?"

Alaric thought for a moment. "I believe it was the day before he vanished. He attended his classes and said he would return the next day, as arranged. Needless to say, he did not attend and I have not seen him since."

We bade farewell to the enigmatic Brother Alaric. Our next destination was the local police station. After a discussion with the desk sergeant, we were shown into the office of Inspector Baker.

"Yes, Mr. Holmes," he said. "We did tell Miss Tomlinson that there was little we could do. After she had gone, I thought I would make a few basic enquiries just to establish what she had told me and see if there was anything to justify a substantial investigation. There wasn't. All I achieved was to rile this Brother Alaric and the staff at Bramble Cottage."

"How did you manage the latter?" asked Holmes.

The inspector leant forward on his desk. "Well, I had to admit that Mr. Tomlinson's final known appearance was strange. Following a search of the house, I was in his garden and noticed that the butler would not leave me alone. He watched me closely. He seemed to get nervous whenever I got near to the grave of the family dog."

Holmes's eye sparkled. "What did you find?"

Baker smiled. "My suspicions were aroused, so I came back with a couple of constables and, in the face of the butler's protestations, dug the area up. We found the dog but it was clear that its death was nothing to do with old age but due to something significant running over it."

"What did you do next?"

"Nothing."

"Nothing?"

"Well, the manner of the dog's death changed little. There was no evidence of foul play towards Mr. Tomlinson."

"How did the butler account for the dog's injuries?"

"He said that his master had accidentally left the door open one day and the dog had run off. It had apparently found its way to the railway station where it was hit, and killed, by a train after wandering onto the tracks. Its body was brought back to the house by one of the station staff, and Miss Tomlinson was told a story it was felt would upset her less than the truth."

"Imbecile," said Holmes, as we left the police station. "Like some Scotland Yarders, our friend Baker can gather information but he does not know how to interpret it. We need to see if we can confirm this story of the dog escaping. If true, it will lend weight to a theory I have formed."

At Holmes's request, our cabby dropped us at a local public house. There, after furnishing the locals with a few drinks, we learned that the Tomlinson's dog had indeed been seen loitering at the railway station. As Baker had told us, the station staff had carried its body to Bramble Cottage where a grateful Mr. Tomlinson had given them some money and asked that they never tell his niece what had happened. They had all been instructed to tell the old-age story if approached.

Holmes rubbed his hands together. "This is good, Watson."

"It is?"

"It is far from a solid case at this point but it's a piece that fits my theory."

"Would you care to enlighten me?"

"That would be premature. Our next step is to talk to the solicitor. We need to return to the police station and get our new friend, Baker, to facilitate an appointment with Mr. Sampson."

We later found rooms at a small hotel and presented ourselves at the office of Sampson and Partners the next day - armed with a letter from Inspector Baker.

We were shown into Sampson's office. He rose to greet us. "How do you do, Mr. Holmes?"

"How do you do?" said Holmes. "We are here to ask about the will of Peter Tomlinson, senior."

"Certainly," said Sampson. "It is a public document now."

"What can you tell us about the terms of the trust for his grandchildren?"

"It is a substantial sum of money," said Sampson. "An equal portion was to be given to each grandchild upon reaching twenty-one. Due to the tragic death of her cousins, Miss Tomlinson is to receive it all in a matter of months."

"Her uncle was the sole trustee?"

"That is correct. Her father was to take over in the event of her uncle's death."

"What access would he have had to the funds in that event?"

"He would have been entitled to sums to cover his expenses as trustee. As long as the expenses could be justified."

"Were there any circumstances under which his access would be greater?"

Sampson frowned. "Only one. If he were to outlive both his brother and daughter, he would receive the entire amount."

I left the building first and lit a cigarette. As I did so, I noticed that Holmes had not yet set foot outside. About a minute later, he joined me.

"Well, Holmes," I said. "I think we have a strong suspect in our client's father."

"You think so?" he replied, with a smile.

Holmes announced there was nothing more to do in Sussex. We therefore boarded a train for London. I had found the county rather bleak so the prospect of our rooms was appealing. We settled into our carriage and the train began to move.

"You have this all worked out, don't you?" I asked.

He smiled. "The matter appears quite trivial. You will recall I left the solicitor's office a little later than you."

"I did wonder."

"I asked if our client's uncle had recently written a new will. Sampson confirmed that it had been discussed but that a document was yet to be drawn up. I also asked for the details of the Tomlinson family doctor. Upon our return to London, I need to send four telegrams. One to the doctor, one to Miss Tomlinson, and one to the Swiss Police."

"And the fourth?"

"That I will keep to myself for the moment."

Holmes was as good as his word. He entered the first available telegraph office upon our return to London. Shortly afterwards, we were back in our rooms.

"What is the next move?" I asked, as I stretched out my feet towards the fire.

He took his seat, opposite me, and began to fill his pipe. "If the answer to my Swiss telegram is as I expect, we will not do anything further for at least three months."

"Three months!" I exclaimed.

"I beg that you trust me and not question further."

"You don't seriously expect Miss Tomlinson to accept that?"

He frowned. "In my telegram, I have done my best to impress upon her the need to accept my counsel. Let us both hope she does so."

Mid-morning the next day, Holmes received a telegram. He read it and sighed. "It would appear, Watson, that you read Miss Tomlinson better than I did."

"I take it she is not happy to wait?"

"Indeed not. She remains convinced that the Brotherhood is behind her uncle's disappearance and she will go there for answers with or without my assistance. I will need to warn Brother Alaric."

"Warn him?"

"Yes. I know who he is and I know he is something of a confidence trickster. Something he is not involved in is Mr. Tomlinson's disappearance. I will suggest he makes himself absent. I will ask our friend, Inspector Baker, to keep an eye on Miss Tomlinson to ensure she does not do anything she regrets."

It pained me to know how distressed Miss Tomlinson was at Holmes's lack of action. At the same time, I knew better than to doubt my friend's motives. Later in the day, a little after midday, another telegram arrived. Holmes read it and smiled. It was a smile I knew well. It was something that confirmed his theory.

"Watson, I need to make a trip to Switzerland."

"Switzerland?"

"Yes. Based on this, I need to visit my contact in the Swiss Police. You won't need to accompany me."

For obvious reasons, the thought of Holmes back in Switzerland filled me with foreboding. He read this in my face.

"Worry not, Watson. I don't believe anyone currently seeks my head."

He left the next day and was away for a week. It was a relief to see him finally walk through the door. I had been under instructions to open any letters from Sussex so I was able to tell him that we had received two notes from Inspector Baker. Miss Tomlinson had been prevented from entering the grounds of The Cedars by his constables. They had successfully frustrated her attempts to reach Brother Alaric three times. Based on her actions, she was clearly getting desperate for answers.

Three months after our last trip to Sussex, Holmes received a letter.

"It is from Mr. Sampson," said Holmes. "I asked him to let me know when Miss Tomlinson's birthday had taken place and the transfer of the trust fund into her name was completed."

"And?"

"It means we can finally bring this to an end. I need to send a telegram on our way to the station."

We presented ourselves at Bramble Cottage a few hours later. Miss Tomlinson was there, as was Mr. Sampson. The solicitor looked rather unsettled.

"I cannot say I am pleased to see you, Mr. Holmes," said Miss Tomlinson. "You abandoned me when I needed you most."

Holmes fixed her with something akin to a paternal stare. "I can assure you that my actions were in your best interests."

At Holmes's suggestion we moved into the study. With the exception of Holmes, we all took seats. Holmes fixed his eyes on Miss Tomlinson.

"I have delayed in order to offer you the best protection. Ultimately it is up to you how you proceed once you hear what I have to say. I will be asking you to choose between the law and your uncle's wishes."

"That makes no sense," said Miss Tomlinson.

"I understand but that will soon change. I must begin with the hardest part. Your uncle is dead. Furthermore, he has been dead for just over three and a half months."

Miss Tomlinson jumped to her feet and began to sway. "Dead? Three and a half months? That's absurd. I have seen him more recently than that."

"With respect, Miss Tomlinson, you have not. Please resume your seat."

Slowly, she obeyed.

"You have to understand how desperately unhappy your uncle was. The event that set everything in motion was the death of your cousin Alice. You said yourself, how your family had been faced with event after event. The accidental death of your cousin Thomas, the grief-induced suicide of your aunt, and, finally, the suicide of your remaining cousin, Alice.

"For you, this was devastating but for your uncle it was far worse. His entire immediate family gone in the space of a few years. From the death of Alice onwards, your uncle wanted nothing more than to join them. Only one thing stayed his hand."

"What was that?"

"You, Miss Tomlinson. He wanted to end his life, desperately. Every day he was alive was a torment to him. He also knew that to end his life, before you turned twenty-one, could leave you at the mercy of your father who he knew would not act in your interests. He resolved to achieve both ends at once. His death without compromising your security."

As Holmes finished the sentence, the bell rang. We heard Wilson open the front door and some muffled words were heard. There was a knock and into the room stepped a man in a monk's apparel, cowl concealing his face.

Miss Tomlinson flushed red. "Have you invited this wretched man, Mr. Holmes?"

Holmes bade the masked figure to take another chair. "This is not Brother Alaric. For reasons that will become apparent, he will need to be kept in ignorance. His order, however, were pivotal to your uncle's plans."

"Please get to the point, Mr. Holmes."

"You will recall that your uncle became well-disposed towards Brother Alaric in the aftermath of your cousin's death. It was because he saw in the order a means to execute his plan. He was determined to join his family before your birthday without giving your father control of your trust fund."

"I don't see how he could do such a thing."

"Your uncle made several financial commitments to Alaric's order. His price was admittance to their ranks. I asked myself what was suddenly attractive about the order to him? Not only enough to fund it but also to join it. I soon came to the conclusion that it was about the monk-like apparel. It provided your uncle with an understandable reason to cover his face."

"I still don't understand."

"Your uncle wanted to die without anyone becoming aware of the fact."

We all paused to take this in. Miss Tomlinson's expression was one of total confusion. Holmes continued.

"You will recall that your uncle prohibited you from visiting him for a period of some weeks. When you later saw him, you thought he had a cold, and he dashed from the room when you queried him."

"Yes."

"The man you spoke to was not your uncle."

"Nonsense, I saw him."

"Only after he returned to the room."

"I'm sorry, I don't understand."

"Your uncle had called in someone to impersonate him. That person had been living with your uncle for those weeks learning how to mimic him. The initial meeting with you was a test. When you queried him, he left the room and your uncle later returned. This was to allay any concerns you had.

"The next piece of the puzzle was Freddy."

"Freddy?"

"Yes. You remarked how the dog kept looking out of the window. That was nothing to do with the valet. He was pining for his master who he knew had left the house. From that point on your uncle was impersonated."

"I cannot take this in," said Miss Tomlinson, as she pulled out a handkerchief from her sleeve.

"You mentioned," said Holmes, "on one of your later visits, that Wilson brought in a telegram to which your uncle replied that all was well. You added that your uncle's reply seemed to sadden the butler."

"Yes."

"Wilson was sad because he knew that response would lead to your uncle's death."

"That implies Wilson knew this plan," said Miss Tomlinson.

"Yes. And he did. Your uncle could not have carried this out without support from those close to him."

"Where was my uncle?"

"He was at a certain hotel in Switzerland."

Miss Tomlinson's face paled. "Not that hotel?"

"I am afraid so. He had asked the impersonator if he were successfully passing for your uncle. The impersonator responded in the affirmative. Your uncle committed suicide as soon as he received that answer. A man answering to his description threw himself from the balcony, and I have recently visited Switzerland to verify the facts."

Miss Tomlinson's attention turned to the robed figure. "Is this the impersonator?" Her face was reddening with anger. Holmes held out a hand and signalled the figure. The individual reached up and removed his cowl.

"Good Lord," I said. "It's Edward Harrison."

"Who?" said Miss Tomlinson.

"He is an actor, Miss Tomlinson," said Holmes. "An actor with a gift for voices. He was on the verge of bankruptcy some years ago when your uncle came to his financial rescue. He was finally asked to return the favour. I take it, Mr. Harrison, that Mr. Tomlinson was the reason for your leave of absence from your successful play?"

The actor did not take his eyes from Miss Tomlinson. It was fear rather than admiration. He could see how angry she was at his deception. "Yes, Mr. Holmes. I had little choice after all he had done for me."

"Did he explain his plan to you?"

"Not in detail. He simply said he had to leave the country without anyone knowing he had gone. I swear I had no notion he intended to end his own life. He had led me to believe that I only had to maintain the pretence for a few weeks. It would have gone fine if my backers had not demanded my return. It was only when I got that telegram and announced my intentions to Wilson that he told me what his master's plans had truly been."

Miss Tomlinson suddenly shouted for the butler. As soon as he entered the room you could see he had been listening and knew what was coming.

"You knew?"

"Yes, Miss."

"How could you involve yourself in something so awful?"

The butler fidgeted. "The entire household understood your uncle's distress, Miss. Of course, we tried to talk him out of it. We explained how much you needed him. When that did not work, we tried to get him to delay at least until after your birthday. For him, even a few more months was too much. He left us well-provided for and, out of loyalty, we played our parts."

It was Holmes's turn to speak. "This is the reason for my silence, Miss Tomlinson. We waited until your birthday and a note from your solicitor to let us know you had control of your money. You now have a choice."

"And what is that?"

"You can go to the authorities and tell them what you have learned. Doing so will run the risk of giving your father an opportunity to mount some kind of legal proceedings. They are unlikely to succeed but you would have to endure them for months. Alternatively, you can remain silent for seven years."

"I don't understand."

"Your uncle was buried in Switzerland under the false name he had travelled with. After seven years you can take steps to declare him legally dead and none of this need come out. Your father will not be able to do anything and you will be free to live as your uncle desired."

Miss Tomlinson sat in silence. After some minutes she raised her head. "I will do as you say, Mr. Holmes. I am not comfortable but I would not wish my uncle's death to be in vain. There is an additional thing that upsets me."

"And that is?"

"In seven years' time I will be forced to hand over Bramble Cottage to that wretched Brother Alaric."

Holmes smiled. "Your solicitor here will tell you that no changes to that effect were made in your uncle's will. He simply told Alaric he intended to do it. Alaric will have no claim."

Not long afterwards, Holmes and I took our leave. Mr. Harrison left with us saying that he had to get back for the evening performance of his play. Holmes had no desire for additional company and told Harrison to go ahead as he had further errands to perform. We took shelter in a public house while we waited for the next train.

"Miss Tomlinson will have to maintain that version of events for a long time," I remarked.

"I'm sure she will manage," said Holmes. "If she has any sense, she will distance herself from her father. She is now amongst the richest women in England."

"What about Brother Alaric?"

"George Bates, you mean?"

"Who?"

"I recognised him as soon as I saw him. He is a petty swindler. This is his most elaborate plan yet, and quite some way beyond his usual schemes. I will let Scotland Yard know where he is. They will make Sussex a little too warm for him. He will not trouble Miss Tomlinson any further."

"It seems to me, Holmes, that the case only came to your attention because Harrison got the urgent telegram to return to the theatre. Had that not come, Miss Tomlinson would never have believed her uncle to be missing."

He smiled and nodded. "That certainly accelerated things. Harrison would have had to vanish at some point. Telegrams, incidentally, were another clue. Clearly, Harrison was no mimic when it came to handwriting. Once Mr. Tomlinson had left the country, all communications to his niece were telegrams."

"I guess that also explains Freddy," I said. "He got killed trying to follow his master who had presumably caught a train to get to the coast."

"The poor dog would have likely been killed anyway," said Holmes. "I think Wilson and Harrison realised that its whining would have excited suspicion had they permitted it to continue."

He looked at his watch. "Drink up, Watson. The next train to London is in thirty-five minutes. We can have an early dinner at Simpson's on our way to Baker Street."

The Adventure of Madame Emmascarar

(Late 1897)

OTABLY, Sherlock Holmes was not a believer in the supernatural. His feet remained firmly on the ground. To even entertain the idea of the otherworldly went against all he believed in. Therefore, the events of which I now write will, perhaps, initially, be a source of surprise.

For the previous few months, the name filling the society pages had been that of Madame Valerie Emmascarar. Her origins were unclear but she had, in a short space of time, established herself as London's most sought-after medium. At the time she emerged, the country was not exactly devoid of mediums and other adherents of what was generally known as Spiritualism. So, you might wonder why Madame Emmascarar had risen so fast in a decidedly crowded field.

The answer to this lay with one Professor Euan Hendry. Hendry, a retired physics lecturer from one of our great universities, had decided to dedicate the twilight years of his life to exposing mediums. He saw them as taking advantage of the bereaved and had availed himself of every avenue to attack them and their practices. One of the national newspapers had even provided him with a regular column where he explained their activities at length. This had attracted interest not only in England but also in the United States where investigators using similar methods had risen to prominence.

The professor should have been happy with this success but he was not. He wrote in his column that he despaired of his fellow men who continued, despite the evidence, to put money into the pockets of, as he put it, "despicable tricksters."

For a few months, he suspended his column, arguing there was no point in continuing. Gossips suggested that the failing health of his wife of forty years also played its part. It seemed more than probable that his exposure of mediums was at an end.

Everyone was surprised when he burst back onto the scene six months later. He announced that he and his wife, who had died in the interim, had agreed a phrase that she would be able to pass to him to prove if she had moved to the other side. He went on to say that any medium who could provide him with its exact wording, under controlled conditions, would not only secure from him the sum of one thousand pounds but also his personal endorsement.

He was asked by the press why he had laid his reputation, and fortune, on the line in this way. In response, the professor had stated that, despite his many successes, he felt he had struggled to make any meaningful impact on the spread of what he viewed as a plague. He felt the financial inducement would bring so many mediums to him that their repeated failure might have the required effect on the public's perception of their ilk.

The unkind members of the press suggested the professor was obsessed and perhaps driven more by grief. To this, he had said nothing. According to most reports, he channelled all his energies into his challenge.

Mediums queued to pick up the gauntlet. Some thirty of them tried, and failed, to convince the professor. Some of them accused him of deception but, as he did not organise or run the séances, this failed to dent his reputation. It also failed to discourage other mediums.

Six months after the challenge had been laid down, Madame Emmascarar stepped forward. The press interest had been on the wane but this had all changed when, at her séance, the professor reluctantly announced that she had provided the phrase in full. Whilst defending his actions, in exposing fraudulent mediums, he said he was prepared to acknowledge a lady of "genuine gifts" and she was presented with a cheque in a ceremony at the Royal Albert Hall.

Such an endorsement from so notable a sceptic catapulted Madame Emmascarar to the pinnacle of London society. The lady found herself besieged by potential clients all seeking to reach their loved ones. She soon became unpopular with both sides of the argument. Sceptics still disbelieved, and practising mediums resented the loss of both limelight and income. Dozens of mediums faded from the personal ads as, presumably, the river of money ran dry.

Madame Emmascarar's way of dealing with her popularity only added to her allure. A would-be client had to seek an audience. Such applicants were vetted and, only if she were satisfied, would she see them. Even then, the séances tended to be arranged weeks, if not months, in advance. It was reported that she saw only one in a hundred applicants and those she did see, without exception, expressed themselves satisfied.

For Professor Hendry, his admission and endorsement came at great cost. The prize money amounted to almost all his savings and he was forced to sell his London home. The scientific community, that had once championed him, now ridiculed him before turning its back on him entirely. Devoid of almost all sources of income, he was forced to retire to his modest family home in the Scottish borders. There, according to rumours, he sat and wallowed surrounded by all the academic achievements that now meant next to nothing. The name which had burned so brightly no longer even smouldered.

My mind was not as closed to the possibilities of the beyond as Holmes's. That is not to say my mind was gaping wide but it was at least ajar. When I had showed Holmes some of the articles about Madame Emmascarar he had snorted with derision. "If people wish to throw their money away on so obvious a fraud, who am I to stop them?"

"But Professor Hendry, Holmes!"

"He was misled, Watson. He is not infallible. He made a mistake or, perhaps, pressure was brought to bear to make him endorse her."

"If you believe the latter, why not investigate?" I had asked.

"Because," he had replied, "I have other things to occupy my time."

In fact, this could not have been further from the truth. Holmes was devoid of clients at the time. I had therefore announced my intention to take a short fishing holiday in the hope he might accompany me. He, unsurprisingly, had declined. He retained his dislike of the more rustic areas of our country. I therefore travelled alone to Euston station two days later.

I was away for two weeks. I breathed the clean air, I ate hearty rural food, and partook of the odd local ale. I was even able to spend some time with an old school friend whom I encountered unexpectedly when chancing my luck in a local river. I was thus rejuvenated when I arrived back at Baker Street late one afternoon.

Mrs. Hudson greeted me in the hallway. As I removed my overcoat, she regaled me with the usual list of woes. Holmes had not been eating, and he had been smoking to excess. I asked if he had anything on hand at present as these activities were more common when he had a case.

She informed me that a lady had arrived to see Holmes an hour earlier. Holmes had been out at the time, on some errand or other, and had returned to find her waiting in the sitting room. They had been in each other's company for ten minutes and she had heard voices raised more than once.

I had no desire to interrupt so I ascended the stairs softly. I passed the sitting room door without pausing. I heard Holmes speaking and a feminine voice responding. I ascended the next flight and entered my room. I placed my case on the bed and began unpacking items and putting them away. Every so often, I paused to determine if I could hear voices below. I wanted to spend the rest of the day relaxing with the newspapers rather than getting drawn into any form of physical exertion. I therefore hoped that the lady would leave before I completed my unpacking. However, the voices continued.

With a sigh, I descended the stairs. I was about to knock on the door when it flew open and a visibly annoyed young lady came out, nearly knocking me over.

"I beg your pardon, sir," she said, breathlessly, her face almost crimson.

"That's quite alright, Miss," I replied. I lowered my voice. "Has Mr. Holmes said something to offend?"

"You don't need to apologise for me, Watson," said Holmes. "Miss Chaplin is put out that I am not inclined to take her case."

Something lurked at the back of my mind. "Are you by any chance related to Dr. Leonard Chaplin of Charing Cross Hospital?"

"My father," she replied.

I lowered my voice, almost to a whisper. "If you would be so good, Miss," I said. "Please let me talk to Mr. Holmes. Perhaps you could return tomorrow."

She nodded. "Thank you." She headed down the stairs and I heard the front door open and close.

I entered the sitting room and shut the door. Holmes had moved to the window. Presumably to ensure that the lady was, indeed, leaving. "What did Miss Chaplin do to rile you?" I asked.

He tutted. "I returned to find her here. She was sitting impatiently on the settee. I had barely one foot in the door before she launched into the reason for her presence. Her manner reminded me of another young lady from a few days earlier. I had returned from a visit to our good barber to find this woman standing by my desk, looking out of this very window. She turned and I could see at once that she was a jilted fiancée in search of answers."

"How did you know that?"

His frustrated expression gave way to a modest smile. "I could see where she had removed an engagement ring. The level of indentation on her finger suggested she had become engaged at least six months earlier. An injury to the same finger indicated she had almost torn the ring from her hand in distress. I explained all this to her. Her response was to flee the room in tears." He gestured to his desk. "Incidentally, I obtained some of your favourite cigars in anticipation of your return."

These occasional flashes of thoughtfulness never got stale. "Thank you, Holmes," I said. I opened the box and took out a cigar. He smiled and accepted when I offered the box to him. We lit them and took our usual seats.

"So, Watson," said Holmes, after filling the air with the first puff of smoke, "who is this Dr. Chaplin and why have you requested his daughter to return tomorrow?"

"Sometimes, Holmes," I replied, "the holes in your knowledge can be decidedly broad. Dr. Leonard Chaplin was jailed after three people died in his care."

"Deliberate?"

"It was briefly considered so and went to court. Several weeks later, a jury came to the conclusion, supported by his defence, that it was caused by his use of alcohol. He was found innocent of murder but guilty of manslaughter. The judge took into account a number of factors and he was sentenced to five years. He was released a few years ago."

"Understood. But why does it interest you, Watson?"

"Because I believe there was more to it."

"You want me to see if she knows anything?"

"I am interested to hear what she has to say."

He drew on his cigar and exhaled. "Whatever she says it is unlikely to be on that subject. In the short time we spoke, I learned the reason for her visit. Her father has fallen into the hands of Madame Emmascarar."

"The medium!"

"The same."

"I thought you had no interest in such matters."

He frowned at me. "I don't. That was the point I was conveying when you arrived. But you have asked her back now. You have placed me into the position where I will have to hear her out."

The next day, at eleven o'clock, Miss Chaplin presented herself. She was calmer than when I had seen her last and I was able to notice more about her. She was in her mid- or late-twenties with black hair, a fresh complexion, and dark green eyes. Her clothing was not the latest fashion and, in some parts, showed a good deal of wear and tear.

"Dr. Watson has mentioned something of your father's history," said Holmes, as the lady took her seat.

"I see," she said, with a look that had all the hallmarks of anger. "I take it, Doctor, you are not the ally that I had at first supposed?"

I felt my face redden. "I merely believe, Miss, that not all questions were answered."

She frowned. "That is a neat way of making it clear where you stand." She turned away from me. "I came here on another matter, as you are aware, Mr. Holmes."

"Miss Chaplin," said Holmes. "Knowing the background of people concerned in any matter cannot fail to be helpful. If you would permit my initial questions, we can proceed to the subject that has brought you here."

With some hesitation, she nodded.

"I have done some research on your father since yesterday and I understand he was pursued by relatives of his patients via a civil case."

"That is true," she replied, her face reddening. "The families were not happy with the length of his sentence. They sought for it to be increased. When this was rejected, they began civil proceedings. Mercifully, their case was thrown out."

"Was the matter pursued after that?"

"Don't misunderstand me, Mr. Holmes," said Miss Chaplin. "I appreciate that these people lost loved ones but my father being imprisoned should have been enough for them. They lost sight of the fact that my mother and I were victims too. I considered it poetic justice when many of them were later bankrupted."

"How so?"

A brief smile, bordering on sinister, appeared on her face. "They had hired solicitors and QCs. People with expensive services. They overstretched themselves in anticipation of success. Some of them were even sued by the men they had engaged."

"I see," said Holmes.

"My mother died whilst father was in prison and I soon realised that my hopes of a conventional future in England were over."

"I take it," said Holmes, "that you refer to marriage?"

She frowned. "You know very well that is what I mean. Potential suitors melted away during the trial. Our family name was tainted."

"Thank you," said Holmes. "I appreciate your candour. Please proceed to the matter of Madame Emmascarar."

Miss Chaplin was evidently keen to do so. "In the immediate aftermath of father's release, we did enjoy some limited peace. We managed to retain a few loyal friends and our lives got about as close to normal as we could hope for.

"Father was unable to work so we were forced to live on the money and investments my mother had left us. He fell apart and turned to drink. The money went out faster than it came in. I am sure, Mr. Holmes, that you have noticed the state of my clothing. At one time I had a father who was successful and a mother who was wealthy. Now I have neither."

"How does the medium enter this?"

"Once the legal side of mother's death had been addressed; I began suggesting to father that we move abroad."

"That may well be a sensible path," said Holmes.

"Father initially refused. He could not see the point of such a course of action. He said his past would follow us wherever we went." She paused to drink some water. "He could not see that it was not just his life that was being affected. The worry started to have an impact on my health and I arranged to see a highly recommended specialist in Harley Street. He agreed that going abroad would be good for me and, with my permission, said he would speak with my father."

"Was the doctor successful?" asked Holmes.

"To an extent. Father did begin to consider the idea. He apologised to me and accepted that I was being affected too.

"Somehow word of the possible emigration got out. We strongly suspected our housekeeper and gave her notice. But the damage was done. It reached the press and newspapers took great delight in mentioning it and accusing my father of running away from what he'd done."

At this point, Miss Chaplin paused to wipe her eyes. My heart went out to her. Whatever her father had done was not her fault.

She tucked her handkerchief into her sleeve. "About two months ago, our home was broken into and vandalised. My father and I were away visiting one of our friends and discovered the damage on our return. Several rooms had been turned upside down and the word 'Murderer' had been painted on a wall. The police showed nothing more than a token interest but I have to confess I was rather pleased."

"Pleased?" I said, astounded.

"I realise how it sounds, Doctor, but this event started to alter father's view. He actively started to investigate the matter of emigration. It was something of a volt-face."

"Miss Chaplin," said Holmes, with some impatience. "Madame Emmascarar?"

She nodded. "I'm sure gentlemen such as you cannot have failed to have seen the coverage that woman has received. My father and I had both studied it with interest ever since she first appeared. Father is an admirer of Professor Hendry and was shocked when the professor endorsed this lady. He began to openly wonder if there might be something in it after all."

"A bizarre notion for a man of science," said Holmes.

"There, we agree."

"Did your father know the professor?"

"No. Not at all."

"Please continue."

"About a fortnight after the events I have just described, a letter arrived. It was from Madame Emmascarar."

"Indeed? What did it say?"

"It claimed she had been contacted by my mother on the subject of 'a significant decision' and asked that he come and discuss it."

"Your father presumably thought this might be connected to the idea of emigration?"

"That was indeed his thought. I was very much in two minds. On the one hand, I don't believe in such nonsense. On the other, if this medium convinced him to emigrate it would be of benefit to both of us."

"Was the meeting at her home?"

"No. Father was expected to meet her at the Langham Hotel two days from the date of the letter."

"You attended?"

"Yes."

"How did the interview proceed?"

"I had to admit that I was rather impressed, Mr. Holmes. It felt like an interview with a doctor or alienist. Madame Emmascarar asked no questions about my mother or her past, nothing that she could call upon later. All her questions to my father concerned how important making contact was to him and to explain how the séance would proceed."

"What was the conclusion?"

"Father said he was happy to continue and she said she would arrange the first sitting for five days hence. She also warned us that the séance would not be exclusive."

"Meaning?"

Miss Chaplin took another sip of water. "It transpired that we could expect to be at a sitting with up to five or six others in similar situations and we would likely make contact with at least two or three people who had passed. My father was expected to pay thirty pounds if contact with mother was made."

I was shocked. Thirty pounds was a nearly a year's salary for many people. I took a look at Holmes. Even Lestrade or Gregson would have been able to read the derision on his face. "I suppose it is hard to put a price on such a *service*," he said. "How did your first sitting proceed?"

"It took place at Madame Emmascarar's house in Clapham. She had given us the details when we left the Langham. When we arrived, we had to ask the cabby if he was sure of the address."

"Why?"

"The house was so ordinary. Shabby, even."

Holmes nodded.

Miss Chaplin continued. "It turned out to be correct and Madame Emmascarar herself welcomed us at the door. She bid us to follow her to the rear parlour. She informed us we were a little late and the room was already in darkness in preparation. Four other people were already around the table."

"How do you know that?" asked Holmes.

"I partially saw them when the door to the parlour was opened."

"Why only partially?"

"Only one dim oil lamp was lit in the room itself. The corridor we were in was lit by gas lamps that were half turned down. Enough light shone into the room for me to count pairs of shoes which also permitted me to determine the number of men and women."

Holmes rubbed his hands. He always admired an observant client. "Who did you ascertain?"

"Only one dim oil lamp was lit in the room itself."

"Of the people sat around the table, there were two ladies and two gentlemen."

"Did you take part?"

"I was not invited to. As father entered, and approached the seat he was directed to, I was asked to wait in the front parlour. There I found a man who introduced himself as Mr. Fowler."

"Was he connected to Madame Emmascarar in some way?"

"No. I learned from him that he was in a similar position to me. He had come with his wife who was seeking to make contact with her late sister. A few minutes into our conversation, we were provided with tea by a slightly surly maid."

"How long was the sitting?"

"It took about one hour. I then heard the sound of chairs being pushed back and a distant door opening. In a few moments, my father burst into the room. He was crying with happiness. A slightly shocked Mr. Fowler excused himself to go and look for his wife. He went out and closed the door. Father said he had spoken with my mother and we would be delaying our plan to emigrate. We were to return in a few days' time for a second sitting."

"Did the other attendees enjoy similar outcomes?" asked Holmes, with an expression that did him no credit.

"I have no idea. I heard lots of conversation in the hall as they were, presumably, bidden farewell. All the voices sounded happy. No one appeared to be upset. There was even some brief laughter. Madame Emmascarar called for respect saying it was not a matter for amusement. I heard the front door open and close and all went quiet. After a couple of minutes, I decided to look for our host. I poured father a cup of tea and said I would return in a moment. I opened the door and stepped into the corridor. It was empty. The other attendees had all gone. I heard my name and turned to see Madame Emmascarar emerge from the rear parlour. She advanced towards me and took hold of my hand. She led me away from my father and towards the rear of the house.

"She was beaming with satisfaction. 'Your father's first sitting was one of the most successful I can recall. It is clear that your mother's desire to speak with him is strong. Please bring him again on Monday.'

"I returned to the front parlour and collected my father. We were shown out and a cab was waiting for us. As we headed home, I asked my father what he had learned. He was so happy. 'Your mother was so reassuring, my dear. She approves of the plan but says she requires time to think about some of the questions I put to her.'"

"I presume there was a similar fee for the second visit?" asked Holmes.

"There was."

"I also presume that you believed your father was being taken advantage of?"

"I did, but he got angry when I suggested it. I was compelled to drop the subject."

"Yet, you are here."

Miss Chaplin frowned. "I am here because there appears to be no end to it. We have been to seven sittings. Each has cost thirty pounds. It is not money we can afford without endangering our emigration plans."

"Have all the sittings proceeded the same way?"

"Not exactly. The number of people in attendance has varied."

"Have the lights in the room always been down on your arrival."

"Only when we have been late."

"How often has that been?"

"On four occasions."

"And were you late?"

She sighed. "I don't believe so. But father was never inclined to question it, and I said nothing because of how upset he would get at any form of interference on my part."

"If the lights were not always down, were you able to see if any of the other attendees were there more than once?"

"Yes. A man and woman have been there more than once."

"Did you learn their names?"

"One was a Miss Jones, who had lost her father. The man was named Frederickson. I believe he was there to make contact with his late brother. There was not generally much time for conversation. Madame Emmascarar did not appreciate people turning up early and discouraged any lingering at the conclusion of her sittings."

There was a pause when Miss Chaplin concluded. Holmes was sat still. His hands rested in his lap. "How do your emigration plans stand now?"

"In limbo. Until the sittings are over, father refuses to proceed."

"What do you wish me to do?"

"I wish you to bring about an end to the sittings. I am not concerned with whether or not she is exposed as the fake I believe her to be. I am concerned with father and I beginning again. Please bring about an end to the sittings so we can leave the country."

Holmes nodded his agreement and I saw Miss Chaplin out.

When I returned, Holmes had lit a cigarette. "I must say, Holmes, that Miss Chaplin's attitude was rather selfish."

"Perhaps," he said, "but it is understandable. Whatever you believe her father to have done, she had no hand in it and yet is being damaged by it. It is only natural that she would wish to start again as soon as possible."

"But," I said, "if, as she thinks, this is fraud, we must endeavour to stop it. Not just for Miss Chaplin."

Holmes drew on his cigarette before flicking ash into the fireplace. "There we have a problem, Watson. Madame Emmascarar has committed no crime that we can prove. We could cry fraud but all her clients appear to be satisfied. We know we can appeal to Miss Chaplin for support and she would give it. Her father, however, would likely disapprove, and endorse Madame Emmascarar. From what we have been told, there were no unhappy attendees at the Chaplin sittings – quite the reverse.

"Added to this is the endorsement from Professor Hendry, which he has not withdrawn despite the personal damage it has caused. If a scientific man such as he is convinced of her abilities, how are we to find a crack in that armour?"

Holmes sat in silence for a couple of hours. He then announced his intention to visit the offices of several of the broadsheet newspapers. He desired no company so I remained in our rooms until his return.

About three hours later, Holmes strode into the sitting room. His face spoke of success. "What did you find out?" I asked.

He went over to the mantelpiece and began to fill a pipe. He lit it and sat down. "I have been forced to spend the afternoon looking into Madame Emmascarar's history since collecting Professor Hendry's cheque."

"And?"

"As you know, she wiped all competition from the board. With the professor's endorsement behind her, all the powerful and influential people, queued up to contact the departed. What is interesting is not only who she worked with but who she did not."

"What do you mean?"

"She clearly had the opportunity to make a great deal of money. Yet she turned down some of the richest people in the country. She arguably made enemies doing so."

"Such as?"

"Sir Richard Castle, the noted industrialist, was dismissed by the lady. He had lost his mother about a year earlier and was eager to make contact. He was not even granted the opportunity to discuss the matter. He wrote an angry letter to *The Times* on the subject. She also rejected Mrs. Jane Hughes, the wife of a prominent member of Parliament, who wished to reach her sister."

"Perhaps she is not interested in the money," I suggested. "Perhaps she desires to help the people who need her?"

Holmes looked at me like I was a foolish schoolboy. "Nonsense, Watson. She helps no one by acting fraudulently. Dismiss from your mind the idea that she possesses genuine gifts. She does not. Money clearly is a factor. Remember what she has been charging Dr. Chaplin."

"Then what is her motivation, Holmes?"

He drew a sheet of notepaper from his inside pocket. "I have compiled a list of the influential people she did agree to see. Two of them are of particular interest and I intend to seek interviews to see what I can glean from them."

"If they suspect you are acting against her, they are not likely to cooperate," I said.

Holmes took himself off to his files to research the names on his list. Later, this done, he sat down at his desk to write some letters.

"Who are you writing to?" I asked.

"Mr. Herbert Babcock and Lady Elizabeth Trevone."

"Why them?"

"They each have a past that brings them into my sphere."

"They do?"

"Yes. Mr. Babcock is stockbroker to the elite and was unsuccessfully prosecuted for appropriating his clients' money for his own enrichment. He not only won his case but sued a few of his detractors for large sums."

"And Lady Trevone?"

Holmes's face darkened. "Lady Trevone is another prospect entirely. She presents a charming veneer but broke many suitors, bleeding them of their fortunes, before marrying Lord Trevone."

"I am surprised Lord Trevone married a lady with a questionable past," I said. "Don't these families investigate people long before the altar?"

"Indeed, they do," said Holmes. "But Lady Trevone was careful. No one could prove anything and she blackmailed anyone necessary to ensure a smooth path to the church."

"You know she blackmailed people?"

"As certainly as if I had been present. But I cannot prove it."

"Do you think they will agree to see you?"

"We will soon find out."

Within a few days, Holmes received agreements from both parties for an interview. Whatever else you could have said about them, they were not afraid to meet with Sherlock Holmes.

Herbert Babcock's house was in Bath and we travelled there the day after his letter was received. The house was made of the distinctive local stone and shone in the sunlight. We were admitted and ushered into the study.

We had been waiting for only a few moments before Babcock joined us. "Mr. Holmes," he said. "I understand you wish to discuss the charming Madame Emmascarar?"

"That is correct," said Holmes.

Babcock waved us into seats. "I welcome any opportunity to sing the praises of that lady. However, I am surprised that a man such as you is interested in matters beyond his understanding."

"That does not surprise me," said Holmes. "I have been commissioned by scientists to speak to satisfied clients to understand her methods."

"With a view to debunking them, I assume?"

"I am not concerned with their agenda," said Holmes. "I will follow the facts. If you know of my reputation, you will believe that."

Babcock smiled. "I have read many of the good Doctor's accounts. I am prepared to believe you. I do wish that these scientists would be content with the word of Professor Hendry. He was her most vociferous critic. If he was convinced, that ought to be an end to it."

"Science never stops questioning," said Holmes.

"Very well," said Babcock. "Ask your questions."

"Why did you contact her?"

"I did not. She contacted me. She explained that my father had been in contact and that she could be of assistance."

"When did your father die?"

"A little over two years ago."

"Did she say if any particular topics were to be discussed?"

"No. I was sceptical but, as she was rather famous, I decided there was nothing to lose."

"How long after her letter was your initial sitting?"

"Six weeks," said Babcock.

"Was it that far away for any reason?"

"When we had an interview, she asked what my engagements for the immediate future were in order to find a time that was suitable. I said I could be ready almost immediately. This was not acceptable to her. She explained that due to her existing commitments it would have to be at least four weeks away. I said the only significant engagement I had was a party at my house for current and potential clients. We fixed the first sitting for one week after the party."

Holmes thought for a moment. "Did Madame Emmascarar attend this party?"

"I invited her, of course. She declined. She said it was vital we had no further contact in advance of the sitting. She did not want to be accused of using social events as a way of gathering information."

Holmes smiled. "Was your party attended by anyone you didn't know?"

Babcock returned the smile. "Of course. I did say it was for potential clients as well as existing ones. I remember struggling to get away from one potential client. He talked endlessly about all manner of subjects. As he was a rather wealthy man, I indulged him. I think I endured his babble for a good twenty minutes. It was a sound strategy as he has since entrusted me with a sizable sum to invest."

"Can you tell me his name?"

"I'm afraid not, Mr. Holmes. My clients are entitled to their privacy."

"Do you always meet your clients in person?" asked Holmes.

"Not always. Some live considerable distances away and those relationships are conducted by letter or telegram. Many are abroad. Mr. Holmes, I fail to see how this is relevant."

"I beg your pardon," said Holmes. "How was your first sitting?"

Babcock was clearly relieved to get onto the subject of the séances. "I travelled to her home in Clapham. I have to admit, when I saw it, I was rather surprised."

"Why?"

"Well, it seemed odd that the toast of London society should live so modestly when she was known to be working with many wealthy clients."

"May I ask what her fee was?"

"Twenty pounds a sitting, if contact was made."

"How many sittings were there?"

"Ten, so far."

"Your relationship continues?"

"Oh yes. The next sitting is in one week."

"May we return to the first? Did anyone travel with you?"

"No. I am unmarried and had no one upon whom I could prevail."

"It was held in the rear parlour?"

"That is correct."

"Were the lights up or down?"

A strange look crossed Babcock's face. "It varied, Mr. Holmes. On the first occasion the room was well-lit. Around the table were three gentlemen. I have to say it was a frosty atmosphere."

"What do you mean?"

"They looked at me as I entered and all of them looked uncomfortable. One of them also looked angry. I was about to introduce myself when Madame Emmascarar entered the room and said we had to commence."

"So, you learned none of their names?"

"No. The next time I went, it was different. I entered the room in almost total darkness. Madame Emmascarar said it was because I was late and she had already begun to prepare the room. The only free seat was furthest from the door. Madame led me to it and the séance began. I believe I sat next to a lady but I cannot say who else was there."

"You were clearly impressed with the results," said Holmes.

Babcock smiled. "I was. Madame Emmascarar is not the first medium I have sat with but she is the first I have ever believed in. I can quite understand why she won Professor Hendry's endorsement."

A few minutes later, with the conversation running out of steam, we made our excuses. A cab took us to the railway station. As we had some minutes to wait for our train, Holmes and I both took the opportunity to smoke.

"What did you take from that interview?" I asked.

"The one thing that is common to both Mr. Babcock and Dr. Chaplin," said Holmes, "is that Madame Emmascarar sought them out. All we have read of her to date has said that people approached her seeking contact with the departed. Now we have two occasions where this was not so. That is telling."

"She was contacted by the deceased and asked to approach the relatives," I said.

Holmes's face darkened. "For the last time, Watson, she is a fraud and, therefore, nothing of the kind happened. For some reason, she targeted these two men who might not have approached her otherwise. Why was it important to see them?"

Just under three hours later, we arrived back at Baker Street. Mrs. Hudson informed us that a lady was waiting for us and had been for a little under an hour.

"Lady Trevone?" I suggested.

"No," said Holmes. "We are meeting her tomorrow at her home." He ascended the stairs.

We entered the sitting room and the lady rose to meet us. She was around thirty-five years of age. She had black hair and a complexion that was suggestive of South America. She was dressed modestly in a dark green dress.

"Do sit down, madam," said Holmes. "How can I help you?"

She remained standing and, in an accent that spoke very much of the metropolis, confidently stated "I am here to help *you*."

"Indeed?" said Holmes. "May I ask your name?"

She smiled. "I suspect you know it."

"Madame Emmascarar?" asked Holmes.

"I am pleased to meet you, Mr. Holmes," she replied, with a slight bow.

"Please resume your seat," said Holmes. As she did so, we took ours. "I am surprised you have come to see me."

"I doubt that," she replied, with a frown that reminded me of a stern nanny. "I have my contacts and have learned that Dr. Chaplin's daughter has called upon you. No doubt, despite my attempts to convince her otherwise, she has accused me of deception and desires you to prove it. I am advising you not to attempt it. You will merely damage your most excellent reputation. You have only to look at what happened to Professor Hendry."

Holmes smiled. "You are not the first person to express concern for my reputation. Rest assured that, while it is appreciated, it is also unwarranted. No such danger exists."

"Such arrogance," she replied. "To presume me a fraud without any evidence is hardly the act of a scientific mind. Professor Hendry tested me thoroughly and was at least noble enough to admit his error."

"To presume you genuine in the absence of evidence would be just as unscientific," Holmes countered. "As for the professor, I am sure he regrets what his involvement with you has done to him."

Madame Emmascarar looked genuinely sad. "That was unfortunate. He should have been lauded for proving my gifts."

"Why did you accept his cheque?" asked Holmes. "After all, you had gained his backing which was surely more valuable."

She frowned. "I thought you would understand that, Mr. Holmes. Many of the people who come to me lack the money to pay for my services. Taking larger sums from the wealthy means I can afford to see the less affluent. This is something I understand you have done in the past. Also, people would likely have been suspicious if I had not accepted the cheque."

Holmes did not answer either point. "Why have you come here, madam?"

She rose from her seat and walked to the window before half-turning to face us. "I came merely to offer you the warning I have just delivered. I have the greatest respect for your talents. I consider us to be much the same. We both help people in distress to get answers. I merely ask that you permit me to continue to do so." She waited for some indication from Holmes. When it was not forthcoming, she smiled a sad smile, bowed, and left the room.

"Most curious," said Holmes, after hearing the front door close. "What did she really want?"

"Perhaps she preferred to see you here rather than have you visit her?" I suggested.

Holmes smiled. "Bravo, Watson. The idea has merit. By coming to me she only gives me herself to draw conclusions from. Had we met at her house she may have been concerned that I would see something that would give her away. But there was no need. I already have a good idea of how her fraud is conducted."

"You do?"

"It is simplicity itself."

"Can you not tell me?"

"It is a little early. I wish to see Lady Trevone first."

I slept little that night. Once again, Holmes the showman was giving nothing away. I only hoped he would tell me more after we had visited Lady Trevone.

The lady's address was in Mayfair. We arrived a few minutes early and were shown into an impressive drawing room. Soon, she joined us. She was a lady in her mid-twenties and tall to the point of being imposing. I found myself rather intimidated by her. I could understand how she had fooled and destroyed her past suitors. Instinctively, I felt she was a lady I would not wish to cross.

"Good morning, Mr. Holmes," she said. Holmes and I both bowed.

"Good morning, Lady Trevone."

She held up an envelope and waved it. "I was intrigued when I received your letter. Given your profession, I must assume you have your doubts about Madame Emmascarar."

"I have been asked to look into her activities, Lady Trevone. I do so without an agenda."

"Very well," she replied. "Please ask your questions. I must say that you have only ten minutes. I deliberately set this interview to be at a time when my husband is out. He would not welcome your presence here."

Holmes nodded. "Did Madame Emmascarar approach you?"

"Yes. It was a few months ago, a short while after my first wedding anniversary party."

"Was that party held here?"

"It was."

"What form did her initial approach take?"

"She wrote to say she had received a communication from my late aunt to say that she wished to speak with me. I was immediately fascinated."

"May I ask why?"

Lady Trevone's face fell. She clearly regretted speaking. "I'm afraid I cannot answer that, Mr. Holmes. It is a private matter."

"But Madame Emmascarar's message indicated that she knew the details of this matter?"

"You may assume so," said Lady Trevone.

"How many sittings have you attended?"

"Five, so far."

"May I ask what you are being charged for each sitting?"

"No, Mr. Holmes, you may not but I'm sure you can hazard a guess."

"Your previous answer suggests that you plan to attend further sittings. Is that so?"

"Yes. I will attend them until such time as they no longer have value."

"I presume you attended these sittings at Madame Emmascarar's Clapham home?"

"Not on the first occasion," replied Lady Trevone.

"May I ask why?"

"I had another appointment that evening and knew I would be late to that event if I was starting from Clapham."

"May I ask where you held it?"

"Madame Emmascarar suggested The Langham Hotel. She would engage a room as long as I was prepared to pay for it."

"Were there others present at your sittings?"

"Regrettably, yes."

"Why do you say that?"

"As I have already intimated, the matter I was interested in was a private one. I had no desire for there to be witnesses. It was the one aspect of our association where Madame Emmascarar did not follow my wishes. She made it plain that at least four people were required for the séance to be successful. If I did not agree she said that the matter could go no further."

"How did you resolve that difficulty?" asked Holmes.

"I said to her that the other attendees would be required to sign papers binding them to secrecy on what they heard."

"What was Madame Emmascarar's reaction?"

"She said it was unusual but that she would convey this to the other sitters. Before the sitting took place all had agreed and signed papers at the office of my solicitor."

"How did that first sitting proceed?"

"There was confusion at the start. The man at reception gave me a room number which turned out to be incorrect. I was forced to return and ask again. He apologised for his error and provided the correct number.

"Because of this, I was a few minutes late to the room. Madame Emmascarar greeted me at the door 'You are a trifle late, Lady Trevone. Please allow me to lead you to your seat.'

"She took me lightly by the arm and directed me to a chair."

"Was the room dark?"

"It was. I could see the outline of three people around the table. It was irritating, but I was late, and Madame Emmascarar had previously told me that she always started promptly."

"Can you tell me anything else?"

"The sitting was successful. We made contact with my aunt and with the sister of one the men around the table. I remember him as he had a peculiarly deep voice. Then I remember a clock in the room chiming and I knew the sitting was running late. I drew Madame Emmascarar's attention to this, which I could tell annoyed her. She halted the séance and led me out of the room."

"Did any of her other clients leave?"

"Not that I noticed."

Lady Trevone suddenly looked over Holmes's shoulder. I turned and saw she was looking at the clock.

"I'm afraid I must ask you to leave as my husband is due home and I would not have him find you here. My last word to you is that Madame Emmascarar is a gifted, if unconventional, woman; and I would ask you to leave her in peace."

We bowed and were escorted out by the butler. It was not a moment too soon as, after we had walked a few paces, we saw the crested coach of Lord Trevone pass us.

Holmes was smiling. "Did you learn what you expected?" I asked.

"I did."

When we arrived at Baker Street, Mrs. Hudson handed Holmes an envelope. He tore it open. "Interesting," he said as he read the enclosure.

I followed him upstairs. "What is it, Holmes?"

He handed me the paper as he went into his room. "Read it aloud, Watson. I need to hear it again."

I looked at the telegram. "Our future sittings have been cancelled. We will leave the country in a few weeks. Thank you, Mr. Holmes. Sincerely, Miss Chaplin."

"Madame Emmascarar was evidently scared off following her decision to visit you," I suggested.

"Possibly," said Holmes. "She may think if she drops the one client whose family has approached me that I will cease to act in the matter. But there is another possibility."

"Which is?"

"That she has got all she needs from Dr. Chaplin."

The next morning, Holmes announced that we needed to visit the Langham Hotel. He brought a large bag from his room which he carried downstairs. We hailed a cab and headed on our way.

"Now, Watson," said Holmes. "I need to look at the hotel register. You need to provide a distraction."

"What kind of distraction?"

He pointed to the bag. "I have filled that bag full of papers. They are mostly sheets of newspaper. When I place my finger to my lips, empty the bag onto the floor and ask for help. The person behind the counter will help you and that will give me time to find what I need."

After about ten minutes, we arrived at the hotel. I took hold of the bag and followed Holmes inside. He strode to the reception desk and began to make conversation with the young man behind it. The subject was evidently not to the young man's taste as he looked decidedly uncomfortable. I remained a few paces behind.

When the foyer was almost deserted, Holmes suddenly turned to one side and placed his finger on his lips. I immediately emptied the bag onto the floor. "Oh no," I cried. "Can someone help me?"

The young man ran from behind the desk and started to retrieve the papers for me. The look on his face was almost comical as he realised he was helping to pick up sheets of newspaper. It took just over a minute to get all the paper back into the bag. I thanked him, gave him a shilling, and left.

I turned onto Regent Street and waited. A few moments later, Holmes joined me. "Well done, Watson."

"What did you learn?"

"I found the booking in the register. It records the fact that Madame Emmascarar booked a suite for the sitting. There was a note added later to say that food would be served for four people."

"Sorry, Holmes. I don't see what is strange about that?"

"It makes it clear that Madame Emmascarar knew that everyone aside from Lady Trevone would be staying for dinner. We have been told before that clients were not permitted to linger after her séances. Why was this different? There was also a note to the effect that one of the guests was not to be served any alcohol."

"I don't see the connection."

"I know," said Holmes, "from the coverage of the time, that Simon Brookes, who was one of Lady Trevone's suitors, was reported as being a member of the temperance movement."

"And you don't think that is a coincidence?"

"No, Watson. I do not. It helps to reinforce my theory."

The next morning, I was the first to rise. I went downstairs and picked up the newspaper. My eyes alighted on the leading articles.

"Holmes! Holmes!"

He emerged from his room pulling on his dressing gown. "What on Earth is it, Watson?"

"Madame Emmascarar has confessed to being a fraud."

He whistled. "That is sooner than I expected."

I continued to read. "It says here that she sent a statement to the newspaper and announced she would be handing herself into her nearest police station within hours."

"Of course," said Holmes. "Pack, Watson."

"Pack?"

"Yes. We are heading for Scotland."

"What about Madame Emmascarar?"

"We have no further need to concern ourselves with her. She is no more."

A few hours later and we were rattling through the countryside en route to the land of my ancestors. Holmes had said little but now chose to speak.

"You realise, of course, that we are going to see Professor Hendry?"

"I assumed so, but why?"

"Because he is a major beneficiary of this."

"I fail to see how, Holmes."

He looked surprised. "Really, Watson? Think about it for a few moments. The professor regularly bemoaned the fact that no matter how many mediums he exposed, the general public continued to flock to them. He eventually despaired and channelled his energies into the care of his dying wife.

"With her passing, he had little left to lose. So, he set up a challenge, to which he attached a significant sum of money. It ran for some time, with medium after medium being discredited, but it still did little to dent the popularity of mediums overall. Suddenly, Madame Emmascarar emerged from nowhere and secured his endorsement."

"But, Holmes," I said, "it ended his career!"

"Yes. But it helped his mission. With his endorsement behind her, Madame Emmascarar removed almost all the competition. No one wanted to see anyone else. By endorsing one medium, he helped to destroy a great many others. Meanwhile Madame Emmascarar builds a larger and larger reputation for herself. She is careful to see only people whose profiles will bring her more attention. Look at her clients. Dr. Chaplin, infamous for the deaths in his care. Then we have our wealthy and influential stockbroker, once accused of significant fraud, with clients losing thousands of pounds between them. Finally, Lady Trevone who has left a number of men broken and bankrupt in her wake. What unites them all is that they are convinced of Madame's gifts and sing her praises, along with the professor."

"But she knew so much about them."

"Oh, Watson," he said. "Dr. Chaplin's house was broken into and vandalised in advance of his first séance. It was not done for revenge but to learn information that could be used later. The vandalism was a distraction from the true purpose. All the late Mrs. Chaplin's papers, photographs, and more would have been there. More than enough to provide Madame Emmascarar with information to use."

"And the others?"

"Our eminent stockbroker told us of a client party. He even said he was compelled to engage with one guest for some time. It is fair to assume that said individual, and one of the other attendees, were on Madame Emmascarar's orders to gather similar information. It was why Madame refused to have the first séance until after that event."

"I suppose it was the anniversary party in the case of Lady Trevone?"

"Precisely. Madame gathers enough, through her associates, to make a significant first impression. It is enough to convince them of her powers. She then uses methods not dissimilar to mine to extract other information from these people."

"All this for the money?"

"Oh no, Watson," said Holmes. "There is far more to it than that. More than two birds are being killed with this stone."

He would say no more despite my entreaties. My head was in a whirl. I could comprehend simple fraud but here was Holmes saying it was more than that. He had also intimated that Madame Emmascarar was dead – a fact on which he had declined to elaborate.

Almost seven hours after leaving London we found ourselves at the door of Professor Hendry's modest home. Given the house's remoteness, Holmes asked the cabby to wait. A young maid answered the door and took our cards. A minute or so later, we were invited inside.

The professor rose from his armchair as we entered his study. "Mr. Holmes, Dr. Watson. It is a pleasure to meet you."

My ability to immediately return the greeting was impeded by the sight of a revolver sitting on the arm of the professor's chair. I immediately regretted not bringing my own. "We mean you no harm, sir," I said.

The professor followed my gaze and smiled. "That is not for you, Doctor. Please take a seat, gentlemen."

We did as he requested, and the professor offered us drinks. We both declined and he proceeded to pour himself a large brandy, which was clearly not the first he had consumed that evening. He lowered himself into his seat and took a sip from his glass. His right hand rested on the revolver under which, I noticed, sat a piece of paper.

"So, gentlemen," he said. "I can guess why you are here. Yes, I am pleased with the result."

"You got what you wanted?" asked Holmes.

"I believe that will be the case, in time, and I am far from the only one."

I could take no more. "Would either of you care to explain?"

The professor and Holmes looked at each other. "After you, Mr. Holmes," said Hendry.

Holmes turned slightly towards me, keeping one eye on the professor. "Some I have already told you, Watson. The professor here worked with Madame Emmascarar. They arranged that she would pass his challenge and he would endorse her. She would get the attention of all the wealthy thus driving much of the competition from the market.

"She would then increase her reputation with success after success until large numbers were convinced of her abilities. Then, as we have seen, she confesses to being a fraud."

"I don't understand."

"It is quite simple, Watson. In a matter of days, the lady's confession will be the talk of the country and, quite possibly, the world. People up and down this great land will conclude that if Madame Emmascarar is a fraud, there is little to no chance of any other medium being genuine. Those not already driven out of business will be distrusted, at best, and condemned, at worst."

I turned to look at the professor. "There was also the Robin Hood element," he said.

"What do you mean, sir?" I asked.

He smiled. "I first met Madame a few months after I had issued my challenge. The newspapers were losing interest and I was no nearer to achieving my goal. In all honesty, I was prepared to give up and consider another approach.

"After one of the many failed séances, she came up to me. She asked me if I were interested in justice to which I naturally replied that I was. I pointed out to her that it was a desire for justice that had driven me in my mission against mediums.

"It was then that she said we could help each other. She went on to explain that she was seeking justice for some poor souls who had been let down by the courts." He sipped from his glass. "She was direct and added that she would be paid by an interested party for what she was proposing."

"I presume it would be too much to expect this party to have a name?" asked Holmes.

"You are correct," replied Hendry.

Holmes nodded. "Nevertheless," he said, "I am surprised she managed to convince you to take part in an obvious fraud."

The professor drained his glass. "Her argument was compelling. She pointed out that I was not having much success with my current approach. She invited me to consider how people would react if they came to believe in a medium so strongly and then had that person let them down, and show them they were fools.

"She proposed that she would become that medium. She wanted my endorsement so it would be easier to lure some wrongdoers into a trap. Once that was successfully concluded, she would deliver on her part of the bargain. I found the idea of a fraud to combat fraud poetic."

"So, this was all about getting money from Dr. Chaplin and the others?" I asked.

Professor Hendry chuckled.

"More than that, Watson," said Holmes. "It was about justice and humiliation. Dr. Chaplin will leave this country poorer and with an even worse reputation than he had before. Even you will see some justice in that. He was a drunk who caused the deaths of three patients and, indirectly, the financial ruin of their families.

"Mr. Babcock's reputation as a stockbroker is likely to be significantly damaged by this. His judgment will be doubted which cannot do him any favours. He too has been parted from a considerable sum over a sustained period."

"But what about Lady Trevone?" I asked.

Holmes snorted. "Ladies like her rely on their reputation and influence in society circles. Everyone will soon be laughing behind her back, her influence destroyed. Unlike the others, she will not miss the money, which will have been considerable, but, in this case, the money is less important than the humiliation when all this gets into the papers."

"I don't follow."

"Think about the séances, Watson. Consider Dr. Chaplin. He was led into a room in almost total darkness. This was not because he was late. It was to prevent him seeing who was there. I am confident that on those occasions, members of his victims' families were present. To use boxing parlance, they had a ring-side seat to witness Chaplin be defrauded. They would have played along and pretended to speak with the departed. This would further fuel Madame's reputation. Chaplin's daughter was kept distracted by Mr. Fowler who was there to do precisely that and, in an emergency, prevent her interrupting the séance. Her father left the séance first, probably at Madame Emmascarar's direction. While he was with his daughter, Mr. Fowler and the others left. You will remember that Miss Chaplin spoke of laughter that Madame Emmascarar stopped. They enjoyed watching him be fooled and parted from his money. I suspect, if we saw their bank accounts, we would see that they all subsequently received money, minus Madame's commission, of course. It is that financial trail we will use to expose this whole plan. Under pressure from the police, they are likely to confess."

"And something similar happened to the others?"

"Exactly."

"What about when the rooms were not in darkness?" I asked.

"Simple. It meant that the people in the room, whilst victims, were not known to Madame's client. Perhaps they were some of Babcock's long-distance clients. Or extended family members of Chaplin's victims who had not met him."

"And Lady Trevone?"

"Madame Emmascarar had to think swiftly there. Forced to meet at the Langham, she had to modify her usual plan. I suspect money changed hands in order to manufacture a delay at the hotel reception which would justify her later saying to Lady Trevone that she was late. At least one of Lady Trevone's former suitors was there. We know that from the note about the menu. At her Clapham home, Madame ensured the audience left before the target of the fraud. At the Langham she knew Lady Trevone was leaving first for an appointment. So, she took the reckless step of arranging a meal for the other guests so they could presumably all laugh, over dinner, about what they had witnessed."

"So, Doctor," said Hendry, "I get what I want and those poor souls get to see the people who hurt them damaged both financially and reputationally. In addition, they get a sizable amount back of the money they lost and a fresh chance at life. Unless..."

"Unless what?"

"Unless I interfere, Watson," said Holmes.

The professor continued. "Mr. Holmes cannot do anything to rescue Madame Emmascarar's reputation. That aspect of the plan cannot be undone, mediums are all but finished in this country. But he can, quite possibly, encourage the police to investigate the finances of Dr. Chaplin's victims and the others. Do they deserve that, Mr. Holmes?"

Holmes sat in thought. Hendry remained in his chair, his hand never leaving the revolver. I waited.

After five minutes, Holmes stood. "Very well, Professor. I must insist on one condition."

"And that is?"

"Your wife must wait for you."

We left the professor's house. On our cabby's advice, we visited a small inn. They had plenty of space and we were soon settled into a small suite of rooms.

"How did the professor know our purpose?" I asked.

"You noticed, of course," said Holmes, "the telegram under the revolver? He almost certainly knew of the confession before we did. Most likely it was from Madame Emmascarar herself."

"Why are you permitting this to proceed?"

"Because this is one of those instances where interference would do more harm than good. A situation where the law would aid the guilty at the expense of the innocent. In any event, the plan will not succeed in its entirety."

"What do you mean?"

"Believe me, Watson. I share the professor's desire when it comes to mediums. Alas, contrary to his assertion, I merely think this plan has set the practice back. The human need for hope will ensure that these people will gain a footing once more. If I expose him, I may accelerate matters.

"I already told you I am convinced of Lady Trevone's guilt but the courts will not touch her. As we know, Watson, the law is not always justice. So, on this occasion, justice cannot be the law. The same applies to Dr. Chaplin and Mr. Babcock."

"What will happen to the professor?"

Holmes's face took on a sad expression. "As he said, Watson, the revolver was not for us. He had every intention of ending his suffering and joining his wife. He was only waiting to hear of the success of the plan. His punishment for his part in these matters is to carry on living. He knows what I could do if he reneges on his commitment. At least he will live in comfort as he will almost certainly get most of his money back. His perceived financial suffering was all part of the plan."

"Surely the police will investigate the death of Madame Emmascarar?" I said.

"You misunderstand me, Watson," said Holmes. "She never truly existed. The lady who posed as the famous medium will return to being the lady who first approached Professor Hendry. She will have returned to her former life with, presumably, a much healthier bank account."

Although uneasy with Holmes, once again, overriding the law of the land, I had to agree. No matter how I looked at it, his approach was the one most likely to cause the least distress. The next day we caught the first available train for London. Holmes spent most of the long journey in silence so I was pleased I had made the decision to purchase several periodicals to stave off the risk of boredom.

It was late-afternoon when we reached our rooms. I asked Mrs. Hudson if she could prepare dinner, before joining Holmes in the sitting room. As I walked in, I saw he was sat at his desk.

"Watson," he said.

"Yes, Holmes."

He did not reply so I joined him at the desk. He was staring into the open drawer. His face was a mixture of surprise and concern. In mere moments, I understood.

An item was missing. An item I feared and which I had persuaded him to lock away when I could not convince him to dispense with it entirely. Amongst the many papers, and a certain photograph, an item that usually rested next to my chequebook was absent.

He looked up. "Curious is it not?"

The morocco case was gone.

The Adventure of the Bad Companions

(Early 1898)

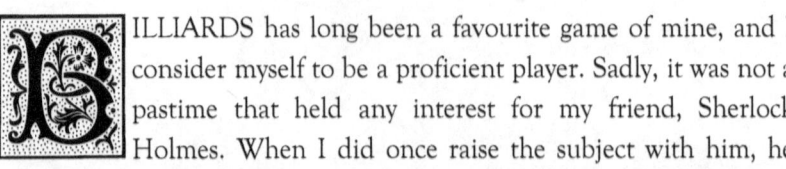ILLIARDS has long been a favourite game of mine, and I consider myself to be a proficient player. Sadly, it was not a pastime that held any interest for my friend, Sherlock Holmes. When I did once raise the subject with him, he reduced it to little more than a mathematics lecture with talk of angles and levels of Newtonian force. As a result, I only played against Thurston at our club. We had been elected at much the same time and, as new members, had naturally gravitated to each other. We soon discovered that we shared a love of the game and were accustomed to playing at least twice a week, for a few shillings, unless other, more perilous, adventures claimed my attention. The billiard room was also where I sought solace during Holmes's less sociable periods.

On this particular occasion, I had left Baker Street a little after two o'clock, following a lunch of delicious devilled kidneys, with the intention of being at my club half-an-hour later. The road was somewhat empty and I had struggled to find a cab. Eventually, I had been forced to venture into the next street in order to locate one. Naturally, as soon as I had secured transportation, the roads had become busier. Consequently, I was late. I hurried into the club, nodding my thanks to the doorman as I passed. I supplied the cloakroom staff with my hat, overcoat, and necessary pleasantries before hastening upstairs to the billiard room.

I was much surprised to find it empty although I could see Thurston's jacket slung over the back of one of the many chairs. I removed my own and placed it alongside. The table was already prepared so I walked over to the rack to select a cue. Having done so, I was in the process of applying chalk to both it and my left hand when I heard loud but muffled voices directly above. No more than twenty seconds later, the door opened and Thurston stumbled in carrying two, unequal, glasses of brandy. It was clear, from the redness of his face, that he was upset. At first, he did not seem to notice me. "Oh," he said, as he looked up and kicked the door closed behind him, "hello, Watson."

"What happened to you?" I asked.

"Conway," he replied.

"Sir James Conway?" I asked.

"The same. You'd think a baronet would hold himself to a higher standard than lesser folk."

"What happened?"

Thurston walked to a table at the side of the room and put down the glasses. His face slowly returned to its normal colour as he crossed to the opposite side to select his cue.

"When it became clear that you were going to be late," he continued, "I decided to go in search of a drink. You're probably familiar with that room directly above this one that is used for private events?"

"Yes, indeed," I said. I had celebrated my engagement there with members of my old rugby club. It was an event marred only by the absence of Holmes who had shown little interest in either the celebration or my engagement.

"What you may not know," continued Thurston, as he withdrew his chosen cue, "is that when the room is reserved, the staff sometimes furnish it with a drinks trolley in advance."

"You haven't been taking advantage, Thurston?" I asked.

"Once or twice," he said, managing to recover his smile. "After all, it is rather convenient. I walked into the room and there was the trolley. I decided I'd sneak two glasses of brandy for us and was in the process of pouring the second when I heard someone shout. I turned and it was Conway. He was in the doorway, dressed head to toe in black. 'Get out of here, Thurston,' he demanded. 'This room is reserved.'"

"What did you do?" I asked.

"I was outraged at his manner but I was hardly in a defensible position, Watson. Had I made a scene it would have been me who would have fallen foul of the committee. He also had witnesses in the form of Dr. Henry Carlton and Mr. Alexander Jackson who were standing right behind him."

"What did you do?" I asked.

"What else could I do? With mumbled apologies, I beat a hasty retreat. I was halfway down the stairs to this room when I realised that I was still holding the glasses." He looked back at the door. "I'm surprised Conway didn't chase after me. In my opinion, he was more upset than the situation called for."

"I wonder what they are using the room for?" I said.

"I had a word with one of the waiters a few days ago," said Thurston. "The staff call them the Bad Companions."

"The what?" I exclaimed.

"I know," said Thurston, shaking his head. "The poor man regretted his indiscretion and begged me not tell anyone else. It was Dr. Carlton who began reserving the room some weeks ago. The three men have used it at least twice a week since. It wasn't all that long after Conway lost that government contract."

"Do you know what they get up to?"

"I'm told they sit round the table, read their newspapers and discuss the day's issues over many cigars."

"But how did it get that name?"

Thurston smiled. "The waiter told me that, on one occasion, he had taken up a trolley and was about to knock but had stopped when he heard raised voices. He stood in shock for some minutes as Conway accused Jackson of taking him for granted and not behaving in a gentlemanly manner."

"What was Jackson's response?" I asked.

"I'm told he rather boldly reminded Conway of the importance of promises and that it was he who was failing to be a gentleman. Dr. Carlton could be heard demanding both men to calm down and lower their voices.

"The waiter told me that, knowing Conway, he expected the men to come to blows. He worked up the courage to knock and all went silent. He went in and the three of them were sat there with faces like thunder. They waited until he positioned the trolley and left. The door was barely closed before the arguments started again. He told the other staff about it, and they came up with the name between them."

Naturally, I remembered the government contract that Thurston had referred to. Sir James had inherited his father's munitions business, based near Dover, and, shortly afterwards, lost a lucrative government contract. At the time, the government had said it was a purely economic decision but within the walls of the club there had been other reasons mooted. Subsequently, Sir James lost much interest in his business. It was understood that he travelled to the factory once a week for board meetings, and other routine matters, but mostly lived by playing whist for high stakes. He was usually successful and was able to live well on the proceeds.

"With regards to Sir James's contract," I said, "I heard rumours that a lady was involved."

"Something like that," agreed Thurston. He placed his chosen cue on the table and returned to the glasses. He tipped one partially into the other, to even them out, before bringing them over. I took one from him.

"After all I went through to get them," he said, with a grin, "we should not let them go to waste."

A couple of hours later, I was on my way back to Baker Street warmed by several, more honestly obtained, brandies, and with a few extra shillings in my pocket. Thurston's form had been shaken by his confrontation and he had failed to win a single game.

As I ascended the stairs, Holmes called out. "You did well, Watson. I can hear the jingle of coins from here."

"Correct, as usual," I said, as I arrived in the room. I took a cigarette from the box, which Holmes had held out towards me, and sat down. "Thurston had a run in with Sir James Conway."

"Ah. The son of the late Sir Hubert Conway, the industrialist."

"That's the man," I said.

Holmes stubbed out his cigarette before lighting another. "Gregson paid me a visit while you were out."

"What did he want?"

"He was called to the house of one Percy Graves yesterday evening. The man's housekeeper found him dead by his own hand."

"If it was a suicide, I am surprised Gregson came here."

"He had good reason," said Holmes. "Graves left a note in which he blamed his suicide on a broken heart caused by one Annabelle Howard who is an actress in the West End."

I was familiar with Miss Howard. "About a month ago, I read that they were engaged. Around two days ago, I read it had been called off."

"What you may not be aware of," said Holmes, "which Gregson and I were, is that Miss Howard is rumoured to be a German agent."

I was staggered. "But why would she be interested in Graves? He was rich but he had no connections of interest to the German government."

"A question I also desire the answer to," said Holmes. "I despatched a note to my brother. He, rather tersely, agreed to a meeting this evening at the Diogenes."

At eight o'clock we arrived at Mycroft Holmes's club in Pall Mall. I had visited a few times but found its atmosphere stifling. As was customary, we made our way through corridors in complete silence and up to the floor where Mycroft had his private rooms. Holmes knocked and entered.

Mycroft Holmes was looking out of the window onto the street below. He turned. "Good evening, Sherlock. Good evening, Doctor."

"Mycroft," said Holmes.

We were waved into chairs. "I cannot say I was surprised to receive your, carefully worded, note, Sherlock. But you must understand that I can only say so much. Most of what I do say cannot go beyond present company."

Holmes nodded. "What can you tell us about this Percy Graves?"

Mycroft Holmes came away from the window and lowered his sizable frame into the remaining chair. "Very little, Sherlock. It was his connection to Sir James Conway and a certain lady that made him of limited interest."

"How so?"

"Conway's father, Sir Hubert, had a lucrative, and sensitive, contract with the government, that is no secret. For more than ten years he had kept our boys equipped to deal with our nation's enemies.

"Just over a year ago, he became ill and it was clear that he did not have long to live. His son had recently reached his majority and was destined to inherit both title and business. Naturally, I commissioned an investigation into him to ensure that he was the right sort of man."

"I presume," said Holmes, "that the report was not favourable?"

"Incorrect, Sherlock," said Mycroft. "It was acceptable. His patriotism appeared both deep and sincere. He was a regular card player but was sufficiently wealthy that we were confident he could not be tempted to any indiscretion."

"Then what?" asked Holmes.

"Sir Hubert died six months ago. Two months later, we received an anonymous letter in which it was suggested that Conway was, shall we say, involved with Miss Annabelle Howard, the actress."

"And suspected German agent," said Holmes.

Mycroft placed a finger near to his lips. "Quieter, please, Sherlock. The letter made plain that their relationship was likely to become an engagement. Naturally, patriot or not, we could not have a man so compromised having any connection to the defence of the realm. I conveyed my recommendation to the Prime Minister and Home Secretary. Conway was called in and told that the contract was to be terminated as soon as legally possible."

"Did he understand the reason?"

"He was left in no doubt."

"How did he react?"

Mycroft Holmes frowned. "I did not deliver the news personally, Sherlock. Confrontation is far too energetic. However, I am told he did not take it well. He denied that their relationship was of that nature and claimed to have no knowledge of Miss Howard's covert activities. In his patriotic anger he declared his intention of exposing her."

"I assume he was told not to," said Holmes.

"Precisely. We have plans for Miss Howard. It was made plain to Conway that he was not to undertake such a course of action. A form of pressure was applied to ensure his compliance."

"That being?"

"We undertook to give a reason for the termination of the contract that would not damage the reputation of either him or his business. The company had other clients and we felt sure he would prioritise his business over vengeance. He understood that any transgression would result in his exposure. He signed an agreement and, as far as we know, has adhered to it. That said, he took little interest in his company subsequently with the result that it is a fraction of what it was. Instead, he does rather well at cards, I understand."

"I'm a little confused, Mr. Holmes," I said. "Miss Howard was engaged to Percy Graves."

Mycroft Holmes smiled at me in an indulgent, patrician way. "Quite so, Doctor. It would appear that she transferred her affections, with ease, to Mr. Graves soon after the events I have described. However, this was kept secret from everyone for some time. Mr. Graves was the heir to a sizeable fortune of his own, and I believe he feared a less than positive reaction from his family if the facts became known."

"But how does Sir James come into this?"

"Because, Doctor, Graves and Conway were close friends. When Graves's father died, quite recently, the news of the engagement was revealed."

"That must have come as a surprise to Conway?" I suggested.

"Tread carefully, if you would be so good."

Mycroft Holmes fixed his brother with a stare. "What do the police know, Sherlock?"

Holmes smiled. "A letter was found with the body, it accused Miss Howard of betrayal."

"But did it state the form of the betrayal?"

"My understanding is that it did not."

Mycroft exhaled and looked down at a side table on which stood a glass of port. "You see that glass, Sherlock?"

"Yes."

"Such small pleasures must be patiently waited for. When the time is right, Miss Howard will prove a valuable asset to this country. Similar patience is needed. Tread carefully, if you would be so good."

After sampling a glass of Mycroft Holmes's excellent port, we found ourselves back on the street. "What do you propose to do?" I asked.

Holmes said nothing and led me away from Pall Mall towards St. James's Square. Once there, we availed ourselves of one of the benches. Holmes withdrew a folded piece of paper from his pocket.

"I took no pleasure in this but I was not entirely honest with brother Mycroft. This is a copy I made of the other letter found with Graves's body. Gregson has retained the original at Scotland Yard."

"Why did you not tell your brother?"

"Mycroft is accustomed to having the upper hand. Remember, Watson, that I was sincere when I said he was my superior in intelligence. It is a rare pleasure to be aware of something that he is not."

"What does it say?"

He returned the paper to his pocket. "That I do not wish to divulge as yet. What I will say is that what it accuses Miss Howard of has nothing to do with foreign powers."

The death of Percy Graves gained a few column inches over the days that followed. The fortune he had inherited passed to a cousin and little more was said of him. Holmes heard no more from Gregson on the matter. This, I put down to Mycroft's influence. All it would've taken was a brief word with the Home Secretary. A fortunate reporter secured an interview with Annabelle Howard. She expressed her grief and announced she would be absent from her current production for a few weeks. It was stated in later reports that she was not to be invited to Graves's funeral. A fact that must have hurt her deeply.

One month after the visit to the Diogenes, a young lady found herself seated upon our settee. Her name was Georgina Morris and she had wired, requesting an appointment, a day earlier. She had walked into our sitting room, nervously. In her hands she held an envelope.

"Thank you for seeing me, Mr. Holmes," she said.

"Not at all," said Holmes. "Your telegram mentioned your former fiancé?"

Miss Morris fidgeted. "Yes. His name is David Greenwood."

"The M.P.?" asked Holmes.

"Yes," she said. "You may have also heard of his father?"

"Yes. Reverend Samuel Greenwood," said Holmes.

"You are correct," said Miss Morris. "A few weeks ago, David learned he was going to be promoted to a sensitive position in the Foreign Office."

Holmes frowned. "How did you come to learn of this?"

"His father had invited me to dinner along with two other guests," said Miss Morris. "David announced his new position during the dinner. I remember he seemed pale and nervous. I assumed the sensitivity of the position was daunting."

"Do you recall any of the other guests?" asked Holmes,

"Yes. A Dr. Henry Carlton and his wife were there. I understood them to be friends of Reverend Greenwood."

"Thank you," said Holmes. "Please continue."

"David announced that he was to commence his new post on a date that is now two weeks away. Everyone around the table was surprised at his rapid promotion, Dr. Carlton especially. In fact, he appeared lost in thought for the rest of the evening. One week ago," she said, lifting the envelope, "this was sent to Reverend Greenwood."

Holmes took the envelope. "Folkestone postmark, dated just over one week ago." He removed its contents. "I see," he said, after reading it.

"It is a foul lie," said Miss Morris, "but it was enough for Reverend Greenwood to demand his son end our engagement. David asked to see me and presented me with this on his arrival. I will never forget the look on his face as he left my house. He looked so distressed, washed-out, and unsteady. He had to be helped out."

"You would like me to look into this matter?" asked Holmes.

"I have no hope of reversing the situation," said Miss Morris, her eyes moistening. "But I need to know who is behind this before they hurt someone else."

A few minutes later, Miss Morris was gone. Having seen her out, I returned to the sitting room to find Holmes standing by the fireplace. His pipe was between his lips and smouldering. His hands were thrust deep into his pockets.

"Would you care to explain?" I asked.

He gestured to the envelope on the table. I took it and read the letter. It was most direct and accused Miss Morris of an over fondness for wine.

"Well, it is certainly rude," I said. "How did this end an engagement?"

"It is far worse than rude to Reverend Greenwood," replied Holmes. "He is a leading member of the temperance movement. Whether true or not, such a rumour could be damaging to his reputation. It is no wonder he forced the severance of any connection between Miss Morris and his son."

"How cruel," I said. "So, you intend to search for this letter's author?"

"Ordinarily, I would not. This kind of hurtful deed is all too commonplace. In all likelihood, Miss Morris has a rival who wants her out of the way. But a number of curious events have occurred over the last few weeks. This one is similar to the first."

"What was the first?"

"The suicide of Mr. Graves," said Holmes. "Both saw the ending of an engagement."

"But under very different circumstances," I pointed out.

"Not at all," he replied. "In both cases an anonymous letter arrived which led to the engagement being brought to an end."

"But only one resulted in a death," I said. "What do you propose to do?"

"Well, we have just had one woman's account," he said. "I suggest we seek out another's."

About two hours later we found ourselves in Belgravia where Miss Annabelle Howard had an impressive home. Holmes had wired ahead and Miss Howard had returned a favourable response.

After being met by her butler, we were shown into her impressive front parlour. We did not wait more than a minute before the lady presented herself. I had seen her in plays before and considered her a most beautiful woman but, framed as she was in the doorway, she took on the appearance of a work by one of the great masters.

"Good afternoon, Mr. Holmes," she said. She left the doorway and advanced towards a settee in the middle of the room. As she sat, she directed us to sit in two armchairs directly opposite.

"I can honestly say I have no idea why you are honouring me with a visit," she continued. "However, when Sherlock Holmes requests an audience, it is too good an opportunity to miss. Of course," she said, turning to me, "it is an equal honour to meet your biographer."

I nodded. "Thank you, Miss Howard."

"Had you not come," she said, returning her gaze to Holmes, "it is likely I would have called upon you before long."

"Why is that, madam?" said Holmes.

"I am sure you will have read of the death of my fiancé?"

"Yes," said Holmes. "Some weeks ago, now. Why have you delayed coming to me?"

"Because I feared you would refuse me."

"On what grounds?"

"Patriotic ones."

"I don't follow, madam."

Miss Howard rose and went to the window. "We should not insult each other's intelligence, Mr. Holmes. I am aware of who your brother is and therefore it is fair to assume you know who I am."

I wondered how my friend would react given Mycroft Holmes's instructions.

"Very well," he said. "You are half-German and, on occasion, work for the German government."

She was not shocked and turned back to face us. Her expression was one of sadness. "Worked, Mr. Holmes. Very much past tense. I do so no longer."

"I am listening," said Holmes.

She returned to her seat. "I won't bore you with my reasons, Mr. Holmes, but I occasionally assisted in helping information of interest to leave these shores. Or I did until I met James."

"You are referring to Sir James Conway?" I asked.

"Yes, Doctor. On the orders of my superiors, I sent him tickets to my play. I was instructed to get close to him, flatter him and learn what I could about his work for the military."

"What happened?"

"I invited him backstage after the performance and he introduced me to Percy. The next day, Percy dropped by the theatre and asked me to lunch. Much to my own surprise, I accepted. One occasion led to others and before I knew it, I was in love."

Holmes's face was expressionless. "Why did you keep your relationship a secret for so long?"

"That was at Percy's request. At first, I was upset but he explained his family would not understand. He feared if anyone learned of it, including Sir James, the facts would come out. If I am honest, I appreciated the irony of getting cross at his desire to keep a secret when I was keeping a significant one from him."

"And what happened to your instructions?" asked Holmes.

"There and then I resolved to cease such activities," she said. "There was no way I could betray Percy by extracting secrets from his closest friend."

"I cannot imagine that this pleased your superiors," said Holmes.

"I managed to put them off with a variety of excuses but eventually they ran out of patience. They decided to cause disruption in another way. Soon after Sir James inherited his father's company, I read that his government contract was to be rescinded. I guessed at once that this was the work of my superiors. They had clearly decided that if secrets could not be obtained, they would cause disruption by exposing me to the authorities here and revealing my connection to Sir James. The cancellation of the contract would, inevitably, result and have an impact, no matter how brief, on British armaments manufacture and distribution."

"Were you aware," asked Holmes, "that the letter sent to the government stated that you and Sir James were on the point of becoming engaged?"

Miss Howard went pale. "No. But it makes sense that our relationship would be exaggerated in an effort to ensure the cancellation of the contract."

"Did you try and contact Sir James?"

"No. I thought that unwise and elected to wait for contact from him. Needless to say, it never came. I expected arrest but that did not come either. You have no idea, Mr. Holmes, what it was like waiting for the knock at the door day after day. Waiting for Percy to learn the truth was harder still."

"Given that you have frequently acted against this country's interests, you cannot expect much sympathy from me," said Holmes.

"I suppose not," she replied. "After a while, I returned to my normal routine."

"Mr. Graves continued to associate with you?" asked Holmes.

"Yes. I tentatively asked after Sir James and Percy told me that he had lost interest in the theatre and was solely focused on cards and his business. This intrigued me as it suggested Sir James had not been told the full reason for the loss of his contract. If he had, he would surely have warned Percy.

"Percy and I dined regularly at Rules in Covent Garden. We had an intimate table on the first floor where we could look down onto the street. The staff are discreet, so we had no fear of rumours circulating. We always arrived separately and left in the same fashion. At one of these dinners, Percy informed me that his father was gravely ill. The two of them had an uneasy relationship and Percy was not as upset as people might have expected him to be."

"I presume," said Holmes, "that he told you it would soon be possible to publicly declare your engagement?"

"Yes. He said he would announce it one month after his father's death. It was a relief. I had been concerned that my past would come back to haunt me, but I had since concluded that the German government was unlikely to waste its time or resources pursuing me, and the British government appeared to have no interest in me."

"So," said Holmes, "following the death of Graves's father, the formal announcement was made?"

"For a few weeks I was happy," she said. "Some of Percy's extended family expressed concerns but, as most of them were looking to him for some form of allowance, they kept their comments to a minimum. Percy revealed to me that he had plans to slowly cut many of them off. He said his father had been too liberal with them and he had a strong dislike of 'hangers-on.'

"Then it all began to unravel. Shortly before his death, we met as usual. Percy was waiting for me and it was clear that something was bothering him. He greeted me without any conviction and we sat down. It was as I did so that I noticed an envelope leaning against the window. He made no reference to it so I did not mention it. As dinner proceeded, we discussed a wide range of subjects but I could not take my eyes from the envelope. At the conclusion of the meal, we were drinking our last glasses of wine when he suddenly said 'I can see you are interested in this envelope.'"

"What happened?" asked Holmes.

"He took it from the window and I saw it was already open. He took out the letter and held it in his hand. 'I received this in the morning post. I was disturbed by its contents.' He held it out and I took it. As I read it, I was shocked. The letter accused me of being solely interested in Percy's money. It painted me as the sort of hanger-on Percy so disliked. It asserted that I had already made substantial commitments in anticipation of gaining access to the Graves' fortune.

"'What do you say, Annabelle?' he asked."

"And what did you say?" asked Holmes.

"I denied it, naturally. I was offended that he would even entertain the notion. I demanded to know the identity of my accuser. At this his face slightly softened. 'I have no notion as to the sender,' he said. 'It is not handwriting I recognise and you can see it is unsigned.' He held out his hand and I passed him the letter back. He announced he was going to think before deciding how to proceed."

Holmes leant forward in his seat. "Sadly, we know what he decided to do."

Miss Howard looked distressed. "I did not hear from him for a day. Then I received a curt note informing me that our engagement was at an end. The next day a note was in *The Times* to the same effect."

"And Mr. Graves was found dead shortly afterwards?"

"The next day."

"Have you pursued the matter since?"

"To the extent I am able but I do not wish to draw any more attention upon myself."

"I am not sure how I can assist you," said Holmes. "But I promise to give it some thought."

With Miss Howard visibly upset, we made our excuses and left. Back on the street, Holmes walked a few paces in silence. On a corner he paused to light a cigarette.

"It is strange isn't it, Watson?"

"What is, Holmes?"

"We have three events that have been brought to our attention. Firstly, Sir James's loss of a government contract and, secondly, the suicide of Percy Graves. Annabelle Howard is the common factor. Finally, there is the end of the engagement between David Greenwood and Georgina Morris. Other than there being an anonymous letter and broken engagement in common, there is nothing to link the first two events to the third."

"True enough, Holmes." I said. "Do you believe it could be a coincidence?"

"It is certainly possible but my instincts are against it. We heard from Miss Howard that Mr. Graves said the handwriting on the letter was not one he recognised. That suggests someone who is a stranger to him. Miss Howard also saw the letter and did not claim to recognise it."

"She could be keeping that from you?" I suggested.

"I have no sympathy with her actions against this country," said Holmes, "but she wants me to discover the truth. Why impede me if that is her aim? I can also reveal that what she said about the letter received by Graves tallies with the one brought to me by Gregson."

"Could it be the German government?" I asked.

"If we were just dealing with Conway and Graves, I'd consider it. But how would Greenwood come into the matter?"

"Well," I said, "there is still a Foreign Office connection."

"Parting Greenwood from Miss Morris has no obvious benefit for Germany. It gains them no discernible advantage. Surely, they would wait for the marriage to take place and try to get to Greenwood through his wife?"

As I pondered this, Holmes marched off in search of a cab.

That evening we were back in our sitting room. Holmes sat in his chair, clad in his dressing-gown. I retrieved the evening paper and began to leaf through it, randomly.

"Holmes," I said. "There's news here of another broken engagement."

Holmes sat up. "What are the details?"

"It says that Miss Julia Wilson, the daughter of wealthy businessman, Bernard Wilson, is no longer engaged to one Mr. Harold Parker."

"Is a reason offered?"

"No."

Holmes sank back into his chair. His face was the picture of disappointment. I turned back to the leading articles.

"Holmes," I said. "It seems we cannot get away from Sir James Conway."

"What is it, Watson?" said Holmes, showing less excitement.

"There is a report here that Sir James has challenged one Walter Fitzmorris to a game of whist with considerably high stakes. It will take place next week."

"Interesting," said Holmes.

"Why is that?" I asked.

"I study the wealthy, Watson, as they are often the focus of crime – sometimes as victims and sometimes as perpetrators. Walter Fitzmorris is a rich banker. His assets have to be valued for insurance purposes and it was once leaked to the press that the combined value of his estate was close to a half a million. I understand he is an elderly, infirm, widower with one son. He has a weakness for many forms of gambling including cards and share-dealing. On more than one occasion he has taken risks and lost considerable sums."

I continued to read. "Here is something more in your line, Holmes."

"Pray tell."

"It's about that Greenwood M.P. It seems he will no longer be taking up his post in the Foreign Office."

"Is a reason given?"

"Well," I said, "the reporter states that sources have told him the position has been withdrawn in connection with disciplinary proceedings."

One week later the big story in the society pages concerned Sir James Conway's whist victory against Walter Fitzmorris. True to past form, Sir James and his partner had taken a substantial sum, rumoured to be around three-quarters of the elderly banker's fortune, and his principal family home. Fitzmorris had wanted to play on but Sir James had refused on the grounds he wanted to leave the man something to pass on to his son. Fitzmorris had underwritten the game so his partner, a former colleague, had emerged more or less unscathed. Opinion was split between those who thought highly of Sir James for refusing to ruin Fitzmorris and those who criticised him for allowing matters to go as far as they had.

Sir James had extended Mr. Fitzmorris a kindness by saying he would give him the right to remain in the house as his tenant. Fitzmorris had refused, as a matter of pride, so, Sir James had, instead, offered him twelve months to vacate the property. This had been accepted.

Mere days later, Fitzmorris featured in the papers again when it was announced that a deal made by him to invest in a wine import business had been cancelled as he no longer had the resources to see it through. The owners of that business were seeking alternative investors. As I read the article, I could not help but feel for the family. To go from such heights to such lows through a single night of cards. I began to understand some of the anger towards Sir James. But Mr. Fitzmorris was a grown man who could not expect to be shielded from his own actions.

Holmes had limited interest in the follies of the wealthy unless a law had been broken. Instead, he pored through the newspapers and smoked incessantly.

A few weeks later the newspapers were buzzing with the news that Sir James and Walter Fitzmorris were to have a further game of whist. Fitzmorris had been demanding a chance to get his revenge but Sir James had been against it, declaring that he had no desire to do further harm. Mr. Fitzmorris had become increasingly forthright about it and Sir James had finally agreed. Mr. Fitzmorris's partner from the previous game had reluctantly agreed to take part as long as, once again, the risk rested with the elderly banker.

As no stranger to a wager, I was fascinated by this turn of events. I also feared for Mr. Fitzmorris who was clearly going to lose what remaining fortune he had. The fact that he appeared to have so little regard for his son's future was rather sad.

Luck was not entirely against the Fitzmorris family. The same newspaper reported that Turner and James, the wine importing company, had suffered a significant fire at their principal premises. An investigation by their insurers had revealed evidence of arson and the fact that the company had been on the point of collapse. The Fitzmorris family situation was not a good one but it had briefly had the potential to be considerably worse.

In the interim, Holmes had, in the absence of other lines of enquiry, decided to contact the Wilson family about the curtailed engagement I had mentioned. He agreed it was tenuous but would not hurt to investigate. His telegram had been answered with a proposed date which was upon us. The interview was to be at five o'clock at an address in Richmond.

The townhouse we pulled up outside of spoke of a degree of wealth. Within a few minutes we were seated in a comfortable study with Mr. Wilson. He seemed more jovial than I would have expected given what his daughter had been through.

"I apologise for the delay in seeing you, Mr. Holmes," he said. "My family needed some time before speaking to anyone."

"I quite understand," said Holmes. "The newspaper reports were short on detail."

"A fact that I am grateful for, sir," said Mr. Wilson. "I come from humble beginnings but have amassed a fair sum of money in the import and export trade. I operate out of the docks at Shadwell. My girl, Julia, had the best education we could give her and her future looked bright."

"Until?"

"Until she met this lad, Parker. He came from a well-to-do family from Chiswick. They seemed a good pair. She had money, he had connections. He was here for dinner around a month ago when he told us he was going to buy a large number of shares in a company that imported wine from Spain."

"Was it Turner and James by any chance?" asked Holmes.

"Yes. That's the company. It seems they were looking for investors. Parker came to me and asked if I wanted to join him as a co-investor."

"And did you?"

"It seemed foolish not to. Young Parker informed me he had been tipped off about the deal by an old friend of his. 'Jack and I went to university together,' he told me. 'If he says it's a sound investment that's good enough for me. He's putting in around two thousand pounds. I intend to match it.' I invited them both to dinner and we discussed it at length. I was surprised to discover that Jack and Julia knew each other from some ball she had been to and they both seemed delighted to renew their acquaintance."

"Given the news in the papers recently," said Holmes, "it is clear you did not invest. What happened?"

Wilson sighed. "About a week later, Parker turned up here the worse for drink. I got him inside and sobered him up enough to learn that his friend had pulled out of the deal and had advised him to do likewise. He said he was convinced Jack had lost his courage. I was asked if, in addition to my existing commitment, I could put up the money that Jack would otherwise have done. If I did not, the deal would fall through. I said I'd consider it and he then left.

"A short while later, I received an anonymous letter. It said the company was not being honest about its prospects. It added that Parker had lost a lot of money on unsafe business deals and I would do well to not get involved in anything he proposed."

"And you took this seriously?"

"I learned long ago to take warnings seriously, Mr. Holmes," said Wilson, "no matter the motivation of the sender. I sent Parker a note telling him I was going to look into the deal more carefully. His response was to turn up drunk, accusing me of letting him down just as his friend had done. Julia was home and tried to calm him down. He pushed her away with such force that she fell and nearly hurt herself. I had him removed from my house and both the engagement and investment were called off. That unpleasant episode aside, I am grateful as my correspondent turned out to be correct."

Holmes nodded.

"Not long afterwards, I was called upon by Parker's friend. He said he had been attacked by Parker and was keen to know if we were safe and well. Julia saw him while he was here and was shocked at how he had been treated. After all, he had warned Parker about the dangers of the venture and was not, in our opinion, deserving of what had happened. They have grown close and I have hopes that they will become engaged before long."

"I hesitate to put the question," said Holmes, "but have you considered that Mr. Parker's friend could have been the author of the letter?"

Wilson smiled. "You are sharp, sir. Yes, I did. I asked Julia to look at it and she said it was not his handwriting."

A few minutes later and we were in a cab heading back to Baker Street. Holmes had declined Mr. Wilson's offer of dinner, and was deep in thought. "There are some names we need to investigate, Watson."

"Who are they?" I asked.

"There is this Jack to begin with. Presumably, he received a similar warning about the dangers of this investment. It would be good to know if he can add anything. Then, going back to the beginning, there is Dr. Henry Carlton who was present at the Greenwood home on the night of that fateful dinner."

"I can help with Carlton."

"You can, Watson?"

"Yes. Dr. Carlton is a specialist in the effects of long-term opioid use, and a member of my club. I have spoken with him once or twice as a professional brother."

"His membership of your club is a fact of which I was unaware, Watson," said Holmes, with a look of reproach. "What do you make of him?"

"He knows his subject inside out and has authored two books in his field. He is, like Sir James, known for his fervent patriotism. Like me, he is a former army doctor and he donates to, and campaigns for, several causes that support former soldiers. He has lobbied many ministers in person and via letter for better provision for invalided personnel."

Holmes stroked his chin. "He sounds like an upstanding gentleman. Can you arrange a meeting?"

The next day, I made enquiries at my club. I learned from one of the cloakroom staff that Dr. Carlton had let it be known that he was away for a week. I asked to be informed the moment he returned.

I was about to go in search of Thurston when the man called out to me. "Dr. Watson. Don't forget, sir, that it's Sir James's whist match this evening."

"I am sure I will read all about it," I replied.

I managed to locate Thurston near the billiard room. Now fully recovered from his encounter with Conway, he managed, over a number of games, to retrieve many of the shillings he had earlier lost. We eventually decamped to the bar and ordered drinks.

"Good health," he said.

"I was reminded," I said, raising my glass, "that Conway is playing whist against Fitzmorris tonight."

"Yes. It's taking place at Fitzmorris's club. He wanted to be on home turf, I'm told. If he loses this time, it's all over. Conway has been walking about saying that he won't be kind a second time."

Later, as I travelled home, I felt full of foreboding for Mr. Fitzmorris and for his poor son.

Holmes was not in when I arrived back at Baker Street so I settled down with the papers. The only story that stood out was one about a medical conference in Edinburgh. Dr. Carlton's name was listed as an attendee. At least I knew where he was and when he was likely to be back in London.

Holmes returned about an hour later and joined me in a cigar. "What have you been up to?" I asked.

"I felt I should finally update my brother on our earlier encounter with Miss Howard."

"Why?"

"He has her on a long leash, Watson, and I assumed her home would be under some form of observation. He already knew we'd called upon her and I knew that he knew. He is not happy with what was discussed but is confident it does not damage his plans for her."

"What is his intention?"

"I think we can presume our government will offer her ample chance to purge herself of earlier sins."

"Meaning?"

"Meaning that he will require her to act as an agent for this country. She is not an unintelligent woman, Watson. Despite what she said to us, the possibility will have occurred to her that our government will want her services. The greater concern is whether it has also occurred to her former masters."

The next day the society pages were dominated by one story. Mr. Fitzmorris had comprehensively bested Sir James at whist. He had not done Sir James any serious harm but had recovered almost all that he had lost. In something of a turnabout, Sir James was reported as being the desperate one, repeatedly demanding further games even when Mr. Fitzmorris was willing to walk away. It was reported that Sir James had resorted to goading his opponent into further games whenever he looked inclined to stop. The newspapers quoted the victorious Fitzmorris as being delighted to have taught Sir James a lesson. His greatest joy was that he had won back his house.

Sir James was reported as having left the club in a foul temper offering nothing but oaths to the few brave reporters who dared approach him.

It was, I have to admit, morbid curiosity that led me to my club early in the afternoon. The building was busier than usual. Clearly every member shared my interest.

Upon arrival, my ally in the cloakroom informed me Sir James had recently arrived but had withdrawn to the private room. I was also told that his friends, including Dr. Carlton, were commiserating with him.

I ventured up to the billiard room. In it, unsurprisingly, I found Thurston. "Hello, Watson," he said. "Come to view the fallen titan?"

"I confess I have," I replied.

As we could not go marching into the private room, we decided to play a few games and listen out for when they left so we could catch a glimpse of Conway. We were only five minutes into our first game when we heard laughter above us.

"They're brave," said Thurston. "I would not mock Sir James to his face."

"Well, it sounds like he's taking it well."

Thurston listened. "You're right. I'd have expected to have heard his angry tirade by now."

We played for almost two hours. During that time no one left the room above. We heard footsteps as the occupants paced about within it but no one left. I checked my watch. "I have to get back."

Thirty minutes later I was back at Baker Street. Holmes was sitting by the fire. His face was one of frustration. "Did you see Sir James?" he asked.

"No. He was with the other Bad Companions."

"I beg your pardon, Watson?"

I explained the origins of the name, as told to me by Thurston, along with everything I had learned. I added, "Aside from Sir James there are Dr. Henry Carlton and Alexander Jackson."

"That is most interesting," said Holmes. "I had noted, of course, that several people in this case were members of your club, but can it be that simple?"

"What is it, Holmes?"

"It's falling into place, Watson. We must pay a visit to Reverend Samuel Greenwood."

It transpired that Reverend Greenwood resided in Kentish Town. Despite not having an appointment, we were admitted and escorted to the reverend's study.

He rose from his desk as we entered. "Good evening, gentlemen. How may I assist you?"

"I would appreciate it if you can confirm some information for me," said Holmes.

"Whatever do you mean, sir?"

"It is about your son and Dr. Henry Carlton."

Greenwood sank back into his seat. "Dr. Carlton is a friend of the family. That is all."

Holmes continued. "Come now, sir, that is not quite true. Some time ago you forced your son to break his engagement to Miss Georgina Morris. I know the reason and am in possession of the letter."

Greenwood was furious. "Blackmail, is it?"

"By no means," said Holmes, who did not look nearly as offended as I was.

"David informed me he had destroyed the letter."

"I'm sure he had every intention of doing so," said Holmes. "Your son, as you know, is hopelessly addicted to opium. You approached Dr. Henry Carlton to treat him. Despite his best efforts, your son has not markedly improved and this got back to the government who rescinded the offer of a position in the Foreign Office.

"Before this, you received the aforementioned letter that informed you Miss Morris had her own addiction. In this case, alcohol."

Greenwood was silent. His face red with fury.

"Your son was your responsibility but Miss Morris was not. You ordered a separation which deeply wounded both Miss Morris and your son. It was your mistake to send your son, with the letter. He permitted her to read it and neglected to request it back. It seems clear that, in an attempt to fortify his nerves, he indulged his vice en route. When he realised his mistake, he lied to you to prevent a scene."

Greenwood recovered his voice. "You have no proof, sir. You have the letter regarding Miss Morris, and conjecture. Nothing more."

"I will soon have more than conjecture, sir," said Holmes. Greenwood started to rise from his seat. Holmes continued. "Don't trouble to rise. Your son is your concern but I will get answers for Miss Morris."

We were soon back in a cab. "What did you learn there?" I asked.

"It was purely a question of confirmation. His pride and his son are his punishment."

"But what about poor Miss Morris," I said. "That letter ruined her life."

"You could argue it saved it. You will recall that I told Greenwood that his son took opium before visiting Miss Morris. That was clear from her account. She described the perplexity and distress on his face. The unsteadiness she described was unlikely to be down to drink. When I learned of the link with Dr. Carlton and, from you, his speciality in opioids, it was a reasonable conclusion to draw."

"So, Dr. Carlton wrote the letter?"

"No, Watson."

I gave up. "What is the next step?"

"When is this singular group next destined to meet?"

"If they stick to their routine, three days."

"Good. I hope you'll be able to sign me in, old fellow."

Holmes said there was nothing to be done until we met the Bad Companions. He had taken to using the term and had already suggested it as the title for any future account. I did my best to occupy myself in the meantime. At Holmes's suggestion, I did not visit my club – in order to avoid giving our hand away. Instead, he had requested that I drop a note to Thurston asking him to alert us to any untoward changes in their routine.

On the day, we received a note from Thurston, in the early afternoon, to say the men had gathered. We seized our hats and overcoats and made our way to the club. I signed Holmes in and we went to the billiard room. Holmes was slightly concerned at the number of people who appeared to recognise him. "We need to be swift, Watson, in case one of your fellow members announces my presence."

At the door of the billiard room, we met Thurston. He assured us the room above had been occupied for the last hour and no one had left. We continued up to the next floor and advanced upon the door.

Holmes paused and knocked. A voice rang out. "Enter."

We swiftly walked into the room. There sat the three men. Cigars were in their hands, glasses of brandy were on the table, but each man had exchanged his earlier good mood for a perturbed facial expression.

Conway got to his feet. "I know you," he said, looking at me, "you're the friend of that fool Thurston." He turned to Holmes. "You are also familiar."

"My name is Sherlock Holmes."

"The devil!" said Dr. Carlton.

"Not so," said Holmes, "but I may be playing the part of his advocate today. Please be seated, gentlemen, and believe me when I say it is in your interests to do as I suggest."

"The hell it is," said Conway, who had remained standing.

"Sit down," said Carlton.

Conway, to my surprise, did as he was bidden, although it was clear he was not accustomed to being spoken to in such a fashion.

Holmes gestured for me to remain by the door. He advanced a few steps further into the room.

"I confess to a certain amount of admiration for some of your actions, and abhorrence at others."

"I don't know what you are talking about," said Conway.

"Then permit me to enlighten you. This all began with the loss of your lucrative contract. When you were called into Whitehall and told of its cancellation, you were also told the reason. That reason being you were connected to a known German spy."

"That damned woman!" shouted Sir James.

"She meant you no harm, Sir James, and refused to act against your interests. Her German masters sent our government a letter, anonymously of course, which caused enough concern to bring your contract to an end.

"You wanted revenge but were prohibited by Whitehall. You were compelled to sign an agreement which can be used to destroy you if you transgress. Later, you learned something you could not endure. Namely that Miss Howard had become engaged to your friend Percy Graves."

Sir James scowled but said nothing.

"He was your close friend and you felt powerless. You did not want him to suffer as you had. So, you decided to interfere anonymously; perhaps taking inspiration from the letter that had damaged you. You explained your predicament to your companions here and one of them agreed to write the letter accusing Miss Howard of being a fortune hunter with debts, and insincere in her affections. You could not, of course, mention her covert activities as that ran the risk of revealing you had reneged on your deal with the government. The consequences of that, you knew, would be severe.

"The letter destroyed Graves. He challenged Miss Howard with it and she denied it. It ate away at him and he called off the engagement. I'm sure when you read this in the newspapers you were pleased.

"Then, within a day, he was dead by his own hand. You were distraught but could say nothing without revealing your involvement.

"Again, you discussed it with these gentlemen. That was when, I imagine, Dr. Carlton reminded you of your arrangement."

"My what?" said Conway.

"He reminded you that they had helped you with Graves. It was not their fault it had ended so tragically. He reminded you of your mutual patriotism. It was your turn to write a letter."

Dr. Carlton sat motionless.

"Dr. Carlton had been called in by Reverend Greenwood in an attempt to rid his son of an opium addiction. Dr. Carlton initially set out to do exactly that but found the dragon had a strong grip on his patient. The reverend was grateful for all Dr. Carlton's help and he became a regular visitor to the Greenwood home.

"Then he attended a dinner where he met, possibly for the first time, Miss Morris, and learned of young Greenwood's imminent promotion to a Foreign Office post.

"He knew that he could not possibly rid Greenwood of his addiction before the commencement of this sensitive post. He also feared for Miss Morris if she were to be bound in matrimony to this unstable young man. He decided to bring that problem to this forum.

The primary goal was to scupper the promotion. If he could also, in his view, save Miss Morris from an unhappy union, so much the better.

"You all decided that two well-placed anonymous letters would likely achieve the required aim. However, the letters needed to be in two different hands to avoid any risk of the matters being linked. Mr. Jackson would write one but Carlton could not write either. His handwriting was known to the Greenwood family and could also be recognised at the Foreign Office due to his comprehensive lobbying on matters relating to injured soldiers. Therefore you, Sir James, wrote to Reverend Greenwood and Jackson wrote to the Foreign Office.

"A fascinating theory," said Dr. Carlton. "What makes you assume it was that way round?"

Holmes smiled. "The postmark on the letter to Reverend Greenwood was from Folkestone," said Holmes. "It is probable that Sir James wrote the letter and posted it during one of his regular visits to his factory near Dover. It would have been no great inconvenience for him to interrupt his journey to post the letter from there. In addition, Sir James was unlikely to write to any branch of government and run the risk, no matter how remote, of his handwriting being recognised."

Holmes smiled and turned to face Jackson.

"Mr. Jackson here had yet to receive any benefit. His request was less noble. He wanted to remove a man who had secured the affections of the woman he loved. Neither of you were keen to assist in such a matter but Jackson knew enough to expose you all." Holmes turned towards me. "I suspect, Watson, that this was the argument about keeping promises that the club's waiter heard all those weeks ago."

He directed his gaze back to Conway and the others. "Your regular study of newspapers during your meetings is well-known. Mr. Jackson told you, when describing his desire, that Mr. Bernard Wilson was a successful businessman who was not averse to investing in other companies. You later came across reports on the Turner and James wine import business and their search for investors. Using your collective connections, you learned of the rumours around its solvency. It occurred to you to get the Wilson family involved using Mr. Jackson's rival as an intermediary. He knew his friend Parker was eager to impress Mr. Wilson and would be too stubborn to walk away from a deal he thought would achieve his aim. It was also fairly certain that Mr. Wilson would be interested. Parker was cajoled into approaching his future father-in-law and to enthusiastically promote the investment.

"Mr. Jackson here later dropped out and you arranged for the warning letter to go to Mr. Wilson. Abandoned on all sides, a drunk and distressed Parker nearly harmed his fiancée and was cast out, leaving the way clear for Mr. Jackson. I already understand from Mr. Wilson that he hopes for an engagement between Mr. Jackson and his daughter."

At this news, Jackson looked up and smiled.

"Thank you for confirming your identity," said Holmes. "If it crosses your mind to deny matters later, I can always get Mr. Parker or the Wilsons to identify you, Jack."

The smile vanished.

"Holmes," I said from the door. "How does Fitzmorris come into this?"

"An unintended consequence, Watson. Mr. Fitzmorris was approached by the owners of Turner and James when the other investment fell through. They knew how desperate their situation was and could not wait for people to approach them.

"Fitzmorris, lacked the knowledge of the company's instability and, true to his risk-taking reputation, boldly announced his decision to invest. These gentlemen realised that by saving Mr. Wilson from the deal, to aid Mr. Jackson's matrimonial aims, they had enabled Mr. Fitzmorris to put himself in financial peril. Sir James here, still feeling remorse for causing the death of his friend, and needing to clear his conscience, demanded they do something."

"So, Sir James challenged him to whist?" I asked.

"He knew the challenge would be taken up. Fitzmorris is no stranger to gambling. Sir James here is fully justified in his belief in his skill and he took enough money from Fitzmorris to undermine the deal. It was then imperative to reverse the damage at the earliest opportunity. That is why Sir James was in no hurry to secure the Fitzmorris family home. He did everything he could to delay the legal exchange. He resisted all calls for a return game until the wine business failed."

"Are you saying he then lost on purpose?"

"Precisely. He handed almost everything back. He did it more for Fitzmorris's son whom he saw as being at the mercy of his father's decisions."

We heard clapping. Sir James rose to his feet. "Wonderful, Mr. Holmes. But what is your evidence?"

Holmes smiled. "Your first mistake was assuming no one would draw a connection between these different events. Had you thought otherwise you could have protected yourselves by the simple expedient of a typewriter. But, because you were confident, nay arrogant, you neglected to take such an obvious precaution.

"Once a connection between these events was suspected, the evidence was easy to find. In fact, you would have struggled to have left more if you tried. We can begin with the letter to Reverend Greenwood. Posted close to your factory, it will match your handwriting. Plenty of specimens exist, many in the records of this club. We have the letter to Mr. Graves which will no doubt match the hand of Dr. Carlton or Mr. Jackson. Finally, we have the letter to Mr. Wilson. We cannot prove the Fitzmorris episode but that is hardly necessary."

While Holmes was speaking, Sir James had resumed his seat. All three men seemed lost.

There was a knock at the door. It opened and Thurston peered round. "There are some men heading up here, Mr. Holmes."

"Ask them to wait a moment, please."

As the door closed, Holmes looked directly at Sir James. "The gentlemen ascending the stairs are from the government. I suggest you be honest with them."

Thirty minutes later, Holmes, Thurston and I were sitting in the billiard room. The Bad Companions had been escorted to offices in Whitehall for some, presumably, difficult discussions.

"I've heard a lot about you, Mr. Holmes," said Thurston. "It was a pleasure to see you in action."

"Thank you," said Holmes. "But I could not have done much without Watson."

"Really, Holmes?" I said.

"Of course. Without your knowledge of these men, and their activities here, it would have been a lot harder. I may have drawn the same conclusions eventually but how many lives would have been upset in the meantime."

"Well," said Thurston, "they did do some good. Look at the fates Miss Morris and young Fitzmorris were saved from."

"But at what peripheral cost?" said Holmes. "Contrary to Machiavelli, the end rarely justifies the means. Miss Morris's influence, had they married, may have saved young Greenwood. There was no evidence that she was in physical danger from him. It was his father's concern for his own reputation, agitated by the letter Dr. Carlton instigated, that caused the only harm. As it is, young Greenwood's career is over before it could begin and Miss Morris is alone with the stigma of a broken engagement upon her. As you know, Watson, I am not a huge admirer of womankind but even I recognise the injustice that permits a man to walk away from such situations with barely a moral scratch while the lady will live under the cloud of his rejection.

"Young Fitzmorris may not be safe for long. If his father plays cards again, or enters into another fateful business deal, he may yet still find himself without an inheritance. I have no idea if a marriage between Mr. Jackson and Miss Wilson will take place - so her long-term prospects are unknown."

We finished our drinks and bade Thurston farewell. In the cab I tapped Holmes's forearm. "I noticed you barely mentioned Miss Howard."

"It would not have been appropriate in front of your friend. She will be allowed to continue her career in the certain knowledge that if this country calls upon her, she must answer. Incidentally, I regret it may be some time before you will be able to publish an account. You will be dependent on my brother's permission rather than mine. I fear the chances are slender."

He lapsed back into silence.

The Adventure of the Six Constables

(December 1898)

CHRISTMAS was an event which Mr. Sherlock Holmes treated with indifference. During the years of my marriage, I had always made the effort to convey the compliments of the season and would join him for a cigar and brandy immediately before or after the twenty-fifth. He would spend Christmas Day alone sustained by his files, tobacco and whatever sustenance Mrs. Hudson was able to prepare for him.

He did once, at my suggestion, arrange to spend some of the time with his brother, who also tended to have a solitary Christmas. He later informed me he was not likely to repeat the experience. They were too alike to endure each other's company for long.

Since my return to Baker Street, we had spent Christmases together except when I had received invitations from friends to spend it in the country. These invitations were always extended to Holmes but he never took them up. A traditional family setting did not appeal to him and I always found myself making his excuses at the homes where I stayed.

This year, I was remaining at Baker Street. My leg had been playing up and I was not willing to put it under the strain of a long journey. It was with some sadness that I travelled to the post office to send declinations to the few kind invitations I had received.

When I returned to our quarters, I found Holmes in an animated state. In response to my quizzical look, he handed me a newspaper which had been delivered in my absence. He tapped on one of the leading articles. It concerned the murderer Abe Moore. Reports of his trial had occupied the pages of many a newspaper for the previous four weeks.

I did not get the chance to read much of the article before Holmes began speaking. "He has been found guilty and is to be hanged on Christmas Eve. A mere two weeks from today."

"Good," I said. "I can think of no better end for so vile a man."

Holmes was positively excited. "That is not the intriguing aspect, my friend. The reporter notes that, following the announcement of the verdict and sentence, the judge ordered that the court be cleared."

"Which means what, Holmes?"

"It means the press and public were barred from being present for anything after that point. The judge was within his rights but he would have needed a weighty reason to prohibit the public from witnessing any statement from Moore. I must endeavour to find out what that reason was."

He threw on his overcoat and I soon heard the sound of the front door opening and closing. When he returned, he informed me he had sent a telegram to Inspector Gregson, who had been the man in charge of the case.

About an hour or so later the response was delivered. Holmes leapt out of his seat, seized the envelope from a startled Mrs. Hudson, and tore it open. His eyes danced over the text and his expression almost immediately became one of both frustration and amusement.

"What is it?" I asked.

"Gregson regrets to inform me that he is not at liberty to answer my question." He smiled and resumed his seat. He held the paper up again, as if to check he had read it correctly, before bursting into laughter. He shook with amusement for at least a minute before calming down and lighting a cigarette.

"I wonder what the reason is?" he said, as he threw the spent match onto a nearby saucer.

"The nerve of Gregson," I said. "He would never have caught Moore without your help." Holmes had spent weeks on the case and was eventually able to predict where the man would be found. According to Gregson, when he had put the handcuffs on Moore, the killer's response was to sneer and ask, sarcastically, for congratulations to be passed to Holmes. The very next day, no lesser personage than the Home Secretary had been seated upon our settee requesting that Holmes not speak about the case, and leave all commentary to Scotland Yard. After a difficult year, the official force needed all the plaudits it could get and was in no mood to share the limelight.

Holmes had acquiesced, as he usually did. What he had not expected was to be barred from all involvement from that point onwards. For the government, it was vital that he not be associated with the case by either press or public. This grated as it meant he learnt all news from the newspapers along with the rest of the country.

"Well," I said, "whatever the reason, it will soon be over for Moore. The perfect present for the families he devastated."

On Christmas Eve, the evening papers carried reports that the sentence had been carried out soon after midday. Moore was reported as saying no final words and was dispatched swiftly. Holmes read the article and put the paper down quietly. He lit a pipe and sat back in his chair. He stared into the distance and his expression was not hard to read. He did not like loose ends and not knowing the full story of the trial was a source of irritation.

"It was simply not his style to go to his grave without a word, Watson."

I had read enough of Moore to know that this was true. "What do you make of it then?"

"I don't know and, unless the official position changes, I may never know."

His voice trailed off as he fixed his eyes on a corner of the room. A few hours later, during which he had barely moved, I decided to retire. "Merry Christmas, Holmes," I whispered, as I closed the sitting room door.

Christmas Day itself was peaceful. My leg was a little better so Holmes reluctantly accompanied me on a short walk after breakfast. There was something about the almost deserted streets that gave the capital a sense of calm. For Holmes, the lack of hustle and bustle was dull, and he made subtle, and not-so-subtle, comments until I agreed to return to our quarters. There we eventually partook of a most excellent goose before adjourning to our seats and cigarettes.

Before we knew it, we found ourselves in that strange void between Christmas and New Year when the country makes a half-hearted attempt to get back to normal before the New Year festivities. Holmes declined to leave the warmth of Baker Street until something sufficiently interesting occurred. As it turned out, he did not have long to wait.

It was the twenty-ninth when we read the sad news of the murder of a constable in Holborn. Regrettably, the police were quite often attacked but deaths were relatively rare. This poor constable, who was new to the force, had been struck down in a dark, quiet street on a night where it had rained without mercy. The only saving grace was he would have known little about it. He was found by another constable who had been sent to search for him when he had not returned to the station as planned. Newspaper reports had been lacking detail but Holmes had simply remarked that it was a sad, but featureless, occurrence. A comment that did him no credit.

On New Year's Eve, at about eight in the morning, there was a frantic ringing of the bell. In a matter of moments, Inspector Gregson was standing in our sitting room. He had clearly been up all night. His clothes were unkempt and even I could see the grime on his collar that told of much exertion. "Have you heard the news about our constable?" he asked, breathlessly.

"Yes, Gregson," said Holmes. "It was in the papers two days ago."

"No," said Gregson. "This was last night."

"A second constable has been murdered?" said Holmes.

"Yes. He was found in Lambeth early this morning. He had been garrotted."

"Don't misunderstand me, Gregson," said Holmes. "But why have you come to see me about this constable when you did not about the first?"

"Because this one had a note pinned to his chest."

Holmes immediately sat up. "What did it say?"

Gregson flipped through his notebook. "The note read 'On this special day, I am feeling lucky.'"

There was a period of silence during which only the sound of Baker Street's traffic could be heard. Without waiting for an invitation, Gregson lowered himself onto the settee. He gratefully accepted the cigarette I offered him.

"I don't mean to sound callous, Gregson," said Holmes, breaking the silence. "But members of the Metropolitan Police have been killed on duty before. As I recall, the unfortunate man two days ago was believed to have met his end less than half-way through his beat."

"That is true, sir," said Gregson. "When Constable Williams was found, his body was soaked. He must have been lying there for hours. All his personal possessions were with him and were equally wet. He was taken to the mortuary where the manner of his death was confirmed."

Holmes nodded. "Now tell me about the second constable."

"Unlike Williams," said Gregson, "Constable Greeves, was found in an alleyway. Rope marks around his neck testified to the manner of his end. The note I read to you was found on his chest. You can see the original at the mortuary."

Holmes frowned. "Gregson."

"Yes, Mr. Holmes?"

"You are holding something back."

Gregson sighed. "As soon as I was called to the scene, I knew what this could be. I managed to secure permission from the Home Secretary to take you and Dr. Watson into our confidence."

Holmes smiled in anticipation.

Gregson appeared to be embarrassed about what he was going to say. He fidgeted in his seat. "We think this could be Moore."

Holmes's eyebrows rose. "Moore? The man you hanged on Christmas Eve?"

Gregson exhaled. "In a manner of speaking, sir."

"Speak plainly, Gregson."

The irony of Holmes demanding a plain explanation was not lost on Gregson. He let it pass. "As you know, the press and public were cleared from court following the verdict."

"Yes. I recall you declining my inquiry on that very subject. The Home Secretary's conditions were strict indeed."

"Sorry, sir," said Gregson. "It was at Moore's request."

Holmes's eyebrows rose. "Why?"

"He informed the judge, through his barrister, that he planned to say something he was confident they did not want the public to hear. The judge was minded to refuse. Moore's barrister persuaded him otherwise."

"You were present following the verdict?" asked Holmes.

"Yes."

"Good. A first-hand account is always preferable."

"I remember it clearly," said Gregson. "After he was found guilty and sentenced, the court was cleared. As people filed out, looking confused, Moore watched them from the dock with an amused expression. How a man just condemned to death can find amusement in anything is all the proof I need of genuine evil. When the court was empty the judge invited him to speak." Gregson flicked through his notebook.

"He said 'Thank you, your honour, for the courtesy you have shown me throughout my trial. I know I go from here to my death. I wish to say that, as payment in kind, I will order the deaths of six constables. They will be killed after Christmas Day and all will be dead before Lent.'"

"Quite the display of hubris. Anything else?" asked Holmes.

"Yes. This is where it gets strange." Gregson stared out of the window. "Something I never quite understood," he said, without shifting his gaze, "was why Moore didn't mention you during his trial. He said your name when I nabbed him but, after that, it never passed his lips again. After weeks of silence, he said that his vengeance would be that the deaths would fool even you and show the public you could be beaten just as easily as the Yard."

"And this was the reason for a closed court?"

"No. Moore stated that we'd know the deaths were caused by him if his words were not public knowledge. The judge took the view that keeping the threat quiet was the best way to ensure the safety of the police."

"Did Moore explain that these notes would be found on the bodies?" asked Holmes.

"Yes. He provided the wording. He said each note would be the same except for the last word."

Holmes leant back in his chair and stared at the ceiling. "I presume, Gregson, you are worried that the first constable may be one of the proposed six?"

"Yes, sir. We found a similar piece of paper on Williams but it was all ruined by the rain. If there had been writing on it, there was no chance of seeing it."

"Have you conveyed this fear to the Home Secretary?"

"Yes."

"I presume that Moore was not permitted any visitors after this outburst?"

"No. We took his words at face value. He had clearly stated he would order these deaths. The implication was he had not yet done so. No one was permitted to talk to him except his solicitor and there was always someone present to hear what was said."

"That leaves many possibilities," said Holmes. "Moore may have lied and issued orders before his capture or before the end of his trial. He could have issued instructions to his solicitor in code."

"I understand that, Mr. Holmes," said Gregson. "That's why I'd like you to come along with me now."

A few minutes later the three of us were in a four-wheeler heading for the mortuary in Lambeth. It was a relief to be outside again even though the motivation was a tragic one.

"Tell me, Gregson," said Holmes. "Was Greeves a new recruit like Williams?"

"No, sir," said Gregson. "He had been on the beat for three years."

"Interesting. That rules out a deliberate targeting of inexperienced constables."

We soon arrived at the mortuary. The daylight streaming through the few windows did nothing to improve the atmosphere. Gregson led us to the constable's body. Holmes studied it closely.

"You can see from his fingers," he said, "where Greeves clawed at the rope." We moved to the man's clothes. "The boots and trousers are interesting. Marks on the boots are clearly from his attacker's shoes. It shows that his murderer kicked at the constable's feet in an effort to bring him down. The trouser knees demonstrate this was successful."

Gregson showed us to a table near the body on which were laid the constable's other personal items. In the midst of them was the note. It was an unusually small piece of paper measuring two inches by one inch. Upon it, in black ink, was written the message that Gregson had already read to us.

Holmes tentatively picked it up. He held it to the light to check for a watermark, there was none.

"Gregson," he said. "You have, of course, noticed that this is not Moore's handwriting. There is both a lack of confidence and a lack of fluidity in the pen-strokes which suggest someone who is not comfortable writing, someone poorly educated. Someone from the lower levels of our society."

"Those were the circles Moore moved in," said Gregson.

"The spelling, however, is perfect," said Holmes. "Two facts that are somewhat in competition."

"What do you infer from that?" I asked.

"Just docket it for the time-being," said Holmes. "The paper size is also of interest. It does not conform to any standard notepaper with which I am familiar. It is also cheap, as indicated by its thinness. Yet it was manufactured this way. There is no evidence of this being produced by tearing or cutting a larger, standard sheet. The lack of impressions on it suggest it was either not part of a notepad or was the first sheet. That may be deliberate to rob us of clues as to the sender. I also note that the paper slightly curls at each end."

He put the note down and briefly looked at the other items. He then looked up with a frustrated expression.

"All we know, Gregson, is someone ill-educated wrote that note on a piece of peculiarly small and cheap paper. Yet, this note ordered the death of Constable Greeves."

"Do you think the writer and the killer are the same person?" I asked.

Holmes stroked his chin. "That we cannot say, Watson. Either the killer writes the note to leave with his victim or someone sends this note to a killer who is instructed to leave it at the scene when the task is done."

"Holmes," said Gregson. "We need more than that if we are to prevent Moore's threat from being carried out. He has four or five more constables on his list."

Holmes frowned. "Clearly a plan was set up in advance of his arrest. The questions are what is that plan's form and how was its commencement initiated? I will think on the matter. Please keep me updated."

A few minutes later, Holmes and I were in a cab heading back to Baker Street. He sat forward in his seat, hands atop his cane and eyes closed.

I decided to break the silence. "What is the next step?"

He tutted, to himself, I believe, rather than me, before opening his eyes. "Do you remember Moore's last murder before he was captured?"

I remembered it all too well. "Yes. He broke into a house and murdered its inhabitant who was a sixty-year-old lady. She was well-known for fostering children. It was particularly cruel and without apparent motive. It galvanised London against him. Every member of the public was on the lookout for him and many members of the criminal underworld were so disgusted that they distanced themselves from him."

"Yes, indeed," said Holmes. "He had no rest from that point onwards. Old allies refused to harbour him. He was forced to move almost every day and find different places to hide. Except for a two-day period just before his capture, barely a day passed without a sighting being reported."

"He didn't deserve any peace, Holmes."

He frowned. "You're missing my point, Watson. How does a man constantly on the move have time to formulate and put in place such an intricate plan? The answer is he does not.

"The note ordering the death of Constable Greeves was not in Moore's hand. Someone else wrote it. You will recall that I remarked on the nervousness of the hand and the concentration. I am convinced the message was either written according to dictation or, and I think this more likely, it was copied from an existing document. It was also decidedly ambiguous, opting to reference a special day."

"What do you draw from that?" I asked.

"It suggests to me there was a fear these notes could be intercepted and therefore innocent sounding words were chosen so as not to arouse suspicion. In turn, this means the recipients understood in advance what form their instructions would take."

"How does that help?" I asked.

"I don't know yet. But all theories must begin somewhere."

Upon reaching Baker Street, Holmes threw himself into his chair and smoked. After about twenty minutes he tutted and dashed out stating, as he flew past me, that he was going to send a telegram to Gregson.

Upon his return he resumed his seat.

"What did you ask Gregson?"

"Something I should have asked at the mortuary. I asked him to check the handwriting of all Moore's known associates. If I am correct, and he did not have time to set up anything himself, someone else must have done so for him. Even though he had been largely ostracised, he may have used associates we already know of. We cannot rule out the possibility that some may not have deserted him. It is worth trying. I also asked Gregson to call upon all Scotland Yard's informants. If plans have been laid for the murder of all these constables, someone will have heard something of it. Gregson will drop by this evening. We need something or, I fear, another constable will die."

It was an unsettling afternoon. The ticking of the clock above the fireplace seemed deafening and I struggled to concentrate on even the simplest task. Holmes sat in his chair, working his way through pipe after pipe. The atmosphere became so poisonous that I was compelled to open a window and suffer the frigid breeze.

At a little after six, the bell rang and Gregson was shown in. Holmes leapt to his feet. "Anything?"

"Nothing."

"Nothing?"

Gregson sank onto the settee. He was clearly exhausted. He suddenly remembered he had not removed his hat. It was thrown onto the other end of the settee in the same manner as a child might hurl an unwanted toy.

Holmes sank back into his chair and lit a cigarette. "Come now, Gregson. Tell us how you have occupied yourself. We may see something you have overlooked."

Gregson sighed and opened his notebook. "We have identified many of Moore's associates over the years. Of the twenty or so we know of, eight are currently in prison and have been since before the murder of the first constable."

"Which likely rules them out," said Holmes.

Gregson continued. "Of those remaining, we have arrested them all at one point or other. We have gathered all the handwriting samples we can and none matches that on the note. Whoever wrote it is almost certainly someone we have not encountered before."

Holmes started tapping his fingers furiously on the arm of his chair - a common occurrence when he was frustrated. "What about your informants?"

"Again, nothing."

"That does not seem credible."

"We have shaken every available tree, Mr. Holmes. Nothing fell out. According to my sources, there has been no whisper of a plan to kill our constables on Moore's orders. The killings seem, to all intents and purposes, random."

"How can you plan and order random murder?" exclaimed Holmes, in frustration. "If there's a plan, and there must be one, it will have structure. With structure must come a discernible pattern. Someone must know something."

"I don't know, sir," said Gregson. "But it does seem like Moore's tense was correct. There is no known plan, yet these killings are being ordered and executed. No one seems to know who or where the next one will be. I don't know how we can stop this."

The beleaguered inspector left soon after. He promised Holmes that the informants would continue to seek information. It was clear he felt hopeless and that another constable's fate was sealed.

"I fear Gregson's pessimism may be justified," said Holmes. "There is one thing of which I am sure."

"What's that?"

"This was not Moore's idea. Be under no illusions, Watson. A new power has risen. Furthermore, it is someone without even the most basic scruples. This man would not turn away Moore even when many worse men refused to cooperate. This is a man who cares about nothing except the challenge, and who will work with, or against, anyone if it offers that challenge."

"Go on," I said.

"It is also, to my mind, the only way to explain the lack of information. Someone has set up a new network of people. One which Scotland Yard's informants have no knowledge of or access to. Moore did not have the time do this and he lacked allies, amongst his former associates, able to do so for him. This points to someone outside of his circle who has had the time to do what he could not."

"Very well," I said. "This man has managed to build an organisation that has proven impenetrable to Scotland Yard's informants. How would Moore have had time to liaise with him when he was the most pursued criminal in recent history? Furthermore, why would Moore not give this person up when he was captured and convicted?"

"Those are excellent questions, Watson. For the first, there was that two-day period when he was not sighted. He was likely taken somewhere safe and told of this plan at that point for there was no other chance prior to his capture. For the second, a possibility is he was offered something in exchange for his cooperation. I would tentatively suggest that my public disgrace could be what he was offered. This would also explain why he did not publicly mention me during his trial. To do so would associate me with his capture and would only enhance my reputation. No, it suited him to keep me separate from his defeat in the eyes of the public. It was one area where he and Scotland Yard were in agreement."

"But what good is your defeat to him?" I asked. "It is not as if he would get to enjoy it personally."

"Very true," said Holmes. "Whomever he dealt with must have had a compelling argument."

In the early hours of the morning, we were both roused by the frantic ringing of the bell. To save Mrs. Hudson the journey, Holmes had answered the door to a sergeant who had demanded our presence. From him we learned that another constable had met his end. A man named Davies had been found dead in Whitechapel. His throat expertly cut.

"This is terrible, Holmes," I said as we rattled our way east.

"Yes," he replied. "But we must make the best use of it. In order to ensure this poor man did not die in vain, we must gather all the facts and see if they can assist us in preventing the next. Moore is up to two or three out of the six, depending on whether or not the first constable is part of the tally."

"Holmes. You are referring to Moore as if he were alive and controlling events."

Holmes frowned. "Apologies, Watson. That is certainly how it appears to everyone else. Ultimately, these murders *are* being ordered. We know the plan is to murder six constables. We are likely at the mid-point. Commissioned murders tend to create paperwork. Yet we have no evidence of any." He smiled. "It is very clever."

"Your admiration is in poor taste, Holmes." I turned to look at the sergeant who had remained opposite us, in silence. His face made it plain he agreed with me.

Our cab soon arrived at the scene in Whitechapel. A small crowd had formed and was being held back by a dozen constables. Notebooks indicated the presence of reporters who were craning their necks for material for the early editions. Holmes was recognised and we were let through. This was not lost on the reporters who franticly started writing.

"We will be part of the story now," said Holmes.

We were directed to a narrow street. Rotten food had attracted a few bold rats who were undeterred by our presence. Here and there were discarded sheets of newspaper. Even though it was freezing cold, first and second floor windows were open so the morbid could lean out to look at the scene. Only their breath, visible by the gaslight in the cold night air, indicated which heads had ducked back inside rooms as we arrived.

We found Gregson a few feet up the street, pointing a battered lamp at the body of his fellow policeman. "I don't see an end to this, Mr. Holmes," he said as he looked up and saw us.

"Calm, Gregson," said Holmes.

"How can I be calm?" snapped the inspector. "Look at this and tell me why I should be calm?"

Holmes took the small piece of paper from Gregson's outstretched hand. I knew what it was but something in Holmes's face as he read it gave me pause. "What is it?"

Holmes handed me the paper. I read it aloud. "'On this special day, I am feeling happy.' Lord! What can it mean?"

"That's not the only reason Gregson is worried, Watson. Look again."

I looked at the paper. "What am I looking for, Holmes?"

Holmes pointed at it. "Different handwriting, Watson."

"I don't see an end to this, Mr. Holmes."

I handed the note back to Gregson. With his cooperation, Holmes examined the scene. As before, the constable had been attacked from behind. The absence of other injuries attested to the fact that he had not had the chance to defend himself. There was no evidence of any attempt to move the body or search it. All the constable's possessions appeared to be present. Holmes walked in every available direction from the scene, in search of evidence. On one occasion, his route took him close to the reporters we had passed on our arrival. They shouted questions at him about why he had been brought in and what he had learned. Holmes ignored them, which in itself gave them something to write about. A few minutes later, he returned, wearing the disappointed expression he had worn on his return from every other direction.

"Appearances suggest," he said, "that Constable Davies was identified and followed into this street." Holmes looked at the wall. "The posters over there are new and advertise a music hall. It would appear our constable paused to read these posters and was attacked from behind. There is some oil from his lamp at the base of the wall. This happened when it was dropped. It is, of course, the one you are holding, Gregson. The constable was killed and laid on his back before the note was positioned. Sadly," he said, looking around, "there is no evidence as to which direction our killer fled in.

"Gregson, do let me know what the police surgeon finds in the post-mortem. Also let me know what your men learn from the residents. Watson and I will head back to Baker Street."

He took a few steps and stopped. "Gregson, may I see the note again?"

Gregson handed it to him and Holmes glanced down. "Happy," he said. "Whitechapel...I wonder." He handed the note back and marched off in search of a cab. As I followed, I turned to look back at Gregson. His face showed both his frustration and despair. I did not envy him.

"What is the significance of the handwriting?" I asked, once we were in a cab.

Holmes looked ahead and spoke. "If the handwriting had been the same there would have been an element of hope. If one person were issuing the orders, according to some diabolical plan, and we identified that person, we could prevent further murders. Now we know there is more than one person giving instructions. It raises the possibility that each murder could be ordered by a different person. That being the case, how do we stop it? This is devilishly clever, and I am currently at a loss as to how to prevent further deaths."

It was not long before reports of the latest death appeared in the newspapers. Holmes's name was mentioned prominently with the press saying Scotland Yard had turned to him in desperation. Unlike many of Fleet Street's utterings, this was not far from the truth. Poor Gregson was the image of desperation.

"Of course," said Holmes, "there is more than one killer."

"How can you be certain?" I asked.

"The different methods employed. If one man were committing all these murders, he would likely kill in the same way each time. Most killers tend to have a preferred method. Also, if one man were responsible for this, someone might have noticed a pattern in his activities that was suspicious. Having many killers, with different approaches, goes a long way to ensure the success of the plan. In the event one gets caught, the killings continue."

"That's appalling."

Holmes continued. "We know the murders began after Christmas Day. That was clearly by design as Moore announced at his trial. It is beginning to look like each is ordered by a different person even though the notes are largely the same. Each note is written by an ill-educated hand, clearly writing to order. What is the significance of the last word in the message? How does it get into the hands of the killer? Oh."

"What is it?"

"A glimmer, Watson. A glimmer."

"Go on."

A smile had broken onto Holmes's face. "I am convinced these notes, or the wording they are to contain, are being conveyed to the killers. There are three obvious possibilities for how this could be done. One is the known criminal underworld. But, if that were the case, there would be some hint of it, no matter how small, through the Yard's informants. Then there is our new opponent's organisation but he is clearly doing his utmost to reveal as little of it as possible."

"So?"

"Think, Watson. Who else can pass a message without causing a single eyebrow to raise?"

"I have no idea."

"Yes, you do. It is your friendly local postman."

"The murders are being ordered by post?" I asked, incredulously.

"Why not?"

"Why can it not be the case that the killers themselves write the notes?" I asked.

"It's not impossible," he replied, "but who is coordinating events, telling them when and where to strike? Who is telling them what to write and how is he telling them? There is someone conducting events but managing to do so in such a way as to make them appear random. I say again, that it is devilishly clever."

The story about the murdered constables was swept from the newspapers the next day. The event responsible involved an even greater loss of life. Thirty-two people were killed when an overnight train from Cumbria to London derailed about two hours into its journey. The many articles painted a horrific picture of bodies amidst twisted metal, burning packages and scorched wood.

As it was not a crime it caused only the faintest flicker of interest from Holmes. He agreed it was tragic but his brain was focused on the matter of murder. At times like this his lack of humanity was startling and all the years I had known him had done little to diminish that.

Holmes was, however, being industrious. Over the week that followed, he had mobilised all resources at his command. His street urchins were crawling all over London looking and listening for anything that might be relevant. They reported to Baker Street each evening but the report was always the same - nothing. Holmes would thank them, give them a few pennies, and send them on their way with instructions to keep going.

After one such visit, I felt compelled to comment. "I don't see that this is getting us anywhere."

"What would you have me do, Watson?" he replied, impatiently. "The first three murders happened in a matter of days. As it stands, we are nearly ten days on from the last murder. The plan seems to have ground to a halt."

"Our constables can relax at least," I said.

"But for how long?" Holmes stood and walked to the window. Once there, he spun round to face me. "As with a certain murderer, from the not-too-distant past, our victims are from a group that have no choice but to be on the streets at night, and often alone. I am convinced that we are up to three victims. The first message was almost certainly rendered illegible in the torrential rain on the night of the murder. Moore promised six deaths. Why would there be a delay now? We must not forget his commitment that all the killings would happen before Lent. Him being dead does not change the fact that he is running out of time to fulfil his promise."

Sadly, the pause ended a day later. The ongoing investigation into the Cumbrian train derailment, was removed from the front pages by the death of another constable. This poor man was found in Camberwell. His death was somewhat different in that he was shot. A clean shot through his helmet brought him down instantly.

Holmes and I were at the location within an hour, following another frantic summons from Gregson. The poor man was visibly aging due to the scrutiny he found himself under. He confided in us that the pressure from his colleagues was far worse than anything from the public. He was letting his men down and felt it keenly.

"This is interesting," said Holmes. "The note is upon the body but the constable was shot from a considerable distance. You will find the bullet is from a rifle. So, our man must have shot the constable and come to the body to position the note. He probably approached, along with members of the public, and affixed it in the confusion."

"The nerve," said Gregson.

"What is the last word on the note?" I asked.

"It says 'pleased,'" said Gregson, evidently disgusted. "Before you ask, different handwriting again."

Holmes stood in thought. "Why the gap in killings? Is this part of the plan?"

"It's all mad," said Gregson, despairingly. "That said, it's not the only mad thing."

"What's that?" I asked.

"I came via Clerkenwell station," said Gregson. "The desk sergeant was doing the paperwork for a man who had been arrested for causing a disturbance at a factory that produces sweets and novelties. He had been physically threatening and had been raving about fraud and the cost of his train ticket from Penrith. When he was arrested, he lashed out and gave a constable a black eye. He's in the cells awaiting his hearing for that assault.

"I also heard," Gregson continued, "that poor old Lestrade has fished two men out of the Thames in the last couple of days. They had been injured in a way that, if you follow me, prevented any hope of identification."

"Interesting," said Holmes, "but we should focus on the matter in hand."

"Of course," said Gregson, somewhat sheepishly.

Holmes continued. "The previous murders were executed in proximity. A cosh, a rope, and a knife. Now it is a gun from a distance. This is not out of a fear of being caught. The killer still had to affix the note to the body. This is presumably a person who prefers a gun or feared he would not succeed in a physical confrontation."

"What does that prove?" asked Gregson.

"For me," said Holmes, "it confirms there is more than one killer. At least two, probably more."

"To my mind," said Gregson, "that is not good news. If, as you say, each person ordering the killings is different and each murderer is different, we stand no chance of preventing the remaining two on the list." He removed his hat and rubbed his left temple. "Moore is, effectively, ordering a series of posthumous murders he cannot be punished for. His men stand virtually no chance of being caught. Even if one of them slips up, there are likely others to carry on."

We left the scene with those words ringing in our ears. Gregson was right. For all our efforts we were no closer to solving the murders or preventing future ones. I feared that this case was destined not to go before the public as one of my friend's successes.

Back at Baker Street, Holmes was in no mood to talk. He announced his intention to smoke and think. "I need to go through all the facts we have learned, Watson. I trust the answer is there somewhere. I will think better in total silence. Please do not speak to me for at least the next two hours."

He gathered almost all the cigarettes, cigars, and loose tobacco around his chair, ensuring all were in easy reach. He donned his dressing gown and sat, cross-legged. After the first hour, he was surrounded by sufficient smoke to give the impression that he was beneath his own cloud.

With nothing else to do, I turned my attention to the newspapers. The leading articles concerned our most recent deceased constable. It contained nothing I didn't already know so I proceeded to the sports pages for the racing. Eventually, I must have fallen asleep.

I have no idea how long I slept for, but a sudden shout came from Holmes. I sat up in my chair. Alas, it was not a shout of realisation but one of frustration. All around him were cigarette ends, and cigar stubs. Several pipes were also on the floor as if he had changed them with each smoke.

"It has been three hours, Watson," he said, sensing my question. "And I have nothing to show for it. The only thing that is settled in my mind is this is, to some degree, the work of our new foe. Something this complex was not in Moore's powers. Moore was clever in his own way but he had neither the intellect nor time to put this together. I fear we will soon be standing by the side of another dead constable."

I had nothing to say in response to this outburst. Holmes resumed his silence and stared into the roaring fire.

I turned my attention back to the newspaper. I felt an urge to break the uncomfortable silence. An article gave me an excuse. "I see here, Holmes, that they have finally cleared the derailed train and inspected the track. Normal service can soon resume. The inquest, however, is likely to continue for some time."

Holmes grunted in my general direction and said nothing. For a few minutes we sat in relative silence. The only sounds being the carriages traversing Baker Street.

Holmes suddenly leapt out of his chair to the rack of newspapers. "Can that be the reason? Can that be the reason?"

"Sorry, Holmes," I said. "What is it?"

"You may have done it again, old fellow."

"I have?"

"Quite possibly."

"How?"

"I theorised that the postal system was being used to convey the orders to kill. We then had the inexplicable delay. How can a plan with no apparent schedule incur a delay? The train that derailed carried letters and parcels as well as being a passenger service."

"I don't see."

He smiled. "It was the major route for the Royal Mail from Cumbria to London. They had to organise an alternative route while the wreckage was being attended to. Letters and parcels originating from all of the north-west to London and the south of England were delayed as a result."

"I am not with you."

"What if that were the reason for the delay? What if the latest order was written and posted in Cumbria? What if they all were?"

"It's quite the leap, Holmes."

"A leap worth making in the absence of other avenues. We also have another Cumbrian link."

"We do?"

"Yes. Gregson mentioned the man being held at Clerkenwell police station. Do you fancy a journey this evening, Watson?"

I soon found myself alongside Holmes heading in cab to Clerkenwell. I'd seen him make leaps before but seldom one as tenuous as this. I was forced to assume that the lack of useful information gained so far was forcing him to consider even the remotest possibilities.

Upon our arrival at the station, we spoke with the desk sergeant. Fortunately, he was the same sergeant who had dealt with the Cumbrian man.

"His name is James Bell," said the sergeant. "He was like a madman when he was brought in. All he would utter were threats. He'd punched a constable after the factory owners called one in off the street."

"Do you have his possessions?" asked Holmes.

The sergeant took us through to a back room. He selected a box and brought it to us. It contained a cheap pocket watch, an equally cheap pocketbook, keys, some loose change, and an envelope addressed to Windsor and Son, 20 Kentish Town Road, Camden.

"That's interesting, said Holmes."

"What is?"

"The envelope is fully addressed. Our Mr. Bell clearly intended to post this from Cumbria before electing to bring it by hand."

Before anyone could say anything, he tore open the envelope. Inside were two small pieces of paper. Holmes handed me the first. It was clearly the man's home address. Holmes paused before handing me the second. As I read it, I felt a sense of dread. It simply read. "On this special day, I am feeling young."

"Well done, Holmes," I said.

Holmes looked at me incredulously. "Don't be silly, Watson. This is not our man. Why on earth would he include his home address if he were the person ordering the killing of constables in London? We need to speak to this man, Sergeant."

We were led down to the cells. The sergeant opened one of the shutters. "He looks calmer now, at least." He opened the door and we all entered.

The man who rose from the bed was about thirty years old. The poor state of his clothes attested to a lack of means.

"May I go now?" he asked, nervously.

"No, you may not," said the sergeant. "You assaulted a constable and will have to answer for it. In the meantime, these gentlemen have come to talk to you."

Bell sank down onto the bed. "More questions."

Holmes seated himself next to Bell. "Mr. Bell, my name is Sherlock Holmes. You may have heard of me. Rest assured I come to you with an open mind. Please explain how you found yourself in your predicament."

Bell sighed. "I came to London to enter a competition."

"Go on."

"It seemed so simple to enter and the prizes were well worth having to someone in my circumstances."

"The prizes being?"

"There were three. Ten pounds, twenty-five pounds, and fifty pounds. The top prize is more than I earn in a year."

"What form did the competition take?" asked Holmes.

Bell's face showed that he feared what he was about to say would not be believed. "On a piece of paper, sir, there were eighteen letters. I simply had to pick one and write on another piece of paper, which was provided, 'On this special day, I am feeling...' and add a word that began with the letter I'd picked. It was to be posted to an address in Camden. We were told to enclose our name and address on a separate piece of paper. If we wrote it on the same paper our entry would be discounted.

"It was a lot of money so I wasn't going to miss the opportunity. I had the letter all ready to go. Then that train crash happened. All post to London was delayed and the competition had a closing date of mid-January. I decided it was worth the money to get to London and deliver it myself."

"We know you still had it. What happened?" I asked.

"The address was in Camden, sir. When I got there, I could see it was a private house and appeared abandoned. It didn't feel right to leave my entry at an empty house so I went to the factory in Clerkenwell to hand it in. When I got there and explained, they said I was mistaken and they were running no competitions. My temper got the better of me. I had paid for an expensive train ticket, and come away from work, apparently for nothing. I got upset and someone fetched the police."

"How did you know where to go when you decided against the house?" asked Holmes.

"I know the factory address by heart, Mr. Holmes. We've been getting our presents and crackers from them for years."

The look on Holmes's face was hard to decipher. He looked both elated and horrified. He stood slowly and indicated we should leave the cell. We waited for him in the corridor. I could see that he asked Bell another question.

As he stepped out, the sergeant moved to lock the cell. Holmes called out, "How many children do you have, Mr. Bell?"

"Four, Mr. Holmes. They cost the Earth. It was another reason I entered the competition."

Holmes seemed satisfied with the answer. He thanked Bell and promised to do what he could for him.

The sergeant was asked to get Gregson to meet us at the factory in Clerkenwell. As we made our way there in a cab, Holmes sat motionless. The only word he uttered was "fiendish."

Upon our arrival at the factory's address, we entered the reception. Despite the hour, the building was still open. We asked for the manager and sent in our cards. It was a matter of minutes before a stout, bespectacled man emerged.

"Mr. Holmes, I am so pleased you are here. Aside from taking away that deranged man, the police have shown precious little interest."

Holmes smiled. "I'm sorry to hear that, Mr.?"

"Windsor. Horace Windsor."

"Well, Mr. Windsor. We are here in connection with that matter. Inspector Gregson of Scotland Yard will be joining us presently. Is it possible to speak in your office?"

"Certainly, sir," said Windsor, with a subservient bow. "Please follow me."

We stepped behind the counter and followed Windsor up a flight of stairs. His office, although spartan, was spacious. We were invited to sit.

Windsor lowered himself into his seat. "Please ask me any questions, Mr. Holmes."

"Have you arranged competitions before?"

A look of exasperation crossed Windsor's face. "No. Never. That is what made it so absurd when this fellow came in. He was polite, at first. He explained to my man in reception that he wanted to deliver his entry in person because of the recent derailment. I was sent for and I explained to him that we have never run such a competition. He started to complain about the time he had wasted and the money he had spent getting to us. I asserted that he must be the victim of a joke. The more I insisted he was mistaken, the angrier he got. I was forced to send one of the lads to fetch a constable. The rest, I suspect, you know."

"I presume you keep records of where you send your stock?" asked Holmes.

"Of course."

"For example," said Holmes. "When it comes to your crackers, I presume you provide different ranges appealing to different pockets?"

"Yes. We have a deluxe range for the more discerning and a low-cost range for the less affluent." The final two words were delivered with a certain amount of disdain.

"In what denominations do you supply them?"

"Boxes of six and twelve for the deluxe. Boxes of six only when it comes to the cheaper range."

Holmes smiled. "That is good. Please provide us with the records of all boxes of six in your budget range."

"Do you have a warrant, Mr. Holmes?" said Windsor, who appeared alarmed.

Holmes smiled. "Alas, I do not. However, given the connection this undoubtedly has to a series of recent murders, I would suggest you cooperate. You are welcome to take it up with the inspector."

On cue, there was a knock at the door and Gregson entered the room.

"Ah, Gregson. Mr. Windsor is hesitant about letting us see his records."

Gregson took the hint. "I can arrange a warrant, sir. It will create a lot of fuss and the press will probably get wind of it."

Windsor paled. "There's no need for all that." He stood. "This way, gentlemen."

We followed him to a room full of files. A young man stood to attention as we entered.

"Simpson," said Windsor. "You are to help these gentlemen with anything they need." He bowed and headed for the door.

"One moment, Mr. Windsor," said Holmes.

"Yes, sir."

"Have you had a break-in here, in the last few months, that you did not report?"

"How did you know?"

Holmes did not respond, and waited. Windsor was all too eager to fill the uncomfortable silence. "Almost two months ago."

"What was taken?"

"Nothing. Which is why we did not take time to report it. We found a broken window and evidence someone had been both in here and in our stockroom. An inventory demonstrated that nothing had been taken. We repaired the window and considered the matter closed."

He waited for a response. When he did not get one, he edged out of the room.

"Nothing was taken," whispered Holmes. "But something was added."

Holmes asked young Simpson for all records relating to sales of the low-cost boxes of six crackers that had been sent out since the break-in. Whilst the young lad worked furiously to locate them, we re-joined Windsor in his office.

"Gentlemen," said Holmes. "It is a sad fact that we will look back on this and say that thirty-two people had to die to save the lives of two constables."

"What do you mean?" asked Gregson.

"It is a simple fact. If that train had not derailed. Mr. Bell would not have attempted to hand deliver a letter to a factory thus exposing a fiendish plan."

"You need to help me, Mr. Holmes," said Gregson.

Holmes smiled. "This was, and is, a plan which I find abhorrent and clever in equal measure. A plan designed to be random to make it nearly impossible to stop. Were it not for that derailment it would likely be proceeding as designed."

There was a knock at the door and young Simpson entered bearing a rather tall stack of papers.

"Thank you," said Holmes. "Now, would you please divide it into records of shipments to the south of England and shipments to the north."

The poor lad placed the files onto the floor and sat down to divide them. When he was done, Holmes leafed through the latter pile before seizing a single sheet of paper.

"Before we left Clerkenwell station," he said. "I did elicit, from Mr. Bell, the name of the shop in Penrith where he bought his crackers." He turned to Mr. Windsor. "I can see that six boxes of low-budget crackers were supplied by you to the same shop. It appears to be the only place you supply in that area."

"We have local competitors there," said Windsor. "The owner of that shop is a former employee of ours and prefers to buy from us."

"I'll wager," said Holmes, "that all the competition papers were in those boxes."

"Can you slow down, Holmes?" said Gregson.

"I'm sorry, Inspector," said Holmes. "When I said it was fiendish, I was not doing so lightly. The full horror will soon dawn on you.

"Two months ago, someone broke into this factory, studied these same records, and headed for the stock room. This intruder skilfully inserted details of a fake competition into a batch of crackers headed for Cumbria."

"How can you be certain it was only Cumbria?" asked Gregson.

"Because the longest pause in the deaths occurred after that train derailment. For almost a week no post made it from Cumbria to London. Some items were destroyed in the crash. Later items had to be rerouted, which added a delay to their arrival in London. If these competition papers had been in crackers sent to the south coast, west country etc. there would not have been such a delay."

"But why pick Cumbria?" I asked.

"I believe it to be a question of distance. They had to be sent to a location where the population were less likely to be familiar with London. Also, far enough away that they would post rather than hand-deliver their entries. Whoever broke into this factory settled on Cumbria as the destination furthest north in the records he found.

"Mr. Bell told us that the competition required you to select one of eighteen letters from the alphabet and write a word beginning with that letter, at the end of a prescribed message, on a supplied piece of blank paper. I am certain those letters were all associated with Metroplitan policing divisions."

"Of course," said Gregson. "H on the paper in Whitechapel. L in Lambeth."

"And Mr. Bell was carrying one with 'young' on it, which means 'Y' for Highgate," I said.

"Precisely," said Holmes. "That is what makes it so fiendish. Members of the public were being used to randomly order the deaths of constables based solely on a letter they chose. This was why the handwriting was always different. There was also no way of telling when the entries would be sent in."

"Wait a moment," said Gregson. "You said eighteen letters. There are twenty divisions."

"Only nineteen, as you know, have single letters to denote them," said Holmes. "The exception being Thames Division. I expect that 'N' was also missing from the options. That, as you know, is for

Islington which puts it in the vicinity of this factory. I don't think they wanted any murders in too close a proximity to this place."

"But why did you focus on the low-cost boxes of six?" I asked.

Holmes frowned as he always did when someone did not see what he saw as obvious. "Surely that is plain? Moore's promise was that all constables would be killed before Lent. Some affluent families buy large boxes of crackers designed to last more than one year. If they carried the competition entries there was a chance the affected crackers would not be used on Christmas Day. Putting them into the small boxes increased the chance of success. Poorer families would opt for the low-cost boxes. They are statistically likely to have larger families thus almost ensuring the single competition paper in each box was found. Each family was unlikely to buy more than one box which meant all the competition papers were likely to fall into different hands. Also, the prize would be too tempting for such families not to enter. Such a prize offered to a wealthy family might be something they would not trouble themselves with."

"Amazing, Holmes," said Gregson. "But how do we stop the remaining murders? The letters could be on their way now."

"We cannot be guaranteed to stop them," said Holmes. "We can, however, reduce the risk. It is possible that not all the crackers were sold. Mr. Windsor here will issue a request to all retailers, who bought the cheaper boxes, to return their stock. He can say they are faulty."

"But, Mr. Holmes," said Windsor, "think of the damage to our reputation."

Holmes ignored him. "Advertisements will be placed in all national newspapers to report that the competition is an error. Anyone who entered will be invited to make themselves known and offered a form of compensation in return for the crackers they purchased. They can be asked to where they sent their entries. Scotland Yard will contact the Royal Mail. All postmen will be instructed not to deliver letters to empty houses in the capital. It seems clear the successful deliveries were to abandoned houses acting as collection points used by the killers. They, of course, had been told what to do if they received a message with the right wording."

It was all carried out as Holmes suggested. One evening, a few days after the advertisements had been published by Mr. Windsor, Holmes directed my attention to a personal ad. It read thus:

"To SH. Very well done. Loose ends will soon be tied up and an injustice corrected."

"What does he mean by that?" I asked.

Holmes thought for a moment and frowned. "You will recall Gregson mentioned that Lestrade had pulled two men out of the Thames. Men who could not be identified. I strongly suspect they were two of the murderers. Not that it can ever be proved. Whether I succeeded or failed they were always going to be dispensed with after they had carried out their orders. It means we can expect two more bodies."

The next morning, just after breakfast, the bell rang. Mrs. Hudson showed in Gregson.

"Good morning, Inspector," said Holmes.

"It may be for *you*," said Gregson. "I assume you have not read today's copy of *The Times?*" He withdrew a rolled-up newspaper from his coat and handed it to Holmes. "The Home Secretary is not pleased."

I moved behind Holmes in order to see the paper. There, atop a lengthy article, was the headline "Sherlock Holmes Halts Constable Killings."

"Did you give an interview to the press?" demanded Gregson.

"Most certainly not," replied Holmes. "You, of all people, know I seldom take any credit."

Gregson continued. "That report not only states our police can relax on the streets due to the killers having been found dead but also gives a full account of Moore's post-trial statement and states that you were responsible for his capture in the first place."

"I can read, Gregson," said Holmes. "I will gladly speak to the Home Secretary personally. If that would help?"

Gregson nodded.

Three hours later, Holmes walked back into the sitting room.

"How did the Home Secretary take your explanation?" I asked.

Holmes sighed. "I told him the story was a Fleet Street fabrication and he accepted it, grudgingly. I suggested that the reporters who were present at the Whitechapel murder site are probably behind the article."

"What really happened?"

"Based on that article, I can only assume our adversary wanted me to have the credit. The question is why?"

Mercifully, there were no further reports of murdered constables, and the arrival of Lent permitted us all to breathe once more. As Holmes foretold, two more bodies were fished out of the Thames. One near Limehouse and one near London Bridge. Neither was recognisable.

I was writing up my notes of the case a few days later and asked Holmes if he were satisfied with how he had uncovered the plan.

His face darkened. "No, Watson, I am not satisfied. Four constables were murdered. As far as some amongst the police and public are concerned, Moore carried out his threat."

A thought suddenly occurred to me and I was undecided about whether or not to voice it. Knowing Holmes valued honesty more than tact, I decided to proceed. "I am loathe to mention it," I said. "But if you were not so averse to the trappings of the season, you may have recognised that piece of paper as coming from a Christmas cracker as early as the second murder."

An expression of unambiguous regret crossed Holmes's face. He took a cigarette out of the box and struck a match. He paused, holding the flaming wood between his thumb and forefinger, and fixed me with a stare.

"I must forbid the publication of this case for now, Watson. It is not one of which I am proud and I don't desire to give our foe the satisfaction of reading it. I will confess that a part of me relished having a formidable opponent again. However, my satisfaction cannot come at the British public's expense. He must be found."